Fall at Once

Also by Nora Everly

THE SWEETBRIAR MOUNTAIN SERIES
In My Heart
Heart Words
From the Heart
Change of Heart
Heart to Heart

HONEYBROOK HOLLOW
Next to You
Make You Mine
By Your Side

THE COZY CREEK COLLECTION
Fall at Once

OH BROTHER!
Crime and Periodicals
Carpentry and Cocktails
Hotshot and Hospitality
Architecture and Artistry

TEACHER'S LOUNGE
Passing Notes

Fall at Once

THE COZY CREEK COLLECTION

NORA EVERLY

An Imprint of HarperCollinsPublishers

Without limiting the exclusive rights of any author, contributor, or the publisher of this publication, any unauthorized use of this publication to train generative artificial intelligence (AI) technologies is expressly prohibited. HarperCollins also exercise their rights under Article 4(3) of the Digital Single Market Directive 2019/790 and expressly reserve this publication from the text and data mining exception.

This is a work of fiction. Names, characters, places, and incidents are products of the author's imagination or are used fictitiously and are not to be construed as real. Any resemblance to actual events, locales, organizations, or persons, living or dead, is entirely coincidental.

FALL AT ONCE. Copyright © 2024 by Nora Everly. Bonus scene copyright © 2025 by Nora Everly. All rights reserved. Printed in the United States of America. No part of this book may be used or reproduced in any manner whatsoever without written permission except in the case of brief quotations embodied in critical articles and reviews. For information, address HarperCollins Publishers, 195 Broadway, New York, NY 10007. In Europe, HarperCollins Publishers, Macken House, 39/40 Mayor Street Upper, Dublin 1, D01 C9W8, Ireland.

HarperCollins books may be purchased for educational, business, or sales promotional use. For information, please email the Special Markets Department at SPsales@harpercollins.com.

hc.com

Originally published as *Fall at Once* in the United States in 2024 by Nora Everly.

Interior text design by Diahann Sturge-Campbell

Mixing bowl and firefighter hat © eva; Vector Tradition/Stock.Adobe.com

Library of Congress Cataloging-in-Publication Data has been applied for.

ISBN 978-0-06-346280-9

25 26 27 28 29 LBC 7 6 5 4 3

Fall at Once

CHAPTER 1

Madi

"No, no, no. Crap, crap, crap. Come on! Please . . ." I muttered as my car sputtered and slowed to a lurching crawl as I navigated the twisty, turny—and I'm just going to say it—treacherous, pain-in-the-butt mountain road that led up to Cozy Creek, Colorado.

I was born and raised in Colorado Springs, where Ubers were plentiful, public transportation was readily available, and when it was nice outside, I could walk. I rarely had to drive myself anywhere. My car was an old hand-me-down Volkswagen Bug, painted a pretty pale shade of pink.

Our mother had given it to my oldest sister after she'd learned how to drive, who then passed it to my second oldest sister, who had passed it to me when I turned sixteen. Mom had bought it when she hauled her booty out of Cozy Creek ages ago after divorcing my dad. She'd insisted we keep it in the family for sentimental reasons; she called it her freedom car.

I should have known it would never make it up here and taken her new Cayenne, as she'd offered. But I was in a rush to leave, and I didn't want to go to her place and pick it up. Seeing her meant I'd have to talk about why I was in such a hurry to get the heck out of town, and I just wasn't ready for the post-mortem discussion of my failed relationship. It was too fresh. And I was feeling too many conflicting things to sound reasonable.

I'd just broken up with the man I'd wasted half of my twenties on, a man my mother wholeheartedly approved of. A man who had no compunction wasting those precious years of time, effort, and love I had invested in him.

But was it really love?

I had thought it was... and *felt* like it was. But maybe I had been willing to simply accept whatever crumbs he threw my way.

With each mile I'd driven away from him and our life together in Colorado Springs, I felt like I was breathing right for the first time in a really long time. Maybe he wasn't who I was meant to be with, and holding on for so long had been foolish.

Or maybe I'd broken his heart, and he wasn't ready to take the next step with me. He cried when I broke it off. He'd sat at our usual table in our favorite restaurant on our fifth anniversary with tears in his eyes as I told him it was over. He had told me I'd blindsided him. Yeah, right.

Blindsided? As if that dinner was the first time I'd broached the question of where our future was going.

It was not the first time I told him I wanted to be married and have children someday. He knew what I wanted from my life. I never hid it. Clearly, our definition of *someday* was not the same. For me, five years had been long enough.

To be fair, that was the first time I'd demanded an answer from him. It was the first time I didn't let him off the hook when he said he liked how things were between us and didn't want to change it. Maybe I was equally to blame for allowing him to lead me on.

But I was currently not supposed to be thinking about him, my life, my feelings, or anything to do with Ross or the fact that I had just turned thirty and was nowhere close to where I thought I'd be at this point in my life. Growing up, I'd thought thirty was so old. I had thought I'd be settled down with a family of my own.

"Damn it." I yanked the wheel to the side, managing to pull safely off the road before the car died completely with an unceremonious mechanical groan.

I scanned the side of the road, watching the cars pass me by. Was it weird that I felt like I was living a life that wasn't my own?

Here I was, newly thirty, newly single, and look at me now—a clueless city girl stuck on the side of a mountain road. I was stuck in a broken-down car while people kept living their lives alongside me.

To be clear, nothing was wrong with being thirty—it just felt like an arbitrary marker in time I'd set for myself and failed to live up to.

Did I have kids? No. *A house?* No. *A husband?* No. Not even a pet to call my own.

I'd always thought by this time in my life, I'd have it all. I wanted a big family. I wanted to go to soccer games and bake brownies. I wanted to curl up in front of fires and read bedtime stories. Driving kids to school and playdates sounded like a great way to spend my time, dang it. My therapist didn't have to tell me that I wanted to create the life I'd always wanted to have while growing up; it was glaringly obvious, and I didn't care.

I had expected to get a proposal at our anniversary dinner. But I didn't. Instead of a ring, I had gotten a sympathetic smile from a random, eavesdropping waiter. I took that as the hint I'd been missing for five fucking years and broke it off right then and there. Five years on the damn dot. Thank god we had never moved in together. I was pathetic; an unsettling mixture of feeling sorry for myself and feeling utterly relieved that our breakup was as easy as me throwing a suitcase into my run-down Bug and hitting the road. I had nothing to collect from his house aside from a change of clothes, a few books, and a toothbrush, and he had left nothing behind at mine at all. It was all so sterile and uncomplicated. Starting over at square one was not part of my life plan at this age.

Shaking off the memories, I inhaled a deep breath to get a hold of myself, but it was neither calming nor cleansing.

I gripped the steering wheel until it creaked, then closed my eyes tight against my confused jumble of emotions and frayed nerves, breathing in and slowly out until I could catch one of my scattered thoughts.

Now what?

I had to call my grandmother. That was first on the list. I was absolutely going to be late for dinner tonight, and she was a worrier.

I was on my way to her place. She'd sprained her ankle while line dancing with her girlfriends and needed me to help her run her bakery until she got better. Gigi's Cozy Creek Confectionery would be my new workplace for the next couple of months. I couldn't wait to get there.

Her accident was unfortunate but a blessing in disguise, allowing me to spend time with her and, at the same time, the chance to get away for a while and clear my head.

Working in Gigi's bakery was the perfect place to reboot my brain. I'd planned to eat my weight in her delicious petit fours, drink pot after pot of her excellent tea, and spend my time mentally checking out while I reassessed my deluded past perceptions about love and marriage and what I deserved from a man. I needed to decide, once and for all, what I wanted for my future and how I wanted to get it.

Cozy Creek Confectionery was Gigi's pride and joy. She needed someone she could trust, she had said to me. I'd grown up baking with her—on weekends, holidays, and school vacations. Spending time with her had always been one of my favorite things, so I jumped at the chance.

I'd spent less time in Cozy Creek while I was with Ross, and I regretted it. Gigi wasn't fond of him. She was always cordial and welcoming, but she felt he wasn't the one for me. Turns out she was right.

With a reach, I grabbed my handbag from the passenger side floor and dug around for my cell—thank god I had a signal. I'd never make it if I had to walk.

I checked my navigation app. I was ten or so miles away from Gigi's neighborhood, and it was all uphill. I looked down at my feet and the beautiful black stiletto-heeled boots adorning them, holding back a wince. In these heels? No thanks.

I tapped my Uber app, frowning when I saw none were available. I'd call for a tow truck next. But first, I had to talk to Gigi and let her know where I was. She was probably already starting to worry, and I didn't want to upset her. I tapped her contact number on my phone.

"Hello, honey. Are you running late? Is everything okay?" I could hear the smile in her voice, and even though this situation was the crappiest ever, I smiled back.

"This day is turning out bad already, Gigi. My car broke down by that big TEN MILES TO COZY CREEK sign. I will definitely be late getting to your place. Calling a tow truck is next on my list, but honestly, I'm so over this car. It can stay here and rot for all I care, the freaking pink monstrosity. Freedom car, my ass."

I glanced out the window, and for a moment, my annoyance faded away as I took in the sight unfurling before my eyes. Goodness, it was pretty up here. The sun was high in the late afternoon sky, leaving the forest dark and intimidating, while the mountains clung to the remaining vestiges of sunlight. The leaves had turned into myriad bursts of ochre, scarlet, yellows, and burnt oranges, mixing in with the lush, spiky peaks of evergreen. Autumn in the Colorado mountains was a sight to behold.

"Why is fall so pretty when everything is literally dying?" I asked Gigi, apropos of nothing.

"It's the way of the world. Things have to die to make room for the new. It's kind of like your breakup with Ross. It's time to start over."

"Ugh, metaphors can be so annoying," I joked.

"And as for your breakdown. You need to call the Huber, honey," she tutted.

"Huber?" I purposefully over-enunciated that first syllable, hitting it hard to make sure I had heard Gigi correctly. "Is this one of those weird small-town quirks that I will have to get used to?"

"Uber doesn't run up here unless you get one at the airport or in the city and start there, but that would have cost you an arm and a leg. I'll call one of the Huber guys to come get you and call for a tow too. Tow trucks take forever around these parts, and I don't want you stuck on the side of the road all night. It wouldn't be safe. You're far too cute to spend the night on the side of the highway."

"I have clearly missed out on the excitement of using the Huber enterprise on my previous visits to town."

"You know what? Never mind. I'll call Cole. He's on his way back to town. I'll see if he's close by. Hold on."

Silence filled the line, and my eyes got big as I contemplated the ramifications of what she was about to do.

Cole? I'd met him a few times. He used to be just one of the three Sutter brothers who lived across the street from Gigi. They were way older than me, always throwing footballs and baseballs around in the street. Who cared about three dumb boys? Not this girl.

But I had spent less time at Gigi's as I grew out of childhood. Between college, work, and Ross, there wasn't as much time for lazy weekends and long holiday breaks at her house.

I'd only seen Cole once or twice in the last few years, and I absolutely did not creeper peep on him while he was working out in his garage from the guest bedroom at Gigi's house. Okay, I totally did, and it was worth it. The man was gorgeous and way out of my league for too many reasons to count.

She clicked back. "We're in luck. He's nearby. Watch for a big white SUV with 'Cozy Creek Fire Brigade' stenciled on the side."

"Oh, okay, thanks, but I can—"

"While I was at it, I called a tow truck for you too."

"But, Gigi, I can take care of my—"

She cut me off. "Don't you worry about a thing, honey. I appreciate you coming to stay with me, and I will help you however I can. Please let me."

"Okay, help away. Thank you." I let it go, deciding to accept her help. It was nice to have someone taking care of me for a change. It felt comforting and warm to be fussed over. "Of course. I'm happy to be with you. Family helps family and all that. Plus, we don't spend enough time together, and this will give us the perfect chance to catch up."

"Pity it took a sprained ankle to get you to take some time off work. It's been far too long since you came up here to stay for anything more than a dinner."

"You know how Mom is. We're always go, go, go at the office." My mother owned a public relations firm in Colorado Springs, and my two older sisters and I worked for her. I was in charge of the business's event and party planning aspects. It was exhausting, but I enjoyed it. Making people's special days the best they could be was the highlight of my job.

Working with my mother and sisters was fun, but I often felt they were far more ambitious than I was. I desperately needed a break and was thankful I had enough savings and my mother's approval to take all the time I needed. She hired a temp to replace me for as long as it took for Gigi to get better.

"I know," she muttered. "She was always such a big dreamer, and I'm as proud as can be, but would it kill her to come visit her mother?"

"As long as Dad still lives in town? Yes, I think it actually might." I huffed out a sarcastic laugh.

My parents were high school sweethearts who married young, with my older sister, Riley, being the unspoken reason for their marriage.

Now, they were divorced and never talked. Dad got custody of Cozy Creek, and Mom got custody of my sisters and me. You couldn't pay her to step foot in this town unless she was sneaking to Gigi's house beneath the cover of night for a holiday get-together or if she knew for a fact that he was out of town.

Their relationship was doomed from the start. Mom was all type A determination as she worked to create the top PR firm in Colorado Springs. At the same time, Dad had become the ultimate ski bum. He owned a ski and snowboarding shop in Cozy Creek with my aunt. She ran it, and he traveled the country, hitting the slopes and leaving a trail of heartbreak in his wake.

I could hardly blame Mom for staying away. Dad had done a real number on her—and on his daughters as well. He was not the type to stick around for anything or anyone. I'd be in Cozy Creek for the foreseeable future, and he wasn't even in the country and had no intention of coming back to see me.

"I know, I know." Her sigh was sad. "They were just too young, and he was completely wrong for her. But enough about them, for now anyway. Did you hear Cole is divorced? It's been final for a couple of months now."

Another shiver shot through my body as my eyes shifted involuntarily to my reflection in the rearview mirror. "Um, no, I did not know that." I pursed my lips and then bit them to add some color. Looking cute never hurt anyone.

"Yep, he's single as could be now and still just as attractive as ever. You're single too. I say it's time for you to get back out there. He's a hero, Madi. He's not just a firefighter. He's now the chief of The Cozy Creek Fire Brigade."

"That's impressive. But I don't need another boyfriend right now. Do not try to fix me up with him, please. Remember how you spent an hour listening to me rant about the guy Riley and Abigail set me up with last week? I'm not dating anymore, Gigi. I mean it. I'm done. It's barely been a month, as it is. I need more time to recover. I tried telling them that, but—"

"That's right, and I told you to let me be the one to set you up next time, didn't I? Hello? They're the ones who fixed you up with Ross in the first place."

They hadn't listened to me, just like Gigi wasn't listening right now. I laughed and let her keep talking. Sometimes, it was easier to nod, smile, and do what you wanted, which was basically how I handled my entire life.

Growing up with a bunch of dominant personalities in my family had made me stealthy. I was so stealthy, in fact, that I barely knew who I was or what I wanted anymore, which was super fun to deal with.

"My picker isn't broken like you girls' is," she continued. "I was married to your grandpa for over fifty years before he passed. You're young and smart and beautiful—"

"You're sweet to say that, but—" She was going to attempt to fix me up with Cole. I knew it.

"Setting you up with a man like Ross, who was too blind to appreciate how wonderful you are, is a travesty. And I don't know who you went out with last week but forget about him. I always say good riddance to bad rubbish. Let the trash take itself out, you know?"

"Thanks, but—"

"You'll see that you're better off soon enough. Ross never deserved you, stringing you along and making you think he wanted the same things you did. Oh, never mind. Lookie here, how fortuitous. Cole just returned my text message. He's about five minutes away, so I'll let you go. Put on some lipstick and check your hair, honey."

"Gigi!"

"Bye for now. See you at the house."

"Wait—" Too late, she'd hung up. "Great," I muttered before blowing an errant highlighted brown curl out of my eye and flipping my mirrored sun visor down to get a closer look at myself.

Apparently, she was going to ignore my newfound vow to forgo dating and fix-ups from my sisters from now on.

Gigi had been right about Ross all along. I wasted too much time on him—five long, fruitless years. The trauma was real, even though my heart wasn't entirely broken.

Perhaps I wanted to be married with kids more than I had wanted to find the right man to start a life with. But I'd keep that little tidbit between me and my therapist. I didn't need the judgment from anyone who wasn't bound by doctor and patient confidentiality laws to keep their dang mouth shut.

No new men in my life were allowed until I met one on my own, the old-fashioned way, like at the grocery store, the park, or maybe a museum if I felt fancy.

Of course, for that plan to work, I'd have to stop having my groceries delivered and commit to leaving my apartment once in a while.

Ugh, whatever.

Maybe I'd never date again.

I pinched my cheeks and fluffed my hair before rolling my eyes at myself in the mirror.

Like you have a chance with Cole, even if she is trying to fix you up with him.

The last thing I needed was to be in another relationship right now. I needed to get my life straightened out. I had to decide what I wanted from a man and not just settle for the scraps he was willing to give me.

Plus, I couldn't help but think a man like Cole would be too much for me to handle.

He was older than me—eight years, to be exact. He had been married and divorced, and, for that matter, he already had kids too. Clearly, he was an advanced adult, while I still felt like I was stuck somewhere in the beginning phase thanks to Ross and my delusional determination to make it work with a commitment-phobic man like him who was too scared to build a future with me.

From what I knew about him from Gigi, Cole Sutter was intense, intimidating, and—based on my scientific guest room window observation—hot as hell. If or when I moved on to a new relationship, I needed to find a man who was his opposite.

Someone safe and nerdy. Someone who didn't require a regular workout schedule and the ability to toss a person over their very broad and defined shoulder to haul them to safety as a job requirement. Not to say nerds couldn't be hot. I'd met plenty of sexy nerds in my day. In fact, Ross had been one. But somehow, guys like Cole were different. I figured having a life-or-death job could do that to a person.

A horn honked behind me, and I jumped in my seat.

Crap, he was here. I could feel my cheeks get hot as I watched him slow down and ease onto the side of the highway.

Hello, Cole. I hope you're ready to get awkward.

After one more peek at myself in the rearview mirror, I opened the door and stepped out, waving my hands over my head as he pulled to a stop behind me and opened the door of his truck.

He was wearing a flannel, and boy, did he fill it out to perfection. I bit my lip to stop the drool from forming as he got out and rolled up the sleeves of the dark blue plaid shirt. His biceps strained at the material as his hands worked the fabric up his muscular forearms.

His legs filled out his jeans very nicely, and the big boots on his feet ate up the ground between them as he approached me. His hair was thick and looked as black as ink in the early evening light. And his eyes, which, if I recall correctly, were as blue as the sky, were selfishly hidden behind aviator sunglasses. Pity.

I had given up on men, but that didn't mean I couldn't still enjoy the view. My stomach dipped and swirled as I took him in. And I knew, based on the butterflies and my shaking hands, that I would absolutely make a stammering, schoolgirl fool of myself once I opened my mouth to speak to him.

A small, friendly smile tilted up one side of his lips.

Wow, he was still as sexy as ever. And let us not forget, he was now just as single as I was and standing *right there*.

My body was reacting as if I'd gotten an extra order of hormones along with my fries and Diet Coke at that McDonald's I stopped at on the way up here. Physical attraction like this, albeit one-sided, was something else. I inhaled a deep, shaky breath.

"You got this," I muttered. "He's just a man."

He was probably used to women throwing themselves at him, and I refused to be one of them.

CHAPTER 2

Cole

I took the last sip of my coffee and stopped behind an ancient pink VW Bug, grinning to myself when I saw a curvy little brunette step out and start waving manically over her head.

Then she turned to face my truck, and I bit my lip.

Damn it.

It was Madison—the cute one and the one I knew the least. I'd been hoping it wouldn't be her. All the Winslow women were beautiful in their own right, but there was something so different, so fascinating about Madison.

My across-the-street neighbor, named Gigi, had three granddaughters: a lovely trio named Riley, Abigail, and Madison Winslow. But she'd neglected to tell me which one I would be rescuing from the side of the highway when she texted me.

I grew up across the street from Gigi. Her granddaughters spent a lot of time at her place throughout the years, on holidays and school breaks. Sometimes, my brothers and I would play out in the yard with the oldest two—they were closer to our age. Madi was always the little one on the porch, with Gigi watching us as we played together.

With a shake of my head to clear it, I waved back.

It didn't matter if it was the cute one since I was most definitely too old for her anyway. Eight years was a lot. At least it would have been back when I was twenty-eight and she was twenty—not that I knew her very well back then. But maybe it didn't mean as much now that we were both in our thirties.

But on the plus side, at least it wasn't the one who started flirting with me the second she found out the ink on my divorce papers had dried; that had been Abigail, the middle. I'd let her down gently. But honestly, her flirting had seemed kind of impersonal anyway, and she was unbothered by the rejection. It was as if I was just single and available and placed in a convenient spot at Bookers Pub for her to talk to, and it was no big deal. It had been a relief, but that didn't mean I wanted to drive her to Cozy Creek to test that theory.

With a shrug and a grin, I stepped out, and slammed my truck door.

Like always, the air was crisp and clean up here. I inhaled deeply and stretched my arms overhead, letting the knot of tension that had built up between my shoulder blades dissipate along with my exhaled breath. I was beyond tired, bone weary, and ready for bed.

I had spent the night assisting on a warehouse fire the next town over. As the chief of the Cozy Creek Fire Brigade, I often helped our neighboring departments if they were understaffed. My entire crew did.

Sleep was the only thing on my mind. My eyes were desperate to close. All I had planned for the rest of the day was to pick up my kids from my ex-wife, grab a pizza, and crash early.

We had an informal fifty-fifty custody agreement that depended heavily on our work schedules. Living in the same town made it easy to facilitate that. Being there for our kids was the one thing we agreed on.

I stood there for a minute, blinking into the sun's glare while surreptitiously watching her watch me. I took in her long, untamed curls, highlighted by the light shining through the trees. Her big, wide eyes looked me over without fear or artifice, though her posture was slightly rigid and timid.

My jaw tensed as I finally took in her tight black sweater and long, lean jeans-clad legs to land on her high-heeled boots.

Then she bit her lip when her eyes met mine, and I had to look away because, damn, she was fucking gorgeous. My hand clenched and unclenched as I realized the word *cute* was utterly wrong when there were so many better words to describe her, like stunning, beautiful, tempting...

What does a few years of age difference matter anyway?

No. She had to stay off-limits.

She was Gigi's granddaughter, and I didn't want to screw up our friendship when I inevitably messed things up like I'd done with my ex-wife.

Pick up the kids and grab a pizza.

Get into bed early.

Do NOT flirt with the stunningly gorgeous Winslow sister.

I knew better than to get involved with her anyway. My dad had always advised against dating anyone you'd be unable to get away from if things didn't work out. I'd lived across from Gigi my entire life. I loved her as much as I loved my own grandmothers. Getting into a relationship with one of her granddaughters was a bad idea.

Don't shit where you live. Dad had said that to my brothers and me as we sat around the table for my youngest brother Tate's thirteenth birthday dinner years ago. Apparently, he'd decided that since we were all teenagers, we were old enough to start hearing the wisdom he'd accumulated throughout his life. Family dinners became vastly more interesting after that night, much to our mother's dismay.

It was good advice, and I should have taken it, considering ever since my divorce from the girl who'd grown up next door to me, I was forced to see her all over town with her new husband, who also happened to be my ex-best friend. The three of us had gone through school together since kindergarten.

They were hot and heavy in a way she and I had never been together, and it stung when I saw them for the first time in public. It's too bad you couldn't legally divide your local hangout places in a divorce.

They'd been carrying on behind my back for months before I caught them together. In my house. In my bed. Going at it like—I forced the mental image of it back outside of my head. Seeing it once was enough. I'd thrown them both out along with that damn bed and filed for divorce as soon as I found an attorney to handle it.

If I'd married someone I had gone to college with or someone from out of town, for example, she'd have moved back to wherever she came from, and I wouldn't have to deal with the awkward sidelong glances from our shared acquaintances whenever we were in the same place at the same time.

Not that I wanted her back; I didn't. I would never forgive him either, for that matter. What a shit friend he'd turned out to be. But after a lot of time and consideration—and a semi-public fistfight in the parking lot of Bookers Pub with said best ex-best friend—I realized we weren't right for each other and never had been.

Bookers Pub and Grill was more than just a bar. You could take your family there for dinner. Unfortunately, my daughter was there having burgers with her best friend's family when the fight broke out.

We'd taken it outside like the upstanding citizens we were, but it was still visible through the window, and Natalie had seen it all.

The look on her face when my fist cracked into the jaw of her future stepfather still haunted me.

I never wanted to be in that kind of situation ever again—a spectacle to be mocked and pitied. I'd been humiliated and, to my shame, had sunken to the level of the people who had hurt me with their dishonesty and betrayal.

But now, I was finally back in a good place. I had moved on. My heart was healed and locked up tight in my chest. No one would ever have the power to break it or put it on display like that ever again.

Needless to say, small-town living was not ideal when you were the center of attention, and everyone you ran into, no matter where you went, knew your history.

"Hello," I greeted once I'd shaken myself out of my exhausted stupor.

"Hi." Her voice was shaky. She was probably scared. Being stranded on the side of the road up here would even make me a bit nervous, and I could absolutely handle myself if any trouble arose.

The stretch between Colorado Springs and Cozy Creek was pretty desolate. Nothing but dark forest and steep drop-offs lined the winding highway that led to town. It would be intimidating for someone who wasn't used to the drive.

"You remember me, right?" I spoke low, soft, and hopefully reassuringly. "From Gigi's. I live across the street." I held my hand out to her. "Cole Sutter."

She took it, squeezing it tight between hers with a tremulous smile. "Yes, I really appreciate you stopping to help me. I'm Madison. Uh, in case you forgot my name."

"I remember you, Madison," I murmured, smiling slightly despite myself when her cheeks turned pink. "Can I grab your things for you?"

"Yes. Please." She dropped my hand like a hot potato and gestured toward the front of the little VW Bug. "The trunk is up here; these old cars are weird."

I watched as she turned to grab her purse from the driver's seat. Her perfume floated through the air as she spun away—vanilla, combined with something earthy that tested my resolve to refrain from asking her out. "Don't forget to lock it," I instructed as I unloaded her bags from the trunk. Gigi said she called for a tow, but getting here would take a while.

"Thank goodness you were available to pick me up. That forest would have started creeping me out once it got fully dark out here."

"Hey, it even creeps out the locals sometimes. You'll be okay. I'll make sure of it." I stowed her bags in the back as she got inside the truck.

"You're a firefighter, right?" she asked after I settled into the cab to join her. "Being the hero must come naturally to you."

"It was my lifelong dream; all I'd ever wanted to do." Too bad I never felt like one. The mistakes and missteps were all too easy to remember, and the successes sometimes felt like luck.

"That's what Gigi said. You climbed onto her roof and rescued her dog, Sir Basil Dungarees I. She still tells that story. How old were you, ten?"

I grinned at the memory. "Yup, ten years old. We may never know how that old mutt got up there in the first place."

"She's on the third, now, you know. The current Basil is a flatulent little thing. Just something to watch out for in case you haven't experienced him crop dusting the living room on his way to the backyard doggy door."

"I have had the olfactory pleasure. I know he thinks it's funny too. Have you noticed the look on his face before he goes outside?"

"I have seen it, and it's truly diabolical. And yet, you still go over there to play poker with her and her friends?"

"Talks about me a lot, does she?" I shifted my eyes in her direction before restarting the truck and found her looking at me.

A fiery blush covered her cheeks. "From time to time—uh, I mean, she talks about all her neighbors. You know how she is."

"Yeah, I know." I cast one last look in her direction before pulling onto the highway. "But I had to quit the game. Mrs. Hadley cheats; losing to her was starting to eat into my beer money," I cracked. "She's worse than the guys at the station. That and—never mind."

She let out a laugh. "Oh, she's notorious, always has been. That woman even cheats at solitaire. And is there a second reason? I need all the warnings. Gigi asked if I wanted to join the game while I was in town."

"Well, her daughter is a little handsy, so you won't have to worry about that. Tate calls her Handsy Hadley. Once I got divorced, it was open season. She'd grab my ass every chance she got. That woman hasn't met an innuendo she doesn't like."

Her eyes widened in dismay. "I'm so sorry. No one should be touched when they don't want to be."

"Yeah, and I couldn't shove her off, or you know, defend myself beyond the words she chose to ignore. I couldn't exactly punch her in the face like I would if it was a guy giving me trouble—anyway." I cleared my throat, embarrassed.

"Does Gigi know? I can't imagine her allowing that to happen."

"No, I didn't tell her. Mrs. Hadley is her friend, so I let it go. It was easier that way. Do you mind some music?"

She patted my arm. "Not at all."

I turned on the radio, grateful she'd let me drop the topic. "Golden Hour" by Kacey Musgraves started playing, and it felt oddly intimate when she unconsciously began to hum along with the melody.

I focused on the road in front of the windshield and my clammy hands on the wheel. She was affecting me in ways I wasn't ready to acknowledge.

She overwhelmed my senses. Between the soft light of the sun setting over the mountains and the sweet smell of her perfume permeating the air in my truck, I was surrounded by her. However, I was surprised by how at ease I felt despite being far outside my comfort zone.

"It's good of you to come to take care of Gigi. I was worried watching her limp around on those crutches all week, and there's only so much I can do to help her out with my work schedule."

"She's stubborn, for sure. I miss her all the time, and I'm happy she picked me to help."

"I'm glad you're here. How come I don't know you? Your sisters always visit Gigi, hang out at the bakery, and Bookers. They're around town a lot. But I rarely see you around."

"Uh, I guess I was just busy with work and stuff. I mean, I was around. Just not as often, I guess."

"Too bad." I shot her a sidelong glance, pleased that the adorable pink blush still stained her cheeks despite my decision to stay away from her.

CHAPTER 3

Madi

Cole was right. I hadn't spent as much time in Cozy Creek as my sisters over the last few years. I'd found it easier to go along with what Ross wanted to do, and he was a city kind of guy. Going on visits to Cozy Creek with me was the last thing he was interested in. I regretted it now that we were over. But at the time, I had looked at it as building my future with the man I intended to marry, hoping I could get him to love it here as much as I did.

I kept my eyes trained out the passenger window as Cole drove, letting them drift along the side of the highway as the forest became one big green blur.

"You awake over there?" he teased.

"Huh? Yes, sorry."

Cozy Creek loomed in the distance, and the highway narrowed as we got closer to town. I sat up, happy that everything was the same. Downtown was even more adorable than usual as it had been decorated for fall. Potted mums decorated the entrances of most of the businesses while autumnal baskets of flowers hung from the light posts. I had to bite my lip and look away when we passed Gigi's Cozy Creek Confectionery. I couldn't believe I would spend the next month or two working there.

When we turned onto Gigi's street and saw her house, I almost burst into tears. I felt a mixture of relief at being off the side of the highway and a feeling of being *home*. Warmth, acceptance, and love filled my heart.

Gigi's place was an old split-level house with a gorgeous wrap-around porch on a large lot filled with tall pines, a lush lawn—that I knew Cole kept mowed for her—and her magnificent rose garden. Of course, she also had a picket fence with a wisteria-covered trellis leading to the backyard and a pair of matching porch swings. Dark-stained wooden shutters and planter boxes stuffed full of annuals and trailing ivy decorated each street-facing window. This house could be a set piece straight out of a small-town movie.

But more than that, Gigi's place felt like home, a *real* home—comforting and cozy, warm and inviting. And after how shitty I'd been feeling about myself ever since my breakup, I needed this. I needed to be around someone who wanted to love me, faults and all, without trying to fix me—well, too much, anyway. Gigi was a fixer, but it was all born from love and a deep knowledge of who I was.

My mother was all about impressing people. She threw business parties and frequently held office staff get-togethers at our house. It was part of her job, and I had always understood that. It was how she earned her living to care for us, after all. But I had to be so careful not to mess anything up. Our house was an extension of her office, and as such, it was very formal. I grew up not being allowed to sit in the living room, eating dinner in the dining room was forbidden to us kids, and god forbid I let my room get messy. What would our housekeeper think?

My sisters had grown up to be her mirror images. Of course, I loved them all; we were close and had all the fun together, but I often felt like the odd woman out. But those feelings could have been related to my inferiority complex. It frequently reared its head to cloud my judgment—at least, that's what my therapist kept telling me.

Anyway, that was not how Gigi lived. You could kick up your feet and curl up with a book on her sofa, and she'd bring you a pillow and a drink, then join you with a book of her own. Formalities meant very little to her. She was more concerned with making sure we were comfortable.

Gigi's house had always been like paradise to me. Think homemade quilts, knitted throws, and cross-stitched pillows on every piece of furniture. Her house always smelled like April Fresh Downy and chocolate chip cookies. Each time I'd visited her over the years, I'd always wished I could stay forever. I could breathe here. I felt free here, and I was myself here—the real me. And I knew Gigi would always be here for me, no matter what.

Relief covered me like a warm blanket as Cole pulled over to park at the curb. "Thanks for the ride," I mumbled, keeping my tear-filled eyes aimed at the house and my face turned away from his.

"Hey, are you okay?"

I swiped the back of my hand beneath my eyes before turning to face him. "Oh, yeah. I'm totally fine."

"Okay." The sympathetic tone of his voice told me he knew I was full of crap. "I'll help you carry your stuff inside. Sit tight, and I'll get it for you."

"Thanks," I murmured, slamming my eyes shut as he opened his door and got out.

"Is that my baby girl I see?" I threw open my door as Gigi burst onto the front porch with Sir Basil hot on her heels, barking his furry little brain out and hopping up and down at her side.

I lost it. Tears ran down my face with abandon as I stepped out and ran to her. The last couple of months had been too much for me. I could admit it now that I was here and safe to let my emotions get the best of me. I needed a hug from my Gigi, dang it. I'd been hanging on by a thread, which had just unraveled.

Gigi was what I always wanted to be like when I grew up. She was fun, driven, savvy, and smart. But most of all, she loved her girls with her whole heart—Mom, my sisters, and I were her pride and joy, and she always made sure we knew it.

We were tall and curvy, just like her, and had brown eyes like hers, but her hair wasn't brown like ours anymore. She had gorgeous, soft silver waves that fell to her shoulders. She was stylish and beautiful and always smelled like Chanel No. 5 and cookies. She felt like home.

"I missed you so much," I cried into her shoulder as she gathered me close. "Oh no! Your ankle." I tried to pull away, but she wouldn't let me.

"It's fine, honey. I need a big squeeze from my Madi, and I'm not done getting it." Basil licked my ankle before scampering into the house, and I laughed.

"I needed this too. I'm so glad I'm finally here."

She pulled back to take my cheeks between her palms, brushing my tears away with her thumbs. "Look at you. Still pretty as a picture. We're going to have fun together, you and me." She looked past me as Cole approached from his truck. "Thank you for getting my granddaughter home safe, Cole. I appreciate it."

"My pleasure." The deep timbre of his voice sent a shiver up my spine. "I'll take these bags inside for you." He nodded in my direction with a grin. Damn, his voice was deep and gravelly, like hot guy ASMR. I could listen to him talk all day. Even though he was nowhere near me, I swear I could feel his heat against my back. Goose bumps raced across the nape of my neck as his voice sent a shiver up my spine.

"Thank you so much, Cole. I owe you a coffee, a beer, or maybe a batch of brownies."

"You don't owe me a thing." He looked at me indulgently. His blue eyes sparkled into mine as if he found me irresistible. "I'm happy I was around to help out. But I am tempted to take you up on the brownies. If they're half as good as Gigi's, I'll be in heaven."

"Uh..." I mumbled at a loss for words as Gigi laughed at my side.

"They're even better, honey. Madi is a wonderful baker. She learned from the best, didn't you, sweetie?" She winked at me.

"I sure did."

He passed with my suitcases, grinning at us as he crossed the yard to the porch. "Would you like these in the guest room?" he asked.

"For now. She'll be staying in the apartment above the bakery soon enough."

"I will?" I followed Gigi to the house, watching Cole walk up the stairs.

"Yep. I have it all ready for you. But I'll show you around tomorrow. Tonight, we're having a girls' dinner together."

"That sounds perfect to me." I inhaled deeply, smiling when I caught the familiar scents of chocolate, fresh laundry, and something else. "Did you make lasagna?" I asked, thankful that it wasn't a cloud of Basil's canine toots I was smelling as he sauntered through his doggie door.

"I sure did. I have all your favorites waiting for you in the kitchen. And you'll need your own space while you're here, so I fixed up the apartment for you. Maybe this time I can convince you to stay in Cozy Creek. I have a good feeling about this visit, and Basil does too. He's been missing his morning walks."

"Ahh, I see. You have ulterior motives. Is your ankle even sprained?" I joked.

"Unfortunately, yes, it is. I took a bad turn on a Cha Cha Slide at the community center and fell hard. I twisted it something fierce. This boot I have to wear is legit, I'm afraid."

"I'm so sorry you got hurt." I winced. "And I'm also sorry I accused you of fibbing about it."

She tossed her head back with a laugh. "No apologies; I've earned that accusation over the years with my sneaky ways. And I'll be okay, especially now that you're here with me and rid of that albatross you've been hauling around for the last five years. Now that he's gone, I can finally make you see that you belong right here in Cozy Creek." Gigi was never fond of Ross, hence her nickname for him, Ross the Albatross.

"Okay, first, it was only five years, which I admit was a colossal waste of my time. Second, sometimes I wish I could stay, but Mom needs me. You know that."

"Your mama can hire another event planner. You only get one life to live, Madi. And if you want to stay here in Cozy Creek after my ankle gets better, you will. I'll make sure of it."

"Wow. That was way too real after the day I've had."

"All in due time, my love. Okay? We have plenty of time to talk everything through."

"Yeah, we have time," I whispered, already half hoping she'd be able to convince me to stay.

Collectively, we turned to the staircase as Cole made his way down. "You're all set in the guest room. Let me know if you need help getting into the apartment tomorrow. I'll be by the bakery in the morning after my jog, Gigi. But I'm happy to stop here and grab your things for you first, Madi."

"You're so sweet. Thank you. But I think I can manage. I don't want to put you out any more than I already have."

"It's no trouble at all. Let me know if you change your mind. Gigi has my number. Have a good evening, ladies." His blue eyes pierced the distance between us, moving over my face before settling on mine, studying me with a curious intensity before featherlike laugh lines crinkled at the corners, and he smiled. *Damn...*

I couldn't help but think we had chemistry. Did he feel it too? Or was this just a bunch of misplaced wishful thinking on my part? Anything to distract from my own problems, right?

Once he closed the door behind himself, Gigi turned to me with a satisfied grin. "He likes you. I can already tell. Just like I knew he would."

"He's a nice guy and your neighbor. Plus, he grew up across the street from you. *You're* the one he likes," I insisted.

"Well, we'll see about that, won't we?" She had mischief in her sparkling eyes. But to be fair, she always had that look about her.

"No meddling," I halfheartedly warned. "Promise me that whatever you have planned in your adorable little head, Georgia Renee Hale, you'll unplan it right now."

"Oh, you full-named me; this is serious," she teased before donning a more earnest expression. "I would never meddle in affairs of the heart, honey. If I were a meddler, they would have discovered Ross the Albatross's body at the bottom of the Cozy Creek Lake eons ago, right? That little turd, stringing you along like he did. I still want to give him a piece of my mind. He better not show his face in this town ever again, or I'll—"

"Fair enough," I cut her off before she could get into an entire rant. Gigi had a temper, and it could get ugly. "You made your point, and I agree—he turned out to be the obtuse commitment phobe you always said he was. But obviously, I'll still be keeping an eye on you."

She held both hands up. "I'm the picture of innocence, I swear. Let's have an early dinner and open a bottle of wine, shall we? Enough talk about meddling, planning, and matchmaking, okay? All I want is for you to be here, spending time with me, happy and content. And maybe—later, not tonight—start planning your future here in Cozy Creek."

"That sounds perfect. I'm ready to get our time together started. And in the spirit of being comfortable and content, I will run upstairs, steal one of your caftans for the night, and dive face-first into a huge plate of lasagna."

I knew she was attempting to appease me by saying she wouldn't try to set me up with Cole, but I didn't care. Gigi was harmless. All she wanted was for me to be happy. Whatever machinations she had dreamed up wouldn't amount to much. I wasn't truly worried.

"I'll meet you at the table, my darling."

"You have yourself a dinner date." I laughed as Basil barked in agreement from his bed in the corner, then flopped over to go back to sleep.

CHAPTER 4

Cole

Against my will, I woke up to my blaring phone alarm. I'd tossed and turned all night and woke in a cold sweat. Anxiety seemed to have taken over my dreams again, and I was getting sick of it.

With bleary eyes, I managed to shower and start a load of laundry before knocking on the kids' doors to wake them for school.

I could already tell this would be a coffee-fueled day as I filled my mug from the pot, which, thankfully, I'd remembered to set the timer on before going to bed last night.

I bought this house from my parents after I got married. They retired and moved to their mountain cabin, and I needed a place to raise a family. I'd lived here my entire life and planned to stay forever. The sprawling ranch house was perfect for raising kids, with plenty of room and a huge backyard.

After helping Madi yesterday, I swung past my ex-wife's place across town to pick up the kids. True to my word, we grabbed takeout pizza on the way home, and then I crashed early.

Though riddled with fits and bursts of wakefulness, sleep had brought a modicum of clarity and made me realize my interest in Madi was exactly as nuts as I had thought it to be. I didn't have the capacity to add another complication to my life. I had two kids to care for, and according to Gigi, Madi was barely thirty. At thirty-eight, I was too old to entertain those ideas about her, no matter how captivating I found her to be.

I needed to focus on my family and repair the damage caused by the divorce. Lord knows my ex wasn't interested in it. Sherry was too busy flaunting her new marriage all over town to care about how it affected the kids. One of us should make them a priority.

"Hey, Dad." My oldest, Natalie, beamed at me as she entered the kitchen and slung her backpack over a chair at the table. She was cheerful, her long brown hair tied in a haphazard knot on top of her head, her big, blue eyes, just like mine, wide awake and raring to go. Who was this kid?

"Morning." I attempted an adequate smile back as I wondered who she had gotten her love of mornings from since it certainly was not from me.

Maybe she got it from my dad. He had always been annoyingly cheery in the morning. He always said life was like a mirror. *It will smile at you if you smile at it.* I flipped the mirror off this morning and had no idea what that said about me.

"Can I drive to school today?" At six-months to sixteen, she was hell-bent on getting full use of her learner's permit. Her hopeful grin made me smile despite my exhaustion as I sipped my first dose of coffee and began packing the kids' lunches for school.

I shook out a plastic bag and stuffed it with the turkey sandwich I had just finished making and aimed a sidelong glance in her direction. "Sure, as long as you remember to slow down on the left turns, okay? Your mom mentioned something about Evan hitting his head on the window yesterday."

She slid onto a barstool on the island, her face apologetic. "That corner snuck up on me. I swear I'll be more careful and pay better attention. I already said sorry to Evan, and he forgave me. He actually said the worse I am at driving, the better he'll look when he starts learning. Rude, right?"

With a chuckle, I took the keys from my pocket and tossed them to her. "You got this," I encouraged. "Steady as she goes, okay?"

"Right. Steady as she goes. Thanks, Dad."

"Evan, it's time to go!" I shouted. "We're running late. And Natalie, listen, even if you're behind schedule, it's no excuse to speed. It's not worth the risk. I've seen the results firsthand, okay? It's better to show up late than maimed or dead. It's grim, but advice you need to take to heart."

"I know. I'll be the most careful driver ever. I want you and Mom to trust me and possibly buy me a car for my birthday . . ."

I huffed a laugh. "You're a good kid, even if you are a bit delusional." A new car for myself wasn't even in the budget, let alone one for Natalie.

"Worth a try." She grabbed her backpack and headed to the door. "I'll get it started and back out of the garage, okay?"

"I'll round up your brother and meet you in the driveway."

Except Natalie wasn't in the driveway with the truck when I arrived outside. She was across the street chatting with Gigi and Madi. "Hey, Dad!" She waved me over and then gestured to Madi. "I never get to talk to this one."

Seeing her again was like a shot of espresso to my senses—jarring, instantly warming my veins to send my heart into an erratic thumping beat in my chest. I watched her on Gigi's front porch, her eyes a little sleepy, with a soft grin gracing her face. I was content to shake her from my mind earlier while I was busy getting our morning started. But being faced with her now, everything didn't seem so cut and dry.

Madi laughed and wiggled her fingers at me. "*'This one'* says good morning and thanks you again for getting her here safely yesterday."

"She has a name, Nat," Evan teased. "I don't remember what it is, but I know it isn't '*this one*.'" He was almost fourteen, and he would go for it any time he had the opportunity to get the better of his big sister.

"I know that," she ground out, embarrassed. "Riley and Abigail are here all the time. I hardly ever get to see *Madison*." She glared at Evan before continuing. "See? I know her name, Ev."

"No worries," Madison confirmed with a laugh. "I knew exactly what you meant, Natalie." Her eyes met mine. "I appreciate you, Cole. And since we'll be neighbors of a sort, you can all call me Madi. Brownies are on the menu today. It's my way to thank you and make you like me."

I laughed inside because I already liked her. Way more than I liked any of my other neighbors.

"We already like you. If you're related to Gigi, then you're cool," Evan assured her. "But we'll still take the brownies."

She burst out laughing, and I couldn't look away. Her hair shone in the early morning light, but her smile was even brighter. She was stunning. "Thank you, Madi." I grinned at her. "As you can see, we have some brownie fans in the family."

Nat beamed at Madi. "I get to drive to school today. I'm going to go pull the truck out. See you guys later. Let's go, Dad!"

She hugged Gigi before running across the street and into the now-open garage, with Evan following close behind her. They'd grown up being close to Gigi, just as my brothers and I had—we all loved her.

"So, I have the day off. Feel free to text me if you need help getting set up in the apartment."

"We may take you up on that, sweetheart," Gigi answered. "Can I give Madi your number?"

"Of course. What's your number, Madi? I'll add it right now."

She gave it to me, and I sent a quick text, grinning when her notification went off. "Gotcha. Don't hesitate to use that number." I flicked two fingers out in a wave and joined the kids across the street at the truck.

"I like her," Natalie announced from the driver's seat after I got inside. "She's super nice and totally funny."

"And she's really pretty too," Evan added. He waited to see my reaction before hopping into the back seat, so I kept my face as blank as possible.

"So pretty," Nat agreed, oblivious to everything since she was currently busy adjusting the mirrors and the driver's seat. "Her clothes are amazing, and her makeup looks like a professional did it. Maybe I can get her to teach me to wing my eyeliner better. Mom sucks at it too. After we went back-to-school shopping, we were cracking up practicing. Remember when she bought me all that new makeup?"

"Yeah, I remember." I did not want to talk about my ex or speak badly of her in front of the kids, so I quickly steered the subject away. "Madi is a beautiful woman," I admitted as Natalie fired up the truck and slowly backed out of the garage.

"So you *do* like her," Evan declared. "I knew it when you got her phone number. That was pretty smooth."

"Wait. What? You got her number?" Nat threw the truck back into park and spun to face me. "Of course, you should like her. I mean, who wouldn't? She's gorgeous. Oooh, you could ask her on a date."

"I got her number if she needed help moving into the apartment above Gigi's. Nothing more. I'm being neighborly."

"Take her to the movies or one of the fall things coming up in town. That's a neighborly thing to do," Natalie suggested.

"You should take her to the Fall Ball," Evan added. "Or the fire department fundraiser. Or to the haunted pumpkin patch. Maybe she'll get scared and hold your hand."

Cozy Creek was not only a tourist destination; we were collectively obsessed with anything you could celebrate—holidays, changing seasons, high school sports. Any event that would warrant a parade, decorations, or a festival of some sort was wildly popular around these parts.

Fall was a favorite, probably because it was so naturally gorgeous here that even the most curmudgeonly of our residents couldn't help but enjoy it.

Even the fire station got into the seasonal spirit: The Cozy Creek Fire Brigade Fall Fundraiser was one of our most popular events, and we raised a lot of money every year. I had a meeting scheduled with the event organizer next week to start the planning process for this year's festivities.

I didn't answer them. I was not in the mood to argue with them or discuss my love life. Plus, what was that saying about protesting too much? If I kept talking about her, my interest would become apparent, and I'd never hear the end of it.

"Earth to Dad," Nat's voice cut into my thoughts. "Ask her out. We don't mind, we both agreed. We think it's time. Move on," she added derisively. "I mean, Mom sure as heck did."

"What? Nah, I'm not quite ready to start dating yet. And I don't think the two of you are really ready for that either. Am I right?"

Her eyes went soft. "I'm sorry, Dad."

I didn't know what was worse. Having her see me knock the crap out of her now stepfather or the pity I saw shining in her eyes as she looked at me from across the truck.

"Hey, don't worry about me. It is what it is, and I'm okay. I promise you."

"He's fine, Nat. He's got us. We're all going to be okay."

"Damn straight, Ev." I turned back to shoot him a grin. "You two are all I need, all right?"

He smirked. "Yup, and when you finally decide to ask Gigi's hot granddaughter out, we'll be there to make sure you don't mess it up."

Natalie burst out laughing and shoved my shoulder. "Heck yeah, we will."

"Let's nip this in the bud. My dating life, or lack thereof, is not up for discussion. I love you guys more than anything in the world, but we won't be discussing this around the dinner table. Do you get me?"

"Sure, we get you, Dad," Natalie mumbled as she turned onto the road that led into town. The high and middle schools were close to home—just right around the corner. Nat was a sophomore, and Evan was in eighth grade. After Natalie got out, I'd drive Evan to the middle school and head to the firehouse.

Was I subconsciously hoping to run into Madi today?

Unfortunately, yes, I was.

All night long, I had been thinking about her. Instead of getting her out of my head, my brain had latched on to her, dissecting, remembering, and appreciating the vivid colors of her hair in the sun, the heady scent of her perfume in the cab, the way her cheeks would blush pink with a shyness I found absolutely riveting. I didn't know her well enough to like her this much—yet. Damn it, no *yet*. There could be no *yet* between Madi and me.

She was Gigi's granddaughter.

She was too close to home.

Above all, I wasn't ready, and neither were my kids, no matter what they said.

It was too bad she was unwittingly about to become part of my daily routine as I, along with most of the firefighters in Cozy Creek, spent a lot of time at the Confectionery. Gigi's coffee was terrible, but her breakfast sandwiches and protein shakes were the best. Plus, it was only a quick walk around the corner from the firehouse.

I was off work today, but that didn't mean I didn't need to get a workout in. After dropping Evan off, I swung into the firehouse parking lot to meet up with my buddy Pace and youngest brother Tate for a run. Both were also firefighters.

"Hey," Tate said, already warming up. "Pace isn't going to make it today. It's just you, me, and the fascinating text Gigi sent me last night. Madi, huh?"

"What?"

"You and Madi. You two are a thing now? I think it's great."

My eyebrows shot to my hairline. I was taken aback. Had someone been reading my mind? "There is no *thing* between Madi and me. I have no idea what you're talking about."

"You sure about that? I didn't believe it, but I do now. You're being kind of defensive." He paused to wait for my reaction, frowning when he didn't get one. "Anyway, Gigi said to ask you about her and report back. I'm letting you know upfront. I'm no matchmaker. I'll tell her whatever you want me to."

"That's good. I'm glad to hear it. Thank you. I have no desire to be match-made."

His lips quirked up at the corner. "No matter how gorgeous she is, right?"

"That has no bearing on anything. Can we run?"

He swept an arm out in invitation. "Be my guest."

I took off down the street faster than my usual pace. The light breeze whipped across my skin as my feet flew across the paved sidewalk. I couldn't get away fast enough.

"Wait up." Tate huffed at my side when he caught up. "It's almost like you're running from something."

"I'm running from you." I shot him a sidelong glare. "I'm not interested in being match-made by you or anyone. And I'm not interested in being psychoanalyzed either, for that matter."

"Touchy this morning, are you?"

"Nope." I ran faster as he burst into laughter behind me. He knew me too well, the ass.

We took our usual path down the center of town and through the park, with him hot on my heels as I deliberately outpaced him. I was in no mood to talk. But ever since the divorce, I never was.

Since my marriage exploded, I have kept everything inside.

Who could possibly want to know how much I still wondered where I'd gone wrong?

Or how much I wish I had done things differently?

Or especially, how deep down, I was glad she was gone.

What the fuck is wrong with me?

She was the mother of my children, and when I realized her cheating upset me for all the wrong reasons, I was ashamed of myself. The hit to my pride felt worse than the hit to my heart. *She* didn't break me, but having everyone know what she did to me almost did.

What kind of husband feels that way? A terrible one.

Had I ever truly loved her? What was love supposed to feel like anyway?

Our marriage had its fair share of trouble, but I had not realized until it was over how unhappy I had been.

The guilt ate at me constantly. I had no idea how I was supposed to feel.

"Wait up, man!" Tate shouted.

We'd made it to the park. I ran off the trail and slowed to a stop. My chest heaved as I panted, entirely out of breath. I leaned forward to put my hands on my knees.

"Damn, bro. You're running like something is chasing you," he accused when he finally caught up to me. "And we both know it's not me."

"Sorry," I muttered without meeting his eyes. "I'm all keyed up this morning. Couldn't sleep worth a shit."

"It's all good." He lifted the hem of his shirt to wipe the sweat from his face. "Don't give yourself a heart attack, okay?"

"I won't. I'm fine. Let's cool down and walk to Gigi's."

"Yeah, you almost killed me. I should have just let you go." He shoved my shoulder with a good-natured grin. "Listen, I'm here to talk about whatever had you hauling ass through town whenever you're ready. We all are."

"I'm fine. No need to talk."

"Of course you're fine. Denial is totally not your go-to method of coping with your problems." Tate's side-eye had been perfected through the years. Even though he was the younger of my two brothers, he was the wisest in many ways.

"Whatever."

I could admit—to myself—I could be a hothead. My temper sometimes got the best of me, no matter how hard I fought against it.

Our middle brother, Quinn, was similar to me in that regard. Poor Tate had years of practice playing peacemaker between us. Tate was a firefighter like me. Quinn was a mechanic and had taken over running our father's auto shop in town—Sutter's Cozy Creek Automotive. He'd been the one to pick up Madi's VW.

"Will Madi be there? She's going to work for Gigi, right?" I didn't answer him as I stalked up the street, sick of this entire morning already. "Did I hit on a sore spot? I didn't mean to."

"It's fine. And yeah, she'll probably be there," I bit out. "She's moving into the empty apartment on the top floor."

"Ahh, I see. So she'll be around a lot then. Hmm."

"Don't get started. I had it bad enough from the kids already today. They seem to think I should ask her out."

"Maybe you should. There's nothing wrong with moving on. Sherry sure did." He backed off with a shrug after catching the look on my face. "Or not. It's all the same to me. But there's no sense in waiting around—"

"I'm not waiting around. Jesus, Tate. It's over with her. After what she did to me, I'd never even consider taking her back—"

"That's not where I was going with this, but good to know." His eyes softened in sympathy, which he knew I hated. "Nobody thinks you're waiting around for her, Cole."

"I don't want to talk about this anymore. Let's get out of here." I ran off, not wanting to hear any more, passing a few other runners on the trail.

"Will you slow the fuck down?" A gasping Tate huffed at my side when he caught up again. "We don't have to talk about the divorce. I'm sorry I brought it up in the first place."

I stopped in my tracks; I owed him an apology. "No, I'm the one who's sorry. I acted like a jerk, and I have no excuse other than I've been so fucking exhausted lately. I hate it when the kids are gone. The house somehow seems to get bigger when they're at Sherry's. And when they're home, I run myself ragged to make them feel like nothing has changed. But it has. Everything is different, and I don't know how to act around them anymore. I don't want them worrying about me, and I don't want them to feel weird in their own house."

"I get it. No more running. Let's walk, or I'm going to drop dead."

"Yeah, sorry about—everything." We walked the rest of the jogging trail leading to the park's edge to the sidewalk.

"It's okay. I get you." He slapped me on the shoulder before we rounded the corner toward Gigi's. "You know I do. Change is hard, and you're in an impossible situation. I don't know what to say other than take it one day at a time and be there when they need you. That's really all you can do."

"You're right. Thanks."

"Of course I'm right. It's what all of us have been doing to handle your grumpy ass. One day at a time."

CHAPTER 5

Madi

Along with her house, Gigi's Cozy Creek Confectionery was my favorite place to be. She'd been in this location on the corner of Creekview and Main Street since I was born. This was more than just a place to buy sweets or order a birthday cake. It was timeless; traditions began here. People came here year after year to order birthday cakes for their children, holiday pies for their parties, or cookies and candies for a quick treat to add cheer to their day.

Gigi had created a gathering place where locals and newcomers always felt welcomed. You could stay awhile, catch up with friends, enjoy a hot cup of tea, and relax with one of Gigi's famous chocolate chip cookies.

Early morning sunlight shone through the floor-to-ceiling plate glass windows lining the front of the stately brick building. I smiled to myself as I took in the way their rays twinkled through the white etched logo that emblazoned the store's name wrapped around an adorable cupcake.

I'd left Gigi at one of the sidewalk tables to sit with her friends while I headed inside. She said she'd catch up after she said hello to them, and I was glad. I needed a moment alone to get the melancholy and nostalgia out of my system.

I'd grown up begging my mom to let me spend my weekends here with Gigi, and she had usually let me. Only in the last few years had I spent less time here, and I regretted it. I'd missed it here, and I hadn't realized how much until we had pulled into her parking space out front.

Sure, there were plenty of weird things about small towns, everyone knowing my business being at the top of the list. But there was a lot of good stuff too. People cared. Last night, I'd spied a stack of casseroles from her book club in her fridge. Having neighbors like Cole, who were willing to pick up a random relative from the side of the road, was on the list too. She had loads of help before I had even arrived in town.

I recalled learning to bake at Gigi's side, decorating pastries and cakes, making candies, and every treat you could imagine. I could run this shop if I had to, and in my secret dreams, I hoped one day I would. Memories washed over me as I moved through the shop, outweighing the negative aspects of small-town life I'd thought of when I was stuck in my car.

My heels clicked over the rustic wooden floor as I wound through the bistro-style tables and chairs toward the display cases and service counter in the rear. Each round table was decorated with various differently colored rosebuds in tiny hand-blown glass vases atop a crisp white tablecloth. It was as gorgeous as ever in here. Gigi had somehow combined the sophisticated charm of a French café with the casual warmth of a small-town diner. It was as cozy as it was gorgeous.

The scents filling my senses were familiar and heavenly—vanilla, spices, chocolate, and fresh-baked bread—if I could bottle the smell and sell it, I'd be a billionaire.

She started as strictly a confectionery, selling various candies and sweet baked goods, but later added fresh bread and other types of pastries to her ever-growing and changing menu.

Over the last few years, she'd added protein shakes and breakfast sandwiches to her repertoire. Now, she was the unofficial breakfast stop for the Cozy Creek Fire Brigade, much to the delight of her older and primarily female early-morning patronage. It was a win-win, she had informed me. Her friends now had eye candy to accompany their tea and scones, and the fire brigade had another place to hang out aside from Bookers Pub.

I froze when I spotted Cole and his brother Tate at one of the tables with breakfast sandwiches and protein smoothies in front of them. They each wore that loose-fitting tank top over tight jogger pants and baggy shorts combo that was popular lately. I watched him, mesmerized. His thick, muscled arms flexed as he raised his shake to take a sip. I bit my lip as his luscious, completely kissable lips wrapped around his straw, and the last traces of sweat ran down his temple.

Say good morning, stupid. Don't just stand there staring at him.

Cole looked up as I got closer and smiled at me.

Why did I have to find him so attractive?

His brother was equally good-looking, but I didn't care one bit about him.

My knees wobbled as I slowed, hesitating to get any closer. So much for my determination to steer clear of him.

"Good morning, Cole. Hey, Tate."

"It's been a while. How's it going?" Tate's sympathetic smile made me cringe inside.

Did everyone in town know about my pathetic breakup? Probably.

I sucked it up and plastered a huge smile on my face. "I'm good, thanks. I'm just happy to be here to help Gigi—"

"Mornin', Madi." Cole's gaze was as soft as a caress. My feet drifted ever closer to his table as if every time I saw him, the pull would be stronger. I had to fight the startling urge to jump into his lap. "Are you working today?"

"No, I'm just here to get reacquainted with the place. I haven't been here baking with Gigi in ages—"

"Hey, girl."

"Kenzie?"

I spun, thrilled to find my cousin Kenzie behind the counter. It didn't matter how much time we spent apart. She was the kind of person I would always be close to. We'd spent our lives picking up right where we left off. Distance didn't matter when it came to Kenzie. She would always be my bestie. Us being cousins was just a bonus.

She was practically my twin with her long chocolate brown hair and heart-shaped face. But she had green eyes lit from within with her naturally effervescent joy instead of brown like mine. She was full of mischief too, like right now, as she spun in a circle and waved at me with both hands. She wore white slacks, a white button-down shirt, and the shop's official pink and white checkered apron. She clearly worked here.

"Kenzie! I didn't know you worked for Gigi! Why didn't you tell me?"

I beamed from ear to ear as I rushed to the counter and wrapped her in a hug. We were the same height, five foot six on the dot.

She was the only child of my aunt Laura, my father's only sibling, and I'd always adored both of them.

"I started last week. I told Gigi not to tell you."

Gigi wrapped an arm around my waist as she joined us at the counter. "Surprise!"

"This is amazing! I'll get to see you every day?"

"Every morning from the crack of dawn until lunch. Midnight Baker takes the late shift. Have you met him? I've never met him. We'll meet him, Madi, even if we have to stalk him. Does he even exist, Gigi? I swear that man never sees the sun, and I find it totally suspicious. Is he a vampire?"

"Midnight Baker?" I questioned. "I haven't had the pleasure. Spill it, Gigi."

Kenzie answered before Gigi could even open her mouth. "He's the mysterious and hopefully sexy dude who bakes all the bread. He's always gone by the time I get here, like *poof*." She waved her hands in the air for emphasis. "He probably turns into a bat and flies away inside of that cloud of delicious fresh baked fumes he leaves behind like a clarion call for all the carb junkies in this town. I'm tempted to hide behind the dumpster to catch him as he leaves. But getting up is hard enough already without adding being early to my sunrise to-do list. I am not a morning person. At all. Ask me how much coffee I've already had today."

"He exists, sweetheart," Gigi replied with an amused sigh as Kenzie held up three fingers, indicating she was already three cups deep. This was clearly Kenzie's latest preoccupation, which she found funny. "He's shy, is all. Don't go chasing him away. Think of the bread we won't be able to eat if you scare him off, my darling. The sourdough alone is worth being discreet. Try for me? Pretty please."

"*Pfft*. Shy? That's it? Okay. I've been building him up in my mind since I started working here. He'd better be hot too, and that's all I'm going to say on the matter, for now anyway."

Gigi and I exchanged a glance. It seemed like Kenzie was still as boy-crazy as ever, or was it man-crazy now? We'd get into so much trouble whenever I was here as a kid, sneaking off to run around with her friends at the park. I'd always had so much fun with her.

"Anyhoo," Gigi said, taking my hand and squeezing it. "Let's get you upstairs. I'll show you around the apartment, get you settled in, and then you can start working tomorrow."

"I heard you'll be the counter girl slash supervisor slash go-to Queen of the Confectionery until the sprained ankle boot of doom is gone." Kenzie nudged my arm with her elbow. "How much supervising you'll actually do is up for debate since this one will be sitting at her table all day taking it easy." She air-quoted the phrase "take it easy," and I laughed. I had no illusion that I'd be in charge and wouldn't have it any other way.

"Queen of the Confectionery?" I laughed.

"Yeah, Gigi does it all around here, but mostly, she makes sure everyone is happy. No one ever notices she's ruling this place with an iron fist."

"Ahh, maybe I can be the princess then. We both know she'll be right over at her table keeping an eye on us."

"You'll be the princess of pastries, and I'll be the cupcake queen. We need those on our name badges, Gigi."

"Okay, girls. Tease me all you want. You know I love having you both here with me. We're going to have such fun, the three of us."

She was a force, and I aspired to be like her when I grew up. Yeah, so maybe I was already grown. I should take a page from her book and start living my life with more purpose.

Caring what people thought of me had gotten me nowhere I wanted to be. I had just turned thirty and was working a job I liked but would rather be doing something else. I was not married, had no kids, and didn't even have a cat or a dog because Ross had insisted he was allergic.

Allergic to pets? Doubtful since he had kept a picture of his childhood dog on his bedside table. I'd since come to the conclusion what he was really allergic to was a real commitment.

I'd let everything I wanted fall to the wayside to keep Ross in my life.

I felt so stupid and frustrated with myself for having fought so hard and so long for a relationship that was one-sided and passionless from the beginning. I should have known better.

Change was afoot, and I suddenly couldn't wait to get started. I decided to be different when I returned to my real life in Colorado Springs.

Madison 2.0 would take charge and be confident in all aspects of her life. No one would dare walk all over me ever again, not this girl. I would get a cat too—no, two cats—I deserved to have something cute and fluffy to love. I was now officially off the market, about to become a cat mom, and it felt freaking great.

"Let's get to it!" I clapped my hands together.

"I'm so happy you're excited about this."

"Wait 'til you meet Kenny," Kenzie said.

My head whipped to the side. "Who? What? Kenny?"

"You'll see. He's the latest."

"Yeah, about that," Gigi hedged. "Um, come on. I'll show you."

"Okay..."

I followed Gigi to the interior entrance of the two apartments above the shop, wrapping an arm around her waist and helping her climb the stairs.

She already had a tenant in the unit across from mine. She'd told me at dinner last night he was one of the town's Huber drivers. Old Jimmy Huber had seen an opportunity and jumped on it. He had a couple of guys working for him, and my soon-to-be neighbor, Noah, was one of them.

"Okay. Listen." She stopped. Hesitating with her hand on the doorknob. "I didn't tell you this at dinner last night, but the apartment already has a few tenants."

Hell to the no.

"Roommates? I—"

"No. Not quite." She threw open the door and waved me through.

Three cats were asleep on the most adorable purple and white striped sofa I'd ever seen. It was covered with a rainbow array of throw pillows and a sunshine-yellow throw blanket that I remembered watching her knit with rapt attention when I was a little kid.

A coffee table was in front of the couch, with a squat vase filled with marigolds in the middle, while a fuchsia wing chair with a tall back sat perpendicular. Its twin was across the room, flanking the fireplace—either chair would be a great reading spot. I could picture myself with a book, feet tucked beneath myself as I read the day away.

"Ahh, Gigi! Oh my god!" I didn't know where to look—at the cats or the newly redecorated apartment interior. It was like she had raided a cottagecore-themed tag sale. Or, more likely, her attic. Grandma chic was the dominating theme in the space, and I had fallen in love with it at first sight.

To my left was a fireplace framed with two massive bookshelves, while straight ahead was an enormous bay window overlooking the street. Soft light filtered through panels of lacy white curtains, and in the distance, I could see the craggy glow of the Rocky Mountains. The window seat was upholstered with the same purple and white fabric as the couch—I could see myself there, curled up with a book and the cats.

To the right was the entrance to the kitchen and a door leading to a half bathroom.

It seemed that Gigi had taken note of everything I'd told her I liked over the years and had stuffed this place full of it.

I spun in a circle, taking everything in. It was a girlie paradise, with pastels, flowers, cozy, overstuffed furniture, and books, so many books. I took note as my eyes scanned the shelves. All my favorites were present and accounted for, from Jane Austen to the Brontë sisters, Nora Roberts to Charlaine Harris. It was all there.

"Gigi, what did you do?" I burst into ugly tears as I rushed to where she stood and hugged her hard.

There was one bedroom and a full bathroom down a short hallway to the left of the front door, and I couldn't wait to see what she'd done in there. The bathroom had a huge copper clawfoot tub, which I'd always loved to soak in whenever my sisters and I stayed with our mom on holidays.

Gigi had redecorated and transformed this place into the apartment of my dreams, and I couldn't help but wonder what I had done to deserve this.

My eyes shot to the shelf next to a little intricately carved bench in the entryway, and I reached out to grab a tiny glass cat figurine. "Hey, I remember this." I sniffled through tears and tried to recall where I'd seen it before.

"I found it at the house, under the guest room bed years ago, tucked into your old Hello Kitty suitcase. You were like a cute little crow, always stealing everyone's stuff, remember that? You'd snatch it if it had sparkles or a cat on it."

"Uh, I forgot I used to do that." I hid my face in my hands. "I'm so sorry. I guess I just really loved cats. This is humiliating."

"Ah, don't worry, honey. It was cute." She hobbled over to the couch to plop down and pet the cats. "We all thought so. Anyway, look around; you might find some memories tucked here and there."

"Oh my god. I'm so embarrassed."

"Pfft, don't be."

I smiled as a sleek black cat wound through my legs. I reached down and scooped her up.

"That's Sage," Gigi informed me. "The Maine Coon is Victor, and the chubby orange tub of trouble is Kenny. Sage started hanging around in the alley, and before I knew it—" She shrugged lightly. "I had a cat to love. But Basil isn't fond of cats, and of course, I'm allergic to them, so I moved her in here."

"And the other two?"

"They're her buddies. Not long after I set her up in here, she got out through the window and came back with Victor and Kenny. I came in to feed her, and they were in a pile on the old couch, sleeping as soundly as could be. I adore them. I'd take them to the house to live with me, but as you can see"—she started violently sneezing—"I can't. Kenzie, Cole's kids, and I visit them every day. It's been a little over a week, and they seem to like it here. The vet said they were not chipped, and they weren't fixed. I checked the local lost pets boards, and they're not on them. So I kept them."

"Say no more. I love everything about this. Why didn't Cole take them? I mean, if his kids like them and all."

"Well, he wanted to, but—" She hesitated before finishing. "Um, I knew you would be coming and, I uh—"

"Ah, I see. You're sweetening the pot with the new décor, cats, lasagna last night, and coffee cake this morning. You're trying to get me to stay in Cozy Creek. Am I right?"

Her grin was infectious. "Perhaps."

"Well, you're scoring points left and right. I already love it here, and I always have. And I love you so much; you're my favorite thing about Cozy Creek. You know that, don't you?"

"I do know it, and I love you too, my sweetheart. And listen, I've taken them to the vet. They're perfectly healthy, have had all their shots and flea treatments, and I got them fixed. There's nothing for you to do. I've taken care of everything."

By this time, I was already cuddling Sage against my chest, grinning as she purred and butted the top of her head beneath my chin. "We're going to be just fine, aren't we, sweet girl?"

"You have to keep an eye on her," she warned. "That one likes to get out and run around the neighborhood sometimes. She has a wild soul. Victor will be on this couch all day long. And Kenny, he's not all there, if you know what I mean."

"What?"

She patted the top of his head and then scratched beneath his chin. I could hear him purring from across the room. "He's an idiot, honey. He's the dumbest cat I've ever met. He's sweet as can be, though."

"Oh, gotcha. I feel like I should take notes or something."

"You'll be great. You're a cat lady with no cats. We both know this."

"Ha, you're right about that. I might be in heaven right now. I love how you decorated in here."

"I knew you would. The kitchen is stocked with all your favorites, and the bathroom has all kinds of goodies. I know you've always coveted that big bathtub. You have everything you'll need for a nice, long soak."

"Thank you. I might have to keep crying for a few more minutes. But I'm trying so hard not to."

"Don't fight your feelings around me, honey. I'm so happy you're here. But beyond that, you're doing me a huge favor. I can't spend one more day at the shop. I need to sit down on my couch with my foot up. I'm supposed to keep it elevated. Speaking of which, I need to get back down there. Kenzie needs to finish decorating the cookies in the back, and my afternoon helper is off today."

"I should get started now. There is no need for me to hang out up here with nothing to do but get lost in my feels. You join your friends for tea, then go home and get some rest, and I'll take over for you at the Confectionery for the day."

"You're sure?"

"Absolutely. Let's go. I can get to know my new kitty cat besties later." I gave Sage one last cuddle before setting her on the floor, and then I found a box of tissue on the shelf, grabbed one, and dabbed it beneath my eyes. "I'm okay. I got this."

Even if Cole is still down there when I arrive.

CHAPTER 6

Cole

She was cute. She was beautiful. Too fucking irresistible is what she was. I didn't know whether to love or hate how attracted to her I had become.

I shifted my gaze to the window and away from her curvy hips and spectacular heart-shaped ass as she walked up the rear staircase with Gigi. Those heels were going to be the death of me. Her legs went on forever, and I couldn't look away.

"You're different around her," Tate accused in a whisper. "Almost like you are around your kids or Mom or Gigi. You're *nice*. Did you actually smile at her? Did it hurt? Is your face going to be okay?"

"Shut the fuck up," I grumbled before stuffing the rest of my breakfast sandwich into my mouth.

I was glad the other guys weren't here today to witness this. Tate was born giving me shit. The rest of the guys from the firehouse should know better, but they didn't.

He burst into laughter before reaching for his drink. "Thank you for making my point for me." He raised it in a silent toast before taking a sip.

"This stays here." I tapped a fingertip on the table for emphasis.

"I've had enough gossip for ten lifetimes surrounding me lately. I don't need any more."

"Yeah, he doesn't need any more gossip, Tate." Kenzie's laughing voice startled me as she passed by our table on her way back to the counter. "Especially about my cousin," she added under her breath as she pointed to both her eyes, then back at him. "I have my eye on the two of you. I'll be back."

"This is great," I muttered. "Just fucking perfect."

Tate waited until she was out of earshot to continue. "Hey, I won't try to set you up with Madi. I wouldn't do that to you, or the kids, for that matter. Dating after divorce is tricky. I know that better than anyone."

I heaved a sigh. "I know you do. But judging by their reaction to her earlier this morning, they'd probably love it."

"I could see that. She's great. But it doesn't matter. I'm a vault, like always. You can talk to me."

"I appreciate it."

"Doesn't mean I won't keep giving you shit, though," he muttered. "I'll just keep it private between the two of us. I give respectful shit, brotherly shit."

An exasperated smile escaped despite my resolve to remain stern. "Do what you gotta do."

"But she could be good for you. I've always liked her. Just saying."

"She would be good for him." Kenzie pulled up a chair and set her coffee on the table. "Gentlemen. I trust your breakfast was stellar, as usual. Gigi's Confectionery always aims to please."

"Delicious." Tate chuckled. "You have a way with egg whites and turkey bacon that is unmatched."

"Of course I do. But we have bigger fish to fry. I'm sure they'll be down any second. There's zero chance of Madi not working the rest of the day, with Gigi hobbling around like she is."

"Okay . . ." The oddest sense of anticipatory dread combined with a spark of hope shot through me. For some reason, I couldn't wait to hear what she had to say.

"Madi has been through a lot lately. It's not my story to tell, but you should know that she's skittish. She's been hurt, Cole. Take that into consideration before you ask her out. Be extra sweet. Like, get her flowers, make a thing of it, make it special."

Who hurt her? I wanted to know his name so I could teach him a lesson. Gigi had mentioned a breakup, but I had my own stuff going on, so I hadn't paid much attention.

"Who says I'm going to ask her out?"

Tate burst into loud laughter. "This is hilarious. You are so obvious. I told you."

"On that note." I slid my chair back with a loud squeak. "I'm leaving. I hope the two of you have a great rest of the day."

Kenzie put a hand on my shoulder. "Nope, stay. She'll be down in a few minutes. You need to say a proper goodbye to her. She needs one more hit of your sexy self before you go. You know, to keep the idea of you fresh in her mind. Give her something to think about for the rest of the day. Do you know what I mean?"

"I do not know what you mean. Not at all." That was a lie. I sort of knew, but there was no way I would admit to it.

"Yeah, keep it fresh, Cole." Tate had tears running down his face from trying to keep his laughter under control. It was more of a spectacle than if he were outright laughing at me.

"You are both ridiculous." I shook my head and tried to dissociate from this entire bizarre conversation. But my happy place had been out of commission since the divorce. I had been living with the pain and the failure for too long.

"We'll keep it subtle," Kenzie tried to reassure me. "Madi isn't fond of attention either."

"You call this subtle? Thanks a lot."

She tilted her head toward Tate. "You need to practice your poker face, bro. Do better next time."

"Next time?"

"Dude, really? I thought we were in this together now."

"This?" His face scrunched in confusion.

Her eyes rolled before closing as she shook her head from side to side. She was the classic picture of the annoyed female praying for patience.

I shrugged, silently commiserating. Tate could do that to a person. But it was best to keep them from getting ideas about interfering in my business.

"Let me get something straight," I interrupted. "*This*"—I waved a hand between them—"is not happening. Just like I told the kids on the way to school, we will not be discussing my love life—"

Kenzie held up a hand with a smirk. "Oh, don't worry, we won't discuss it *with you*."

"I give up. This is too much. I'm out of here. Talk to you later, Tate. Kenzie, it's been a real pleasure."

"Toodaloo." She waggled her fingers at me before slugging Tate's shoulder. "Let's get down to business." I overheard. "We have plans to make. He's grumpy, but he's the only single guy in this town I'd trust with Madi, and she needs to move on from her dickhead ex."

I grabbed my smoothie and spun toward the door, thinking I might continue my run when I was finished. All I knew was I had to get away from all these nutcases.

The fresh air felt good as I sat at one of the outdoor tables, frowning when my text notification pinged with an incoming message.

> **TATE:** Don't worry. Kenzie went back to work. I told her I was not planning anything behind your back. We're too old for this ridiculous high school bullshit. Madi is a sweet girl, though. Maybe you should think about it.

I didn't bother to reply. But I did manage to relax a bit.

He knew better. Yeah, he'd keep giving me crap, but there was no way he'd let Kenzie get out of control and meddle in my personal life, and I didn't honestly think she would get that carried away, at least not in a harmful way.

I would be fine, totally fine.

Totally fucking fine.

I snagged a table and mindlessly scrolled through my phone while I finished my smoothie. I avoided the eyes of the local passersby; I was in no mood to talk to anyone. Then, I tossed my cup into the trash and headed toward the station. Although I was off today, I often checked in after my workouts.

I heard a slam and a stream of creative cursing as I approached the alleyway behind Gigi's.

Was that Madi?

"Is everything okay back there?" I called out. "It's Cole!"

Never sneak up on a woman. That was one of the many pearls of wisdom my father had doled out to us boys over the years.

I rounded the corner and stepped into a cloud of white dust.

Was that flour?

Madi turned blindly in my direction, her lips pursed as she blew a breath, and a poof of flour hit me in the chest.

"Oh shit. Are you hurt? Let me help."

"I'm not hurt. I spilled a huge flour bin in the kitchen, and it got all over me. I swept it all up, and then the bag split when I dropped it in the can. I should have let Kenzie take care of it like she offered." She laughed and wiped her face with the clean underside of her apron. "This flour is a metaphor for my life. I swear it is. Messy, flying in a million different directions, unsettled, just like me. Never mind. Is it in my hair?" She patted the top of her head. "It is. Isn't it?"

I stifled a laugh as a tiny cloud floated out of her bun. "Uh, pretty much. It's in your eyelashes too. Let me help." I closed the distance between us and reached out to tuck an errant strand of hair behind her ear. I zeroed in on her face. Flour was everywhere.

With a light touch, I ran a finger down the slope of her nose, the dip of her chin. I brushed the flour from her cheeks with my thumbs, all the while holding my breath, not quite believing I was this close to her.

"Hold still. Close your eyes." I blew gently against her face to get the rest off. "There you go."

Rapidly blinking, pretty brown eyes met mine, and I cleared my throat and stepped back. I had to. All I wanted was *more* when it came to her.

"Thanks." There was laughter in her voice, though I could tell she was embarrassed. "There you go, rescuing me again. Is this our thing now?"

I shook my head, unsure how to answer. "If you grab the broom, I'll help you get this cleaned up."

She sighed as her cheeks turned pink beneath the light dusting of remaining flour. "Fair warning, Cole, I'm a lot. It's been what? Twenty minutes tops since I officially started working, and I've already made a mess. I'm a human calamity. A walking disaster."

"No, you're fine. Let me help."

She ran a hand down her apron, brushing off some of the flour to create a powdery white storm between us. "Take the side of the road yesterday, for example. I should have known better than attempting to drive up here in that car. Then, let's see, last month, I locked myself out of my apartment, wearing only my bathrobe, I might add. Then, I had to wait in the hall for my mother to show up with the extra key. That was fun. I've been in too many precarious hiking situations to count, so I've given up the hobby. I've been banned from the gym in my apartment building—treadmills and I do not get along. You know what? I'll stop talking now. Explanations will not be necessary. I'll be in town for the next four to six weeks, or however long it takes for Gigi's ankle to heal. You'll find out for yourself, and I apologize in advance for whatever's gonna go down. You're a firefighter; I can guarantee there will be at least one call while I'm here that involves something I've done. You can ask Gigi all about it—"

"Nah, I don't need to ask her. I've heard a few things throughout the years." I was teasing her to lighten her mood. But the look on her face gave me pause. I'd put my foot in my mouth and felt terrible.

"So, you already know what a mess I am. That's good, no surprises." She cringed. "I'm already mortified, and it's only my first full day here. I'm so sorry." Her voice sounded a long way off. It was small. She was embarrassed, and I hated that I was partially the cause of it.

"No worries, okay? Any time I run into you, it makes my day. I mean it. I'm sorry I embarrassed you. That was not my intention."

"It's okay. You didn't embarrass me. I'm just perpetually embarrassed, and it's not your fault."

"Please don't be embarrassed around me. I've been a spectacle before. My divorce and how it went down was fodder for local gossip for weeks. I know what it feels like to want to disappear; trust me. But, like my dad always says—shit happens, and it doesn't discriminate. We've all been there. Let me help you clean up."

Reaching out, I gently brushed flour from her cheek with the back of my hand, sucking in a huge breath to contain the temptation to pull her in for a hug. It seemed like she needed it. Vulnerability radiated from her like sunbeams. All I wanted was for her to feel better.

"You really are a sweet guy." She breathed. "Just like Gigi said you were. And now you're all floury too. I am so sorry."

"You apologize a lot. You don't need to, not to me."

"Well, I seem to feel sorry a lot." She watched me through lowered lashes before casting her gaze off to the side. "I wish I didn't."

"You have nothing to apologize for. What's a little flour between friends, right?"

"I guess so. I'm sor—"

I quirked an eyebrow, and she laughed instead of finishing her apology.

"Good. Shit happens, don't forget that."

"I won't forget. You're right, nobody is perfect."

"Say it so I know you believe it."

Her eyes lit up with humor. "Shit happens."

"Attagirl." Now, let's get this mess cleaned up. Point me to a broom."

"Thanks, Cole." She broke into a wide grin, momentarily disarming my resolve to keep her at a distance. Her lips were full—kissable, biteable, luscious—and I wanted them on mine.

She was too fucking tempting.

"You're welcome," I answered before following her to the supply area and taking the offered broom instead of sweeping her into my arms and kissing the hell out of her like I wanted.

CHAPTER 7
Madi

After spending a good couple of weeks in town, I couldn't help but think I might have finally found my groove here. The Cozy Creek Confectionery was basically heaven on earth—from the customers to the coworkers—I loved everything about it.

I discovered that Gigi's schedule was not a typical nine-to-five or five-to-lunch like Kenzie's. She kept her own hours and told me I could do that too. She had plenty of employees. What she wanted from me was someone trustworthy and responsible to ensure the place ran smoothly while she was incapacitated—she wanted the freedom to cut her day short or not come in at all. Popping in at odd hours, occasionally working the counter, and getting to know her employees would accomplish that.

She also encouraged me to sit with her and her friends whenever they were at the shop for tea, scones, and chats about what was happening in Cozy Creek. They were amazing.

I drove Gigi's old PT Cruiser to her house every day, bright and early, to take Basil on his morning walk. She'd let me borrow it since she couldn't drive with her booted foot. My car was still in the shop. According to Quinn, the mechanic who was also Cole's brother, the ignition coil needed to be replaced, and the part was on order.

Escorting Basil around the neighborhood and through the park had replaced my morning trek to work in Colorado Springs. I was making my own hours, making new friends, and having the time of my life. *Ross who?*

And it must be said, walking in Colorado Springs did not have the added benefit of Cole sightings or various other fire department members either. Getting my steps in while enjoying the show they unwittingly put on was a bonus I hadn't expected. Those guys liked to work out, and they gave the citizenry of Cozy Creek plenty to gawk at. How anyone got any work done here was miraculous, considering the many sexy distractions walking, jogging, or sprinting through town at any given moment. And don't get me started on the stretching or pull-ups on the exercise equipment in the park.

I still wasn't ready for dating, but nevertheless, I found myself primping in the mirror every morning before making my way to Gigi's place to get Basil. My brand-new pale pink Lululemon set was the outfit of the day for this morning's excursion. It was skin-tight and did amazing things to my boobs and booty.

I decided to forgo makeup this morning for a change, only adding a slick of pink lip gloss to match my outfit. I always showered after walking Basil, but applying makeup before and after walking him was getting old. I could admit I was high maintenance, but it was starting to get ridiculous, and I was over it. Pulling my hair into a high ponytail, I stuck my tongue out at my straightener.

I spun in front of the mirror to ensure the back looked as good as the front, smiling in anticipation when I imagined Cole's reaction if I saw him. I liked how it felt when his eyes were on me. It felt like he really saw me, not like he was checking me out. He wasn't winking or being flirtatious. He was paying attention and learning who I was; it was a heady feeling. I craved it.

I was playing a dangerous one-sided game, but I couldn't find it in myself to care. Talking to him made me feel good. It gave me a lift I desperately needed after spending the last couple of years begging for scraps of affection from Ross. The trouble was that after each conversation Cole and I had, I liked him more, no matter how innocent it was.

Kenny wound through my feet as I contemplated my life choices in front of the mirror. He was a morning cat, always up at the crack of dawn. Victor and Sage were still sleeping on my bed. I could hear Victor snoring from there. "Hello, you." I picked Kenny up to cuddle him. "Don't cause any trouble while I'm gone, you hear?"

His meow was not convincing. This cat was made to cause drama. I set him down and grabbed my keys on the way to the door.

Saturday mornings were busier than weekdays. Cozy Creek was a tourist destination as much as a homey small town. A few years back, a social media influencer called Cozy Creek the best, worst-kept secret in Colorado, and it stuck. Weekends were for brunching, shopping, and wandering around Main Street, where visitors and locals alike could peruse the marquee at the visitor's center to find all the latest town announcements.

I stopped at the marquee to see the fundraiser for the Cozy Creek Fire Brigade announcement pinned to the top. I stood there lost in thought for a minute, imagining Cole in a dunk tank, wet T-shirt contest, or shirtless for some random yet totally valid and not at all gratuitous reason. They should have hired me to plan it. Oh well, maybe next year.

I let my eyes wander as I headed down Main Street for a fast-paced walk. Fall was in full effect, with haystacks, pumpkins, happy scarecrows, and colorful pots of mums placed up and down the street, decorating doorways and staircases in numbers too big to count.

I turned the corner toward Gigi's house, waving at Natalie as I approached. She was sitting on her front porch and did not look happy at all. "Are you okay, sweetheart?" I called to her.

"Hey! I'm fine. Are you going to walk Basil today?" She was a sweet girl. After school, she sometimes visited Gigi's shop with her friends for lemonade and cookies.

Occasionally, throughout my time here, she'd catch me early in the morning at Gigi's house or come up to the counter to chat about makeup and boys and sometimes in-depth topics like college choices and what she should do for the rest of her life. For now, she wanted to be a veterinarian, and I thought it was a great idea. She was great with the cats, and Basil adored her. She made me remember how I was at her age, and I missed it.

Where did all my hopes and dreams go? That wasn't the right question. Why had I set them aside to work for my mother and settle for a man who wasn't sure if he even loved me? I had let other people steer me in the directions that benefitted them, which was what I needed to think about. But later—I could think about all that when I returned to Colorado Springs. Cozy Creek was supposed to be my respite from all the complicated feelings I didn't want to deal with.

"Can I come with you?" Her voice broke through my reverie.

"Oh, of course, you can if it's okay with your dad. Go ask him, and I'll grab Basil, then meet you in the front yard."

I watched her run through the garage door before crossing the street and letting myself into the house. Gigi was already at the Confectionery. Her friends had picked her up early today for their standing brunch date.

Basil came running to greet me at the door, leaving a trail of canine gas behind him. I quickly hooked his leash to his collar and grabbed a few bags to clean up after him.

I smiled at Natalie as she darted across the street to meet me. "He said it's okay!"

"Want to go to the park? I mean, after Basil finishes."

"Yes! I wanted to talk to you."

"Oh yeah? About what?" Basil found his way to his favorite mulberry bush and lifted a leg. He was fine, so I focused on Natalie. I'd make sure she ended our time together feeling better. It was my morning mission.

"Dexter Ryan. How do you get a boy to ask you out? I can't ask my mother. She's too busy lately."

I glanced at her out of the corner of my eye. From the tone of her voice, it seemed like her mother was her biggest worry, not Dexter Ryan and their potential date.

"You're fifteen, right?" I decided to cut to the chase. "Are you allowed to date? I don't want to encourage something your parents would disapprove of."

"Yeah, I can go to dances and stuff with my friends. Not car dates, whatever that is."

"I see. Nothing with just the two of you?"

"Exactly." She rolled her eyes. "Like I'm some kind of baby. All my friends can date. And my mom has no business telling me what to do when—never mind. It's embarrassing. I'm over it."

"You can talk to me if you want. My parents have been divorced since I was a baby, and I rarely see my dad. Have I heard from him since arriving in Cozy Creek? That's a big fat nope. Awkward is the nicest way I can describe being around both of them. Rare is another word. They avoid each other like it's their job."

"I'm sorry, that sucks. And, yeah, it's awkward, all right. I hate it, and I'm sorry you have to deal with this crap too." We turned our focus to Basil. "Is he going to let us go for a walk or just nose around in the grass?"

"He has to start his business in his own front yard. Picking a prime spot is part of his process. Part two will be in the park, somewhere behind that big group of aspen trees or near the gazebo. It is not for us to question. Basil has his ways."

She laughed, but it seemed forced. "Got it. Dogs are weird. Boys are weird. Mothers are weird too." Her chin wobbled. "Like, she was supposed to pick us up this morning to take us to brunch, but she canceled. Apparently, Todd's kids are more important. They're not ready to be a family or a stepfamily or whatever the hell we're supposed to be since she cheated on my dad and busted up our family. So she went to the Skytop Diner with them and left me and Evan here. Supposedly, she's going to talk to them and smooth things over. But who cares about us, right? Her own kids? Ev is inside playing Xbox with Dad. Like, she wouldn't dare go to Gigi's with them for brunch. Gigi would give her that look and probably kick her out."

"She totally would." I kept it light. I wasn't sure what she wanted from me yet—sympathy, distraction, or the freedom to vent her feelings and have someone impartial to listen. "I've seen that look; she always gave it to my ex and sometimes my dad. Her judgy face is legit. I'm so sorry this is happening to you, Natalie—"

"It's okay. I'm okay. I mean, did she ever ask if Evan and I are ready to have a stepfamily? Nope. We're supposed to go along with whatever she wants. But his kids can throw a fit and get their way." Her head shook from side to side as she seemed to realize what she'd shared with me. "God, I didn't mean to dump all that on you. I'm so embarrassed."

She needed someone to talk to, and that was obvious. "Don't be. It's fine," I reassured her. "I'm glad I could be here for you. Please don't worry. I know how much this sucks. Believe me, I get it."

"I can't talk to my dad about this. I know he's still mad at Mom and Todd, and I don't want to make things worse, especially after what happened at Bookers. He's trying so hard to make everything all right for Evan and me—"

"But it's not," I deduced. *What had happened at Bookers?*

"Nope. Not one freaking bit."

God, I saw so much of myself in her, and it broke my heart.

"Your dad said something to me the other day when I was upset and embarrassed. You've probably heard it before, but it's worth repeating."

Her lips tipped up in a slight grin. "Shit happens? Grandpa says that all the time."

"Yeah, shit happens—to all of us. But most importantly, you are allowed to feel what you feel. I don't mind at all if you want to talk more about it, and I'm honored that you trusted me enough to open up. I'm in no place to judge anyone. Nobody is. Obviously, the divorce and your feelings about it are more serious than a simple *shit happens*. My point is, don't be embarrassed when you get overwhelmed by your feelings and have to let them out."

"No, I get what you meant, totally. Speaking of shit—" Her eyebrows shot up as she gestured to Basil with a tilt of her head. He had just finished part one of his daily business. "We can walk now."

I held my hand to her, honored when she took it and squeezed it.

"Let's get a move on. Want to do the honors?" I offered her Basil's leash, and she took it with a grin. "I'll be on clean-up duty." I held the bags up as Basil barked happily at her side. "I'll get that one when we get back."

"What kind of dog is he, anyway?" she asked.

"According to Gigi, he's almost a beagle. She rescued him from an animal shelter when she was at my place in Colorado Springs. He's not purebred by any means."

"Like Snoopy?"

"Maybe a bootleg, street dog version of Snoopy. Basil has seen some things out there on the streets. He's kind of nutty."

We power walked through town, falling into a comfortable silence as we basked in the fresh air and bright yellow sunshine.

"Thanks, Madi. I didn't think I could feel better after my mom called to cancel." Her whispered voice carried through the light breeze and warmed my heart. I loved that I could be here for her to talk things through, just like Gigi had always been around when I needed her.

"Any time, honey," I answered as we approached the park.

We spent the rest of our time watching Basil run around, barking and yipping at the falling leaves in the breeze while we chatted about lighter topics.

As I walked them back home, I thought about Cole and his divorce and whether or not I should tell him I knew some of what had happened between him and his ex. I would hate it if he knew all the pathetic details of my breakup. Ross hadn't cheated on me, but keeping me dangling on a string while he put up with my affections and fed my hopes for our future was still pretty bad.

Oh crap, what if he knew about everything already? I had previously doubted Gigi would spill anything genuinely personal, but who knows? She considered Cole a good friend and was obviously trying to push me in his direction.

Oh well, what did it matter if one more person knew how sad and desperate I had been?

CHAPTER 8

Madi

When I returned to the apartment, I ran a bath. Coffee and a bubble-filled soak in the tub sounded like the perfect way to spend the rest of my morning before heading to Gigi's to work the counter and keep an eye on things.

But was I in the bathtub right now?

No.

I was up a tree.

Literally.

Let's rewind to about ten minutes ago, and the decision now ranked somewhere in the top five of the running list of bad choices I've made in my life.

I'd gone into the kitchen after the tub had filled to pour my coffee, and while I was in there, Kenny managed to wedge his fluffy orange butt through the window I'd left open to let the steam out.

I'd returned to the bathroom to find the window flung wide open, then heard him yowling from the big branch that brushed against the side of the building.

How he'd done it, I would never know. He was a fat cat, and it had been, at best, a three-inch gap with a dang screen that he'd somehow knocked to the ground.

"Come on, Kenny. Come back inside where the cat treats live." I tried coaxing him back through the window, but he was terrified and stayed stubbornly stuck in place with his butt against the trunk and his big golden eyes locked to mine.

He yowled at me, and I jumped, sloshing my coffee on the pink and white tiled counter. I set it down, trying to determine if I would fit through the window. I decided I wouldn't. Plus, getting stuck halfway through a window would be way more embarrassing than someone seeing me climb a tree to save a cat.

"Fine, have it your way. I'm coming to get you. I have to go down to the sidewalk and climb up. Don't move."

He meowed plaintively, digging his claws into the bark.

"Damn it," I muttered. I grabbed my backpack and dumped the contents on the wing chair by the fireplace, wincing when Sage and Victor jumped up to start pawing through it. Whatever, that was future Madi's problem to deal with.

I made it to the sidewalk and managed to climb the tree. Lucky for me, there were plenty of sturdy branches to use; it was almost like a ladder. It was precarious, but I wasn't worried I would fall—not yet, anyway.

But Kenny was stubborn and scared. He refused to budge, so I was now straddling a branch about two stories off the ground, wondering what the hell to do.

I was way too high to look down. I tried not to panic while also trying to convince Kenny to get into a backpack so I could strap him on and climb down, but he was not having it.

Gigi was right. This cat was an idiot. But I'd fallen in love with the fluff-brained little demon, so I was not about to let him yowl his way into an early death stuck up in this freaking tree.

"Come on, Kenny. I won't let you fall," I singsonged while trying to inch close enough to grab him and stuff him in my backpack.

I hadn't adequately thought this through. I had one hand on the branch above me for balance. How the heck was I supposed to climb down with him, let alone get him into the damn backpack?

"Need any help?"

I slammed my eyes shut.

It was Cole.

Because, of course, it was.

I was a makeup-free, hair in a ponytail, sweaty mess. And my cute Lululemon set had gotten filthy on my way up the tree; I'm pretty sure I snagged it on something too. Pale pink and dirty tree bark did not mix.

I was joking when I said his rescuing me was our thing. Lesson learned. No more jokes were allowed.

Still, I managed to shrug slightly before looking down to find his brother Tate and friend Pace standing at his side.

I had an audience.

Even better. Damn it.

"Cat up a tree. This is classic," Tate joked. "Who's going up to get them?"

Pace slugged his arm. "We're happy to help. Can I go inside? One of you can pass me the cat through the window."

"Good thinking, thank you," I shouted down. And yes, it's unlocked. Go right in." I'd met the entire Cozy Creek Fire Brigade. They were all good guys, but that didn't mean I wanted them to see me in all my calamitous glory.

"I'm coming up to get you. Hang tight," Cole announced before hopping up to grab a branch and rapidly scaling the tree until he was suddenly straddling the branch across from me and a little above.

"Hang tight." Tate chuckled at his accidental pun. "It's going to be okay, Madi. I'll stand right here and catch whoever falls first."

"This is so not funny," I hollered down to him.

"It's a little funny," he countered. "One day, we'll look back on this and laugh our asses off."

"Doubtful," I muttered.

"Ignore him. I find it best that way," Cole said. "I've got you both, I promise."

"Okay..." I looked down, then quickly shut my eyes, squeezing them tight as I tried to stay calm.

"Madi. Hey. Look at me, and don't look down. It's going to be fine."

A surge of courage steeled my spine. "You're right," I agreed. "I got up here with no problems, and now that I have help with Kenny, I can get down too."

"That's the spirit."

I sucked it up and tried to find my sense of humor. Making jokes would be better than acting like a wuss about the situation.

"You're rescuing me again, Sutter. We're going to have to stop meeting like this," I teased as I looked up to find him staring at me. The tenderness in his expression surprised me.

"You have freckles," he blurted.

My eyes whipped to his. "Yeah, I usually cover them up."

"Why would you do that? I mean—you're so beautiful. I—"

"Thank you," I murmured as a surge of warmth turned my cheeks red.

"You're welcome. Uh, pass me the backpack."

"I don't know what I was thinking by climbing up here like this," I confessed once he had taken it from my outstretched hand.

His gorgeous blue eyes met mine, and I smiled back when they crinkled at the corners, and his lips tipped up in a grin. "It's obvious to everyone who's met you that you have a good heart. When you love something, you don't think. You do whatever it takes to help them, and that includes cats. Right, Kenny?"

"I—don't know what to say." Tears stung at the back of my eyes. It was like he saw straight through me to my heart and liked what he saw.

"You don't have to say anything." He smiled softly. "Can you help me hold the backpack open? I think I can reach him."

"Yeah, I think I can." I let out the breath I'd been holding. "Give me a second."

"Don't let go of that branch."

"Okay."

He locked his thighs around his branch and wedged his feet on either side of the trunk. Gently, he took hold of the scruff of Kenny's neck and shoved him into the backpack, zipping it up tight as I held on to it with my free hand.

"Thank you," I whispered.

"Yup. Don't let go, Madi. Grab it, Pace."

From the corner of my eye, I saw Pace leaning out the window, ready to take the wiggling backpack from Cole's outstretched arm.

I looked down and saw Tate observing as if he really would catch me if I fell.

"Don't worry. I got you, Madi, I swear," he confirmed. "We'll both most likely need medical attention if you fall, but I won't let you hit the ground. I promise."

"Thank you." The words were almost inaudible, but he shot me a grin and a mock salute anyway.

"Look at me, Madi." I met Cole's eyes. He was calm. He was cool. I would be okay. "Do you think you can climb down with me? If not, Pace can help you get through the window."

"I can climb down. Believe it or not, I used to be great at climbing trees as a kid, back when I wasn't afraid to fall. Trying to back through the window feels more daunting. Plus, it's a small window, and I have a booty on me. I doubt I'll fit through it. How embarrassing would it be to require the jaws of life in addition to this impromptu rescue mission?"

"No way, you have a great ass. You'll fit through just fine," he earnestly protested before slamming his eyes shut with an apologetic grimace. "Ah, shit, never mind. That was inappropriate. I'm so sorry. Sometimes, stuff comes out of my mouth before my brain can filter it."

"Hey, it's okay. Never tell me you're sorry for complimenting me," I joked to cover the riptide of emotions that were about to pull me under. "Shit happens, right? It's all good." I was off my game. Okay, I had no game. I was going out of my mind for so many reasons I couldn't seem to focus on one at a time. Cole overwhelmed me in all the best ways. Add my newfound fear of heights, and I had become an utter mess.

"Nice." He nodded his approval at my use of his dad's words. "I'll start down first and spot you. Feel free to grab on to me if you need to."

There was nothing more I wanted now than to grab him, anywhere, everywhere. I couldn't mentally choose a spot since every inch of his body was perfection.

Dirty replies butted against each other in my brain at his unintentionally loaded statement. Instead, I reassured him that I wasn't offended as we slowly climbed down, with him going first to keep me steady if I faltered.

The drop to the ground from the lowest branch was more intimidating on the way down. I hesitated.

"I got you." He held his arms up to me.

My hands landed on his big shoulders, and he held me above my hips, so close to the underside of my breasts that I inhaled a sharp breath. Our eyes widened at the contact as I slid down his front until my feet were on the ground again.

He took a step back.

I dusted off my hands.

No big deal.

Once they confirmed we were okay, Tate and Pace took off, leaving me alone with Cole. They were on shift soon; they explained after Pace assured me Kenny was okay. He'd drained the tub for me, and the window was now closed and secured.

"Are you sure you're okay?" Cole asked. "You look pale."

"I'm fine, I think." My whole body was trembling, from my fingers to my toes, from a mixture of undiluted fear and pure adrenaline. I was not okay. My head spun, and my breathing was choppy; black spots danced before my eyes. "Oh, crap. I'm not fine. Nope."

My body erupted in tingles from head to toe as he swept me up like a groom would a bride. My arms encircled his neck as he held me close. Our eyes met, and he whispered softly. "I got you. You're okay..."

I shut my eyes, burying my nose in his neck. I didn't mean to, but I breathed him in. He was warm and steady and smelled so good, like clean laundry and fresh air.

He carried me through the outdoor entrance to my apartment. I stifled a gasp as he continued carrying me straight up the stairs and to my front door.

His chest was rock hard, nothing but solid muscle. He carried me like I weighed nothing at all. I felt like I was being held against a wall. But walls weren't warm. Walls didn't ruffle your hair with their breath as they walked or whispered in your ear, telling you that you would be okay, they wouldn't let you go, and how brave they thought you were.

I could feel his biceps flex against my waist, and if I wasn't already swooning from the triple threat of mental exhaustion, worry for Kenny, and lack of food, being this close to Cole would have done it all on its own.

From beneath the backs of my knees, he twisted the doorknob and kicked it shut behind us after he strode through my living room, not stopping until he was at the side of my couch, where he placed me down gently and covered me with the yellow throw blanket I kept on the back.

"Have you eaten anything today?" he demanded. His brow furrowed in concern as he studied my face.

He wasn't even breathing hard. His stamina was incredible. I imagined what it would be like to go to bed with him and felt myself turning red.

"No, not yet. I was going to grab a late breakfast downstairs. I had just run a bath when Kenny decided to make a break for it. I was halfway up the tree before I thought better of it. Then it was all, in for a penny, in for a pound, you know?"

"Pretty brave of you. Do you realize how high you were?"

"No, and I don't want to."

"Fair enough." He chuckled.

Speaking of Kenny—he let out a plaintive meow, then jumped from the windowsill adjacent to the couch to land in the center of my chest. I let out an *oof* as he spun around on my boobs before settling down to rest with his head against my neck.

"He owes you a huge apology. Don't you, Kenny?" Cole moved aside a stack of books and sat on the ottoman in front of the couch. He reached out to scratch beneath Kenny's chin, grazing the side of my cheek with the backs of his fingers.

I let out a soft hiss as sparks shot between us, and our eyes met and held.

"Yeah, he sure does, but I'm afraid this is the best I'll get out of him. Too bad he can't make me a cup of coffee to replace the one I spilled all over the counter, clean up the mess in the bathroom, or anything else useful."

He laughed softly as Sage and Victor cuddled against my side. "He's pretty cute. You're lucky you're adorable, Kenny." His tone was something I'd never heard from him before. It was light, filled with humor and warmth. "Are you sure you aren't a Disney Princess?" he teased. "You resemble Belle right now with all these books everywhere and your pretty brown hair," he murmured. "Plus, everyone seems to have fallen in love with you since you got here. Natalie talks about you every morning after she gets back from walking with you and Basil."

My heart fluttered to a crescendo of giddiness that almost overwhelmed me. "That makes me happy to hear. I just adore her."

"It's mutual. I'm glad you're in town, Madi. She needs positivity and fun so much right now. And I'm—"

"Hey, it's okay." My heart broke at the concern for his daughter shining in his eyes. "Divorce is hard on a kid. I know all about that firsthand."

"I'm so sorry. Thank you for being there for her—today, especially. It meant a lot."

"You're welcome. However, spending time with your sweet girl is no trouble at all. She's good company."

He cleared his throat, and I watched, entranced, as his eyes grew lazy on mine, crinkling at the corners, while his lips tipped up in an intimate smile. "I'm pretty good with a coffee maker. Can I make you a cup before I head to the station?"

"Oh, you don't have to do that," I protested. "I can get another one when I get to the bakery."

"We both know Gigi's coffee is crap, even she won't drink it. I insist. Plus, you need something to eat before you go down. I'll fix some toast too. Do not move a muscle."

"Okay. I can't believe I got lightheaded like that. I'm so sorry."

"It happens to the best of us, sweetheart. No apologies." He reached out and ran his finger gently down the bridge of my nose where, for all my life, I'd mistakenly thought I had been cursed with freckles. "So cute. Stay put, you hear? Let me take care of you so I don't have to worry about you passing out later."

I nodded. "Okay, yes. Thank you, Cole. It's good to know I was right about you."

He turned back to face me. "Oh yeah? How?"

"You're a hero. Are you sure you aren't a Disney Prince? Wait, you're already a firefighter; that's even better than a prince, except for Prince Eric because he has a dog."

His cheeks turned pink above his stubble. I watched, entranced, as he drew his lower lip between his teeth and looked away. "Are you sure you didn't hit your head on something while you were up that tree?" he murmured.

"It's funny how we never see ourselves as others do. Gigi says that all the time. Kenny and I owe you big time."

"You don't owe me a thing. But I could say the same about you. I bet she tells you things you don't see about yourself too, doesn't she?"

My eyes drifted toward the window. "Maybe she does."

"Maybe you should listen to her. You're wonderful, Madi. Believe it."

My lips parted as I inhaled a sharp breath of disbelief.

I had no words to answer him. But he was gracious enough to head into the kitchen and let me off the emotional hook. Or maybe we both needed to be let off the hook.

"How do you take your coffee?" he called out.

"I have vanilla creamer in the fridge. Would you like some too? You could join me."

"I wish I could. But I have a meeting I can't miss in about half an hour." I could hear him rummaging around in the fridge. "Found it. Hey, I drink this one too. Anyway, planning for the station's fall fundraiser starts today."

"Oh! How fun. That's what I do back home. I'm an event planner."

He popped his head through the kitchen entrance. "I know. I heard you're pretty good at it too."

"Gigi talks about me a lot, doesn't she?"

"Yup."

"Is there anything you don't already know about me?" I closed my eyes, not wanting to see his face as he answered.

"I only know the facts. She doesn't gossip about you. She's proud of you. I know you just turned thirty. You're an event planner. You love books and cats. You bake amazing brownies—which my kids and I devoured in one day, by the way. And today, I discovered you are fearless, have a face full of adorable freckles, and can climb a tree if the need arises." He punctuated that sweet statement with a wink, and I'm pretty sure I almost died.

"Oh. My." The words left my mouth with all my breath because he had taken it away.

"Be right back."

"Okay."

He bustled around in my kitchen while I ran over everything he had just said in my mind.

That was flirting, wasn't it?

The winking? The compliments about my freckles and tree-climbing skills? He thought I was brave and not dumb for climbing that tree—that was the best part.

I heard the coffee start bubbling as it brewed into the pot. Then the toast popped up. The scratch of the knife across the bread told me he'd be in here again real soon.

Nervously, I bit my lip.

Cole Sutter was totally flirting with me, and I didn't know how to feel about it.

Lie.

I was thrilled that the sexy Cole Sutter had flirted with me and was already contemplating how to get him to do it some more.

He liked my freckles? From now on this girl lived in freckle city—no more concealer.

I should bake him another batch of brownies. No, a strawberry rhubarb pie was my specialty. I'd bake him one of those, I decided, while mentally preparing a grocery list.

Warmth surged through me when he appeared in the living room carrying a steaming mug and plate of toast. "I noticed some grape jelly in the fridge. I could add some if you like?"

"No, thank you. Just butter is fine."

It wasn't quite breakfast in bed, but it felt almost as intimate because of the way he looked at me as he set the toast on the coffee table and handed me the mug. His eyes were warm on mine, crinkling at the corners as he smiled at me softly, saying without words that he was worried.

"Here you go. I want you to eat every bite of that. You need to get your strength back up."

"Thank you." I breathed.

He sat on the chair perpendicular to the couch. "My pleasure. Make sure you're feeling one hundred percent better before you go downstairs."

Reaching out, he placed his hand against my forehead and drew it back like it was on fire. "Oh god, I'm sorry. It was a force of habit. I check for a fever when my kids don't feel well."

"It's okay. Your dad instincts are strong."

"Yeah. Usually, when I'm delivering food to a coffee table, it's for a sick kid laid up on the couch watching cartoons. My mind must have subconsciously forced my hand to your forehead."

"My dad was not like you at all. If we were sick when it was his turn with us, he'd ship us off to Gigi for her to deal with. My mother was like you, but she kissed our foreheads to check for fevers. Then, after, she'd get the thermometer to make sure she was right. Um . . ." My voice trailed off when I realized how much I had given away about my life and the fact that I had some major daddy issues I was still dealing with. "She read somewhere that lips are more sensitive to heat or something like that. Uh, not that I expect you to kiss my forehead or anything. I mean, obviously, I'm not sick or feverish, and that would be um . . ."

His watch started beeping, distracting him. "I've heard of that." He flicked his wrist to turn it off. "I have to get to my meeting. Please make sure you're back to one hundred percent before you go downstairs, okay?"

"I will. I promise." I took a bite of toast and chased it with a sip of coffee. I held the mug aloft for emphasis.

"Good. Don't make me rat you out to Gigi. We both know how she can get. Unless you'd like to spend the day in bed being fussed over with chicken soup, Sprite, and a stack of *Good Housekeeping* magazines." He paused to grin at me. "That sounds pretty good right now, not gonna lie."

"I'm already feeling better. I'll save a sick day for later."

"I'll see you soon, Madi."

After he left, I finished getting ready for the day, forgoing a bath for a quick shower. It was funny how, since arriving here, my accident-prone ways had led to good things rather than eye rolls and annoyance.

While contemplating my face in the mirror, I used a light touch with my makeup so my freckles would show through. Then, I chose my prettiest yellow sundress and a pair of high-heeled strappy sandals. I wanted to look like Belle if we ran into each other again today, a sexy Belle who wasn't afraid to show a hint of cleavage. I wanted him to remember our moment on the couch, so maybe I'd get another one.

And if I didn't see him, I felt beautiful and needed to feel good about myself again. I'd spent the last few weeks before arriving in town doing some serious moping and lying around in my apartment. I think I'd watched almost everything that existed on Netflix and was on a first-name basis with every DoorDasher in Colorado Springs. It was time to pick myself back up again.

I fed the cats and ensured the windows were closed tight before heading down to the Confectionery to work.

CHAPTER 9

Cole

It was clear, bright autumn perfection as I jogged up the street quickly so I wouldn't be late for my meeting. Leaves crunched under my feet as my sneakers pounded over the sidewalk. Tourists were fucking everywhere, and I had to weave around them as I ran up Main Street to the station.

The Cozy Creek Fire Brigade Station took up an entire block. The structure was designed to serve as a gathering place for services and a shelter for our community in emergencies.

The brick building had four double-deep and two single-deep apparatus bays on the ground floor and a reception area. The second floor held administrative offices, a conference room, a turnout gear room, and a storage area for our emergency medical supplies.

We had ten bunk rooms, each with a bed, desk, and storage cabinets, and five unisex bathrooms with private showers surrounded by a locker area.

We spent most of our downtime in the newly remodeled kitchen and seating area of the station. When we were in town, the Cozy Creek Confectionery and Bookers Pub were some of our favorite haunts.

With a combined force of paid and volunteer firefighters, we were always ready to help wherever needed throughout the county.

My office was on the top floor, where I would meet our event planner. I had barely enough time to shower and change before we got started.

I scowled as I crossed the parking lot toward reception. My heart was still flying circles in my chest from my interaction with Madi, and I couldn't think straight.

Interaction? Right, what we'd had was no simple interaction. I'd shamelessly flirted with her. I told her I liked her freckles, for fuck's sake, and compared her to Belle. I think I even winked at her.

How was I supposed to resist someone like her? She was like fucking sunshine, and I was nothing but a grumpy, dark cloud. But worse, she seemed into me, and I fucking loved it.

I wanted to keep running, blow past the station, blow off my meeting, and run until these fucking feelings I was developing for Madi were gone, and I was back to feeling nothing again. *Nothing* was safer. I could deal with nothing.

With a shove, I opened the door and stepped inside, hoping to make it to the locker room without talking to anyone.

"Cole! Bad news." I stopped short. The last thing I needed was more to deal with.

Our administrative assistant, Monica, a pretty redhead who was a year behind me in school, stood behind her desk to greet me as if she had been waiting. The look on her face said it wasn't just bad news; it was terrible.

"I don't wanna hear it," I joked. "No, thanks."

"Jenny canceled." Our event planner. Great.

I closed my eyes, praying for patience. "Please tell me she only canceled today's meeting."

She tapped her fingers on her desk. "You're going to find this hilarious."

"I seriously doubt that," I answered as I walked slow circles around the lobby to catch my breath and cool down.

"She took a temp job in Colorado Springs. They offered her twice what she'd make freelancing here. She's filling in for Gigi's granddaughter."

"No shit." I barked out a laugh.

"None whatsoever. Ironic, isn't it?"

"We're screwed. We're already selling tickets online and in town; it's on the marquee, Monica. It's official. It's a done deal. We can't cancel, and there's no way I can plan this myself. Not unless we want to grill burgers and watch football. I mean, what the hell?"

"I don't know. That sounds pretty fun to me."

"I don't have time for this. *You* don't have time for this either."

"I know, Cole. I'll make some calls and see what I come up with. I'll let you know by the end of the day."

"I appreciate it."

"Of course." She waved me off and picked up her phone. "I'll call around. Or maybe I'll get in touch with Gigi or one of her friends. Those ladies know everybody in town. Word of mouth is key here. We don't want to hire just anybody to replace Jenny. We need someone who can handle this on their own."

"Yeah, and this is all Gigi's fault too, for spraining her ankle." I laughed. "She owes us."

"Ha! I'll be sure to mention that to her," she joked as she dialed. "We'll be okay. I'll find a replacement as soon as possible."

"Let me know if you need me to call around too. Thanks, Monica."

I made my way into my office and sat at my desk. I leaned back in my chair and put my feet up. I needed time to think. I only had a month to get everything ready.

Maybe I should call Madi.

Or not.

She probably had her hands full helping Gigi. The irony was not lost on me here.

But what if she could be the one to save my ass this time?

A lot of the fundraiser was preplanned to cut costs. The timing stayed the same. People were desperate to donate for the tax write-off toward the end of the year. We had a standing reservation at Cozy Creek's Veterans Hall, and our caterer knew when to expect our call. The only real tasks were to decide on a theme, activities, something to auction off, and a menu—all of which usually ended up being fall-related—and decorate the place accordingly.

I pulled a yellow ledger pad from my desk drawer and a pencil from the cup.

If it came down to it, I could do it all myself. We could have a chili cook-off or host a poker tournament. I jotted down and crossed both ideas out. Gambling was a terrible idea for a fundraiser, and no one would want to be around the crew if we'd all eaten chili. People would demand refunds for their tickets.

I wrote down ideas as they came to me.

Touch football?

A ride through town on one of the trucks with the lights and sirens blaring?

Auction off slides down the fire poles?

I tossed the pad on my desk.

I could not do this.

We had set a precedent. I had standards to uphold. The Cozy Creek Fire Brigade Fundraiser was a classy event. People dressed up, for fuck's sake. Who was I to take that away from the town?

I pulled out my cell and called Gigi myself.

"Cole! I was just about to call you. Meet Madi at Tres Chicas," she ordered me without preamble. "Buy her some tacos and finish convincing her she can do this. I already talked to Monica."

Relief flooded through me. Gigi was one step ahead of me, and I was grateful. I was also intrigued by the thought of bringing Madi on board. I'd get to see her more often and on my turf. The idea of her knowing what I was all about felt good. I'd save the contemplation about why I felt this way for later.

"Where is it?" Tres Chicas was a food truck that was almost always open. The only trouble was finding it; they parked all over town according to where they determined the taco cravings would be the strongest. For example, it could often be found across from the fire station after a call. We were all shamefully addicted to their food.

Gigi and her friends tried to keep the location updated on the town's Facebook page, but the Tres Chicas ladies were too fast for that.

"They're at the end of the street, near the park. It's Mommy and Me day at the playground. Madi is hangry and stressy. So far today, she's only had toast—delicious toast, I might add—thanks for helping her out of the tree and feeding her breakfast, by the way. That Kenny is a dang menace; he's lucky he's so cute. Anyway, you have to hurry before they move the truck. It's almost lunchtime at the high school, and you do not want to wait in that line. She's leaving now! Go! Cole! Go!"

"I'm on my way." I shoved my phone in my pocket and didn't hesitate.

"I think I have a solution!" I hollered over my shoulder as I passed Monica's desk at a run.

"Oh, you do? *You* have a solution?" She scoffed. "You're welcome, Cole!" she shouted to my retreating back.

"Thank you!" I yelled, grinning when she burst into loud laughter behind me.

CHAPTER 10

Cole

I booked it down the street, only stopping once I saw Madi.

"Hey," I huffed, all keyed up and full of adrenaline as I skidded to a stop in front of her.

Was it because of the fundraiser emergency or because I had an excuse to spend time with her?

It was her. I couldn't lie to myself anymore. I liked her way more than I should, and I'd already flirted with her way past the boundaries of friendship. I had to knock it off.

"Hi! You're fast."

"Yeah, I ran all the way here." I took a deep breath and let it out with a low laugh. "I'm not sure why."

"Gigi got you all pumped up. She's good at that. I heard her side of the conversation," she added as an aside.

I could tell she was excited too, from the sparkle in her and the flush spreading across her cheeks. I couldn't help but notice that while she was wearing makeup now, I could still see her freckles, and it did things to my heart that I was not ready to admit to. Her dress was amazing, and it was all I could do not to do a full scan of her gorgeous body. Was she in heels? I didn't dare let my eyes wander to her feet to check.

"She is good, isn't she?" I turned my smile up a notch, relieved she didn't think I was a weirdo for running over here like I did.

"Look at my situation; I'm on a leave of absence, living in the cutest apartment ever and working in a carb lovers' paradise while I care for my adorable grandmother and her dubiously sprained ankle. I'm also about to plan the Cozy Creek Fire Brigade's Fall Fundraiser pro bono. The woman has skills. No one says no to Gigi."

"It's not pro bono. We have a budget. I'd never ask you to work for free."

"Even better. But I must insist on a bachelor auction. I've always wanted to plan one, and everyone always says no."

"I'll think about it. I do not relish the idea of being sold to the highest bidder." Unless I could somehow get her to bid on me, I would be entirely on board for that.

"Yay! We're working so well together already. Now go buy me tacos while I snag one of those picnic tables over there." Her satisfied laugh was infectious. It was impossible to be in a bad mood around her.

"Yes, ma'am," I agreed through my smile. "Something to drink?"

"Surprise me."

"You got it."

I stepped into the line and watched her walk to the picnic area, the smile never leaving my face as I looked forward to the rest of my day—something I hadn't done in months. She was indeed wearing heels; her legs were amazing, and that ass was something out of a dirty dream. I wanted to take a bite out of it.

I brought our food to the table and slid across from her, trying to control my attraction, but it was almost impossible. That yellow dress was doing things to me that would be inappropriate for her to know about at this point in our relationship. *Relationship?* I caught myself, frustrated that I couldn't get control of my feelings for her.

"How are you feeling?" I asked.

"Starved. That smells delicious. And you?"

I want you, and I shouldn't.

You're gorgeous, hilarious, smart, and funny. My kids adore you, and I hate that I want you so bad.

I cleared my throat and popped open my Coke. "They make the best tacos in town. Let's dig in while it's hot."

We each finished a taco before she broached the bachelor auction topic again.

"I don't think any of the guys would go for it."

"I get that. But it would be simple and fun. We will make it totally innocent. We could hold a dinner the next night in the same place for the date. It could be a planned event that everyone in town could attend—and it could be ticketed."

"So that means it would raise even more money."

"Exactly. Double the money. Who wouldn't want to show up to see how the dates turn out?"

"Okay, let's add that to the list. How bad could it be?"

"It will be totally innocent, I promise. And no one would have to be alone with their date at any time. That would be icky."

Icky. I nodded my agreement with a smirk as she pulled out a tablet and added it to a list she'd already started. I tried to take a peek, and she pulled it to her chest with a shake of her head.

"No peeking. We need party favors to sell. How about a Cozy Creek Fire Brigade calendar? Featuring twelve of your most smokingly hot fire dudes."

"No way."

"Do you want to make some serious money for the station? Or whatever you're raising it for."

"Of course I do."

"What is the money going to, anyway?"

"Gear, food for the station, various charities we sponsor, station tours for kids—they love stickers and those plastic fire hats—the holiday pancake breakfast, a bunch of stuff. I could email you the itemized list from last year if you think it would help."

"No, that's okay, I don't need it. Oh! We could create trading cards with your pictures on them. Think of the kids in their little hats, Cole. Kids love trading cards, and their mothers would too—I'm just saying."

"Do you really think those would sell?"

"I've noticed two things this town loves more than anything. Carbs and eye candy. Do you know how much attention you and the rest of the Fire Brigade attract when you're at Gigi's, drinking your smoothies and eating those sad little egg-white breakfast sandwiches? Plus, tell me you've seen all the heads in town whipping to the side whenever one of you jog by on the park trail."

I flattened my lips together so I wouldn't laugh. "I have no idea what you're talking about."

"Sure you don't. Okay." Her eyes shifted to the side as her lips pursed to stifle a laugh. "I'll humor you on the off chance you really don't notice. Try paying attention next time you are out for a run, and you'll see it for yourself. I can promise you that. Trust me, anything with your pictures will sell like hotcakes."

"Okay, maybe I just don't want to pose for any pictures, and at least half of the guys won't either."

She laughed. "Fair enough. But you have to admit, selling a firefighter calendar is pretty standard. Lots of firehouses do it."

"Fine, you're right. I'll talk to the guys but don't count on it. And no trading cards. I do not see that happening at all."

"How about a wet T-shirt contest, then? You could all wear those cute pants with the suspenders hanging down and your blue Cozy

Creek Fire Brigade T-shirts." Her eyes lit up with mischievous, smug delight as she awaited my reaction.

Shocked, I burst out with a startled laugh. "No. Not happening. No way."

"Dunk tank?" Her head tilted to the side speculatively.

I crossed my arms over my chest. "Nope."

"Shirtless car wash?"

"Oh god, no."

"I know. I think I have it this time."

I bit my lip and shook my head from side to side as I waited to see what ridiculously hilarious suggestion would come out of her mouth next. "What is it? Come on. Don't hold back on me now."

"We could line you all up and auction off a chance to spray you down with the fire hose."

I threw my head back with a laugh. "You are oddly determined to get us all wet, aren't you? What would Gigi think?"

"Oh, please, half of these were her idea. The woman is shameless, and so are her friends. Do you think she started serving protein smoothies and healthy breakfast options with no ulterior motive? Nope. She did it to get you guys into the Confectionery every day. But listen, I was joking about most of those suggestions." She grew momentarily serious. "Please, tell me you know that."

I covered her hand with mine. "I know. Don't worry."

Her eyes twinkled mischievously in the sunlight as her lips tipped up at the corners. "I bet the calendar idea looks pretty good now, right?"

"Okay, fine," I answered with a chuckle. "We'll do the calendar. It's the most normal thing you've suggested so far."

"Yay!" She tugged her hand away and held it up for a high-five.

Instead, I pulled it toward me and kissed the back, pleased when her cheeks turned fiery red. "You're amazing," I murmured. "I haven't laughed like this in months. I enjoyed having lunch with you."

"I don't know about amazing. But there is definitely something wrong with me."

"Nothing is wrong with you. You're brilliant and hilarious. You saved the fall fundraiser, and I can't thank you enough."

"You're too sweet."

"Can't say I've ever been accused of that before."

"I enjoyed everything about having lunch with you today. We're going to have so much fun planning this. I can't wait to see what we can come up with together."

"Same. I'm looking forward to it now."

"Good. So, are the bachelor auction and calendar a yes then?" She fluttered her eyelashes in mock flirtation before tapping something on her tablet's screen.

"Do you always get your way?" I couldn't fight it; my smile was etched across my face. Maybe it would be permanent. The urge to pull her across the table and kiss her was overwhelming.

"Hardly ever. And I have the feeling you don't give in easily, so I'm feeling pretty good right now. And deep down, you know a calendar and an auction will raise a ton of money."

"Nah, I think it's just you. I don't want to say no to you."

"Ahh, that could be dangerous." She was smiling, radiant, and completely correct. She was an absolute danger to my heart.

CHAPTER 11

Madi

I was flying high after Cole and I finished lunch and said goodbye. There was no denying he was flirting with me this time. He kissed my hand! He called me amazing. And no matter what he said to deny it, he was sweet.

I walked the short distance back to my apartment with a spring in my step that had been missing for—gosh, a few years now.

Cole was the amazing one, and I knew it for sure now. He was everything Gigi had ever said he was.

The smoldering hot guy vibes that had intimidated me before had disappeared in a puff of imaginary smoke when I realized he was an undercover sweetheart. He felt my forehead to check for a fever—my father had never even done that, for eff's sake. And he made me toast, *and* it was delicious.

Memories of being carried up these stairs by Cole this morning clouded my mind as I walked up to my apartment. I spun in a circle and held the hand he'd kissed up to the hallway light once I reached the top. It was a good thing I had a fresh manicure.

It was happening.

I was officially crushing on Cole.

He was hilarious and delicious, and I was about to spend all kinds of time with him.

My phone went off with a text notification at the same time Noah, my across-the-hall neighbor and driver of Hubers, stepped into the hall.

"Hey, Noah." I grinned at him.

"Hey, Madi. You look happy."

"Thanks! I'm feeling good today. What are you up to?"

I took a glance at my phone.

> **Riley:** We have to talk about Ross. I'm coming over this weekend with Abigail. We'll all have dinner together and have a good chat.

Shit.

Dejected, my face fell.

They probably wanted me to take him back. They were the ones who introduced us, and he was part of their circle of friends. It must have been awkward for them, considering how I broke up with him at our anniversary dinner and hadn't spoken to him since.

I was hurt and angry, and it was ruining my mood.

"Bad news? Is everything okay?"

"Yeah, I'm fine. I—uh, you know what? I'm not fine, and I'm pissed off all over again. I came to Cozy Creek for two reasons: to help Gigi and to forget about my ex. Breakups just fucking suck."

"You got that right. I've been there. Sometimes, it hits you out of nowhere."

"Yeah. I want my good mood back, damn it. Not this crushing sense of doomed reality that has plagued me off and on ever since I got here."

"Fuck that guy. Seriously. I don't know him, but I know you deserve better. Don't let him ruin your day."

"You're good people, Noah."

"Tell that to—never mind."

I tilted my head questioningly. "Fuck that girl?"

"I wish."

"Ahh, gotcha."

"But in a nice way," he clarified with a grin. "A respectable way."

"You're a true gentleman. All a lady wants is a respectable fuck and someone to make her days better." I made jokes whenever I was upset. It could not be helped.

He burst out laughing. "Well, I hope you get what you want."

"It's not going to happen today, that's for sure. Later, Noah."

"See you around." Since he was going and I was coming. I waved goodbye before entering my apartment.

The rest of the week was going to suck now that I knew my sisters were coming to drop some bomb on me about Ross. And knowing them, they wouldn't tell me over the phone—the drama queens.

Whatever. I didn't want to hear their opinions anyway.

These situations are what books and wine were for. And cats, I had cats to love now. I'd think about everything later, including Cole.

Or maybe it was best to only think about Cole when I had to spend time with him, like during the next meeting we had scheduled to finish planning the fundraiser.

Now was not the time to catch feelings for someone. I was clearly not over my breakup—I was definitely over Ross—but the leftover feelings of resentment about all the time he had stolen from me and how I had let him take advantage of me were still there. I had some shit to work through. I would be nobody's doormat ever again.

It was probably best to stick to strictly business with Cole, especially since I'd be returning to Colorado Springs after Gigi's ankle healed.

Kenny greeted me with a plaintive meow as I headed into the living room to plop on the couch. "Come here. I forgive you. It wasn't all bad. I found out I could still climb a tree. And I was carried up the stairs by the hottest man in existence—which I'll be writing all about in my journal later, and I owe it all to you." I scooped him up and settled him on my chest, remembering how it felt to have Cole taking care of me in here earlier today.

"Damn it, Kenny. I like him too much. Make it stop."

Victor raised his head from the chair by the fireplace to acknowledge my presence, then promptly fell back to sleep with a soft, trilling snore. "Good to see you too." He was sweet but mostly uninterested in me unless I was filling his food bowl or bribing him for attention with a cat treat. He reminded me of Ross in that way. Rude.

Sage hopped up and nudged her body between Kenny and my neck to rest her head on my chin. Her golden-yellow eyes glowed into mine, and I couldn't help but feel a bit judged.

"Well, what do you want me to do?"

She placed a paw on my cheek and purred.

"Okay, fine. Spending the rest of the day moping around the apartment is a bad idea. I guess I could go back downstairs. Kenzie is always good for a laugh."

I swear Sage meowed her approval. It was almost like she was a tiny, wise old lady trapped in a cat's body, not just a simple creature Gigi had rescued from behind the dumpster.

I loved cats, but some of them could be totally creepy.

I narrowed my eyes and studied her expression. "I'll go change."

She jumped off me to land on the ottoman as if she understood, then smacked Kenny on the head and hopped up to the windowsill with him following behind her.

After donning my best jeans and little black T-shirt combo—I didn't do uniforms, which Gigi agreed to before I got here—I threw my hair into a messy bun, put on my Converse, and left. No more dressing up to impress Cole. I had been playing with fire earlier by wearing that dress, and I should have known better. And I needed to quit it with the high heels. My feet were freaking killing me.

A couple of hours left before closing meant that much less time would be spent being stuck in my head tonight. Yay.

Plus, Sage was right. I'd done enough moping around over men. I needed a new outlook on life. Which was what I was supposed to be working on this entire time, damn it.

A rueful laugh escaped as I pushed through the door to the bakery's kitchen. "Kenzie, where are you hiding?" Gigi was already home for the day.

"Oooh, you look pissy." She popped out of the walk-in refrigerator and then eyed me up and down. "Tell me all about it."

"I'm fine. I came back down to help out."

"No need. It's under control, as you can see." She swept an arm out, and yeah, she had it covered.

I sighed and didn't elaborate, even though she could always read every emotion on my face.

"I can see you're upset. I have two working eyeballs and the sixth sense of a psychic, don't I? Do you want me to comfort you? Or bring you treats and leave you alone?"

"Both."

"Ahh, this requires chamomile and your favorite petit fours. Today, we have strawberry cream and chocolate peanut butter. Which would you like?"

"Both."

"I see. Is Ross getting you down? Or possibly the emergency

taco lunch with Cole at Tres Chicas that has you all stressed out and grumpy?"

"Both." My lips shifted up into a grin.

"You'll spill your guts, and I will make you feel better. One-word answers will not suffice." She eyed me speculatively. "Listen, I have a date tomorrow. Can I borrow your pink cashmere sweater and brown leather bomber jacket?"

"Fine, respect. You got me. I'll talk. But I won't start ranting about clothes right now, no matter how funny you think it is." I never let anyone borrow my clothes. I'd learned my lesson in high school when Abigail ruined my first designer little black dress by spilling red wine all over it. It was gorgeous, and I loved it. I'd saved up for months to buy it. I didn't loan out my books for the same reason. I was generous with other things—things you couldn't break. Except for my heart, I'd been generous with that, and Ross hadn't cared one bit.

"Ha! I got you talking. Two things to consider. One—Ross is a giant douche, and we hate him. It would have been a shut-up ring if he proposed to you that night—like a 'will you marry me and shut the fuck up about it' kind of thing. He would have been one of those wedding reception cake-smashed-in-your-face guys, Madi. It wouldn't have been holy matrimony. It would have been holy shit, what was I thinking? And you know it. You did the right thing by dumping his ass and running away. You dodged a huge bullet."

"Don't hold back. Tell me how you really feel."

"I'm glad you're here. That's how I feel."

"I'm glad I'm here too."

"Two—Cole is something else entirely, and I'm intrigued. Tell me all about your lunch with him."

"He—"

She held up a hand. "Wait. Let me gather the supplies. Go, grab us a table, and I'll be right there."

"Oooh, the petit fours. I need a lot, Kenzie. Like, too much."

"Got it."

I stared out the window, letting my mind wander, until I heard a throat clearing beside my table. I turned to find a tall drink of hot guy, who told me his name was Andrew, standing there.

"So, Andrew, what can I do for you?" He seemed shy. He was giving me non-creeper vibes, so I smiled at him.

"You're Kenzie's cousin, right?"

I sat up, narrowing my eyes. "Maybe."

He shook his head. "I'm not here for anything nefarious, or stalkery, or—" Frustrated, he ran his hands into his hair and let out a low growl. "She's driving me crazy. I just need her to talk to me."

"Yeah, I can see that. Driving people crazy is one of her superpowers."

He laughed, dry and cynical. "Why won't she listen? Are running and hiding her other superpowers?"

"No!" I turned to see a rage-filled Kenzie stomping through the Confectionery. "Uh-uh. Nope. You don't get to be here. Get lost, Drew." Kenzie set our food down and glared at him before turning to me. "We dated a few months ago. Zero stars. Do not recommend."

"Oh." I perked up. "This is Drew. *The* Drew? He said Andrew, and I didn't make the connection. I remember now. Hi." Kenzie had told me all about Drew—the man who had cheated on her and broke her heart—over a wine-filled phone call not long after it happened.

"I just want to talk to you—" he told her.

"No. I don't talk to lying, cheating, scumbag men."

"Will you give it a rest and talk to me, please?"

"You give it a rest, asshole. And now you want to talk to me? Fuck that, you had your chance, and you didn't want to talk. Plus, that's my cousin you're hitting on. You have a lot of nerve."

"She thinks I cheated on her," Drew informed me. "And I did not."

"Yeah, right." Kenzie was practically apoplectic, but she also looked sad.

Beneath the anger and bravado she was hurting, you'd have to know her as well as I did to be able to tell. Plus, she'd never been serious about a man before. I wanted to hug her. I wanted to take her upstairs and make it all better with a glass of wine and maybe a movie to veg out over. But I knew better. Getting mushy would only piss her off more.

"Leave. Now," she yelled at him. "I'm going to hurt your feelings or your face, Drew. It's up to you and totally depends on what you choose to do next."

"Fine, I'll go."

"Good. Leave. Bye."

"Great. Perfect. I'm out."

"What the hell, Kenzie?" I hissed as she sat and shoved two petit fours into her mouth.

"I'm pretty sure I'm in love with him," she mumbled while chewing. "I'm so stupid."

"You're not stupid. You're breaking my heart, Kenzie. Can I hug you?"

"Ugh, no. I don't want to talk about it. What's the deal with Cole? You have to talk to me now. Tell me all the things. I need a distraction so I don't go running after his stupid ass."

"Um, okay. I like Cole. Too much, and I need it to stop."

"I can help with that." She nodded emphatically. "I got this. Men, in general, are huge disappointments in most areas. Case in point, both of our fathers, Ross and Drew, Riley's ex-husband—you get the picture. Ask him what his favorite book is. Or his favorite dish to cook. Ask him for laundry tips. Tell him you need to get a grease stain out. And you'll like him a little less when he can't come up with a solution for you, right? He doesn't know about laundry, Madi. None of them do."

"That's not a bad idea. Well, he can make good toast. His coffee was pretty good too."

"Toast is not food. And any idiot who wakes up in the morning can learn to make a decent cup of coffee. Those are basic life skills. Come on, Madi. Just get him talking. The more words that come out of his mouth, the dumber he'll probably sound. Then, boom. Your crush will be deactivated."

"It's worth a try. Can I help you with Drew?"

"Nope. There's no more help for me. I've given up on men, especially that one."

"I think I have to."

"No, not you. You can't give up. It's not too late for you."

"Yeah, I think it is."

"Madi, no. You have a big heart and a lot of love to give. It was wasted on Ross. You'll get your hope back once you move out of the pissed-off phase, unlike me, who will be pissed off for the rest of eternity. No one cheats on me and gets away with it. I'm bitter. I'm jaded as fuck now, and it's never going away."

I sent her a side-eye. She was mad, and she'd get over it, but arguing with her was useless. She was the most hardheaded person I'd met in my entire life.

"If Ross can trigger me with just a random thought and whatever news—that I don't even know yet—coming from my sisters, then I'm a lost cause. I don't want to put myself out there anymore. I don't want to get hurt."

"I beg to differ. Take that yellow dress you were wearing earlier today. I was with you when you bought it, and I know what it's for.

It's a take-it-off-me-dress. You wore it for Cole, right? That equals subconscious hope, which means you still have it."

"Maybe. Okay, I wanted to look cute in case I ran into him. But I didn't want him to take it off. I don't know what I want from him, and that's my problem. Therefore, I now want nothing. It's logical. If I can't have love. Then I want logic."

"Logic, shmogic—don't be boring. You have plenty of time to decide what you want. But listen, I am the true face of hopelessness. Don't be like me. There are no take-it-off dresses in my closet anymore, and cute undies are a thing of the past. I'm wearing granny panties right now. I have no hope, and I'm all out of time, patience, and the will to tolerate any more bullshit from some dumbass man. I used to be like you—wearing cute clothes all the time, and cute undies too. But that was back when I thought getting laid was a possibility. Now I'm like, sweet, these come in a six-pack, and I get two more pairs for free. And I'm thinking these thoughts at Costco, Madi. I'm going to die alone. Just me and my jumbo-sized jar of cheese balls, sitting around in my granny panties, binge-watching *Bridgerton* on my couch. All alone. I'm done with love."

"Oh, girl."

"I know. It's bad. Don't let yourself turn out like me. You dumped your bonehead, and you'll move on eventually. I'm still—"

"Pining?"

"Fuck yes, I'm pining. But it will never work out with him. I can't be with a cheater. And I can't stand liars."

"No. You're right, and both are unacceptable. Did he really cheat, though? Are you sure? He seemed pretty earnest."

"Thongs do not lie. Men do."

"Yeah. I guess you have a point about that."

"Plus, he won't explain anything. He says he doesn't know how it got there and expects me to trust him. Like, hello? Do thongs grow in Corollas? Do they pop up between the seats like freaking spring flowers? I think not. Thongs generally only find their way into a back seat when they're bodily removed from someone's tush, in this case by a horndog, lying cheater. Am I right?"

"I mean, probably..."

"Good. We agree. Back to Cole."

"Oh god."

"I think Cole might be a good guy for real. One of the very few left in existence. He's always in here, and I've gotten to know him and his kids. But I get not being ready to move on. I accept your reasoning, and it's sound. I even agree with it. I'll help you avoid him whenever he's in here. There will be no more teasing. No more pressure. No more nothing."

"Thanks. I appreciate that."

"Not until you're ready."

"Oh, I won't be."

"But you will."

"I won't. I'm done too. You can come to Colorado Springs with me when I go back. We'll be roomies; we can shop for caftans like Gigi's and eat midnight cheesecake whenever we're stressed out. I'll bring the cats—the only men we need in our lives are Kenny and Victor. It'll be great."

She rolled her eyes. "Okay. We'll see."

"Yeah, we will. We'll see me, still single as a Pringle when Gigi's boot comes off, and you with your anger issues under control because we're gonna work on that—riding off into the sunset to Colorado Springs. Together. Me. You. Three cats. Pow!"

"Enough, there is no way I'm moving to Colorado Springs. I am Cozy Creek for life. Born and bred, baby. I'm never leaving."

"Okay..."

"As your friend, it's my duty to comfort you. But as your cousin and blood-related family member, it's also my duty to kick your ass into gear too. You got hurt, Madi. You can't keep it all inside. Feelings fester if you don't let them out. They'll rot you from the inside. I don't want that for you."

"You're trying to tell me about what's healthy? Hypocritical much?" Ignoring her excellent advice, I focused on something I could argue with. "Are eternal granny panties and cheeseballs good for you? Binging *Bridgerton* is completely healthy, so I'll let that one pass. But you said it yourself; you've given up. That is not healthy at all."

"Are my feelings a mystery?" she shot back. "Do you ever wonder how I feel? About anything?"

"No, you're an open book, Kenzie. But I'm not like that. I don't want to talk about Ross with my freaking sisters or you. What's wrong with that?"

She heaved out a sigh. "When you're ready, I'm here to listen. But the longer you wait, the more alcohol we're going to need to get through it, just saying."

CHAPTER 12

Cole

The week went by in a blur of kids' activities, work, and the various minutia of life. I saw Madi most mornings at the Confectionery when I was there for breakfast with the guys from the station or when she stopped by Gigi's to walk Basil with Natalie. But it was always brief, and I was unable to get any time alone with her—which was good since I was not supposed to want to be alone with her, damn it. The lack of discipline in my mind whenever she crossed it frustrated me.

We had a fundraiser meeting next week, but I didn't want to wait that long. I craved another conversation with her. I wanted to hear her laugh, and I missed her smile.

"Dad! Can I put it here? Pumpkins are just too freaking heavy," Evan grumbled as he hobbled from the back of my truck to set his armful down next to me.

"Yeah, bud."

October had rolled into Cozy Creek, bringing in burnished shades of red, orange, and deep golden-yellow. The town square was decorated to the nines for the season, and I, along with the rest of the Fire Brigade crew, were doing our part to keep the station festive.

Leaves blew in the light breeze as Evan and I added pumpkins and scarecrows to the pots of marigolds and mums decorating the old red 1950s GMC pumper truck parked in front of the station. It no longer ran, but it was a piece of our history that tourists loved to sit in and pose for pictures with.

Long-standing Cozy Creek tradition dictated our décor. A few crew members were outside the station on ladders, hanging garlands and festive lanterns.

I waved as Mac McCreedy drove by on his tractor, pulling a trailer full of happy-faced locals and tourists through town on a hayride. He donated pumpkins to the station every year. His family's ranch had been around forever.

"Can I go on the next ride?" Evan asked.

"Yup, find Nat, and she can go with you."

"Yes! Thanks, Dad." He ran into the station to find Natalie, who was busy helping Monica decorate the reception area. Each year at Halloween, we passed out candy and gave station tours.

"Cole!"

I spun to find Madi hurrying across the street toward me with a huge camera bag slung over her shoulder. She wore tight jeans, a gold-colored V-neck sweater, and high-heeled booties. Her long golden-brown waves flowed over the opposite shoulder to tangle in her necklace and fall into the delicate line of her cleavage.

The breeze carried her perfume to me, like when I picked her up that first day on the highway: vanilla and spice. I wanted to pull her in and smell it up close. I wanted that scent on my skin. I wanted too much.

Fuck me, she was stunning, and I couldn't look away. She radiated sunshine. Even her walk was filled with cheerfulness.

"This is perfection." She patted the truck's hood, slamming into me with the heavy bag as she approached.

I let out a breath and rubbed my hip bone.

"Oh god! I'm so sorry."

"I'm okay." Her nearness was overwhelming. She could run me over with her car, and I probably wouldn't mind too much.

"Did I hurt you? This bag is huge." Her delicate fingers struggled with the strap, which had become tangled in her hair.

"Let me help you. Hold still." Our foreheads touched as I leaned in to disentangle her. "Sorry," I mumbled under my breath.

"No, it's okay," she whispered back. "Thank you, I'm a mess. We can do the photo shoot for the calendar right here by the truck. It's like you knew I was coming. It'll be so pretty with all the flowers and the decorated station in the background." The slight chill in the air flushed her cheeks pink, and her parted lips were stained a deep burgundy rose. It was all I could do not to kiss her.

I cleared my throat. "Damn, I was secretly hoping we'd run out of time for that. It's short notice, isn't it?"

"Nope." She beamed at me. My heart boomed in my chest, and I knew I was about to do anything she asked me. "I know a guy who owes my mother a favor. His specialties include everything last minute and cheap, and he just texted me back. He can get the calendar formatted and printed in time for the fundraiser—as many as we need—if we send him the pictures of you guys by the end of the week." She gestured to the camera case I'd set on the truck's hood. "I was hoping to stop by and grab a few shots."

"Great. Should I take my shirt off right now?" I teased, tugging the hem of my T-shirt up a couple of inches.

"Uh—" She froze; her face turned bright red as she stared at the sliver of abs I had bared, and I grinned as her mouth dropped open. It was like she'd glitched. "I—"

"Dude, you broke her," Kenzie called out from across the street, where she'd just parked her car. She carried a ring light and her phone. "I'm helping out today. I told Madi a surprise mission was for the best. I know none of you guys want your picture taken. Am I right?"

"It's for a good cause," Madi, who had snapped out of her stupor, argued.

"The mental picture of all you guys sans shirts must have short-circuited her brain when she brought it up. Is that it?" Kenzie teased. "Madi, you were practically drooling."

Madi slugged her arm lightly. "No. I'm fine. I'm good. I'm a professional." She huffed. "I took a bunch of photography classes in college. I know what I'm doing, okay? And no, none of you have to be shirtless. I mean, unless you're comfortable with it, that is."

"It never crossed my mind to question your abilities," I said pointedly. I couldn't stand to see anyone embarrassed, even if the joke was good-natured like Kenzie's was. "We all trust you."

"Thanks. See, Kenzie?" She stuck out her tongue while Kenzie laughed. "They trust me."

"I'm sorry, Madi. My filter is faulty. I didn't mean to embarrass you. I'll go see who wants to be shot today," Kenzie offered, passing me the ring light and leaving Madi and me alone by the truck.

"It's been a while," I said to change the subject. "I mean, since our lunch at Tres Chicas."

"Yeah, I've been busy. Working at Gigi's keeps me on my toes. Plus, her doctor said she needs to keep her ankle elevated. She's been on the couch all week. Kenzie and I have been bringing her dinner and hanging out every night."

"Understandable. So, about the meeting, I'll have the kids tomorrow—"

"Oh, do you need to reschedule?"

"No. That won't be necessary. I thought you could have dinner with us at the house instead of meeting at my office. Natalie wants to discuss something with you—something about winging her eyeliner? Anyway, I'll cook. You can talk makeup or whatever with Nat. Then we'll all eat, and you and I can have our meeting after. If that's okay with you?"

"That's fine with me. What time? And should I bring anything? I could whip up another batch of brownies?"

"How about six o'clock?" I suggested, and she nodded, saying that it was okay. "Normally, I'd say I had it all covered, but if I turn down your brownies, the kids will kill me."

"Uh, what's your favorite dish to cook? I could help you make dinner?" she offered.

My eyes darted to the side, where Kenzie stood, not quite out of my view, as she talked to Tate and gave Madi an approving thumbs-up before going inside the open bays to speak to the rest of the crew. *Weird.*

I turned my focus back to Madi. "Do you like rib eye? My mom has an amazing herbed butter recipe that goes great on steaks—with thyme, garlic, and fresh cracked pepper."

"That sounds awesome."

"Excellent. I'll pick up the steaks on my way home tonight. I like to use my grandma's old cast iron skillet and baste with butter halfway through. You'll love it. We can go out to my greenhouse with the kids and pick a salad if you're interested. My garden has gone wild. We could make ranch dressing with fresh herbs to go on top."

"Oh. Wow. I've never tried that."

"It's important for kids to know where their food is coming from."

"I agree. I have always enjoyed baking with Gigi ever since I was little. Do they cook too?"

"Yup. They've been in the kitchen with me since they were tiny. They love it."

Kenzie shouldered her way between me and Madi. "I am both jealous and impressed with your dinner plans. Listen, we have five of Cozy Creek's finest willing to pose right now. Today. Boom! Add Cole, and we will have half the year covered. You're welcome."

"This is perfect." Madi was back to all business. "How about you guys wear the suspender pants and T-shirts? Would that be okay?"

"Uh-uh, nope." Kenzie shook her head. "Tate wants to be shirtless, and he insisted on hanging from a pole like a stripper."

Madi burst out laughing. "I mean, he deserves January for that. Start the year off right."

"Pace also agreed. No shirt."

"Really?" I raised an eyebrow. Tate, I believed, was a total ham. But Pace?

"I'm totally persuasive," Kenzie insisted. "Okay, fine. It's probably the sprinkle cakes I bribed them all with. And the friendly reminder that it was for charity. I didn't say anything untoward, not really." She shrugged. "Strong-arm tactics, what? Threatening to cut off their breakfast sandwich and protein smoothie supply, who? Not this girl. Oh, and they're doing us a solid, and some of the crew that are off will swing by. We might be able to get the whole year today." She took a bow. "You're welcome, Madi. Tell me I'm the best assistant ever."

"What can I say?" Madi grinned at her. "I couldn't do it without you. You're the best ever."

"I see." I chuckled. "Threatening to cut them off at Gigi's, blackmail, and bribery; I respect your tactics, Kenzie. It makes complete sense now. I'll change and round up the guys. Be right back."

"Girl, I heard almost everything he said to you," Kenzie whisper-shouted once I'd turned my back. "He cooks. I should have known. That was a complete and total failure of a question. Find a way to ask him about books when you have dinner at his place. Or spill something and see if he knows how to clean it. I don't know. He might be the perfect man. Like, look at him. Look at all of them. Damn. Today is going to be fun. Helping out friends is so worth it sometimes."

"Right. You're so freaking helpful," Madi whisper-shouted beneath her breath. "Jeez, Kenzie." Her voice oozed with sarcasm. "You were supposed to be my flirtation prevention buffer. But instead, you accused me of perving out at the thought of shirtless firefighters, then ran off. Thanks for making this so much easier."

"Hey, I came back as fast as I could. I made a few threats and got the job done. We'll get six pics today. What more do you want?"

"Fine, you're right. Thank you."

I couldn't help but eavesdrop as I walked away. *Did she have feelings for me?* It sounded like she did. *Flirtation buffer?*

I wanted to stop and listen to the rest of their conversation, but I was already being too obvious with how slow I was walking, so I forced myself to go into the station instead.

Tate was already shirtless and rubbing lotion on his chest when I found him by his locker. "I need to wash my hands before I head out. Don't want to slip off the pole, bro."

"You're—"

"Oiled up and ready to rock?" He flexed in the mirror.

"Not the words I would choose, but all right."

"I want to be Mr. January, or maybe February—Valentine's Day. This could be good for me."

"I'm glad you're excited, but I'm not sure I'm up for this, to be honest. And a bachelor auction too—"

"You don't want the attention. Yeah, I get it."

"What's that supposed to mean?"

"You've been lying low since the divorce. This will put you back out there. Then there's the whole Madi situation."

"Yeah. That. I mean, her. The situation."

His eyes flicked to mine in surprise. "You're admitting there's a situation now. Wow. That's good. You're making progress. I'm proud of you."

"Well, I can't stop fucking thinking about her. Does that mean there's a situation?"

He shrugged lightly as he grinned at me. "Pretty much."

"She's young," I grumbled. "Too young for me."

"She's thirty years old, Cole. She's hardly a kid. You had a wife and two kids by the time you were her age."

"Fine, point taken. But she's eight years younger than me. Isn't that creepy?"

"Ask her and see what she says about it. Eight years means nothing when you're both in your thirties. Besides, I've seen how she looks at you."

I didn't want to ask, but I had to know. "Uh, how does she look at me?" He was going to give me so much shit for this. I knew it.

He leaned in conspiratorially, relishing being in the older brother role. Usually, I was the one giving all the advice. "Well, it's not so much the *how*. It's the fact that she doesn't stop looking once she catches sight of you. The second you step into the Confectionery, you're like a hunk of metal, and her eyeballs become magnets. It's cute watching her try to look away, though. Pay attention next time you see her."

My heart went into orbit at his words. This felt like—I didn't even know what it felt like. I tried to recall how I'd felt when I had asked Sherry out for the first time and couldn't.

"Maybe I'll ask her to dinner. I mean, on an actual date. Not at my house with the kids present. Should I?"

"Hell, yes. Now take off your shirt and get your ass outside. Go for it." He tossed me his bottle of lotion with a grin.

I caught it, then tossed it back. I'd be keeping my shirt on, thank you very much.

"I haven't asked anyone out since Sherry, Tate." The smile slid from my mouth along with the words. Why was admitting my insecurities out loud worse than when they were just torturing me in my head? "I have no idea what I'm doing."

"Other than falling for her, am I right?"

I waited a beat, taking a deep breath through my nose before exhaling loudly to gather whatever courage I had left. "Yeah." It felt good to admit it. Scary. Real.

"Being in a relationship is not like riding a bike," he stated. "You don't do it once, and the rest are the same. I don't have to tell you this, but I'll say it anyway. Women are elusive—all of them are different. There is no such thing as a game plan for love, and anyone who says there is is a fool. The good thing is, you've been getting to know her. Think about Madi and what would touch her heart and go from there."

I stared at him for a second.

Where was the sarcasm?

Where was the joke?

"That's actually good advice."

"You sound so surprised." He laughed. "Should I be offended?"

"No. I know you're a good guy, Tate. You've just been—"

"Broken? Bitter? Extremely disgruntled? The last couple of years have been bullshit, you know that. You were there for it. Divorce sucks."

"It sure as fuck does." I took a deep breath in and let it out in a whoosh. Like letting go of a weight I'd been carrying around. "But that doesn't mean we can't move on, right?"

"Damn straight. It's time." He slapped me on the shoulder.

"You don't think it's a mistake? She's Gigi's granddaughter. What if it doesn't work out?"

"But what if it does? Look at it this way. You've already fucked it all up by having feelings for her. What are you going to do? Will you watch her date someone else? Watch her bring some dumbass to Gigi's place for the holidays? No. You need to be that holiday dumbass, Cole."

"Another good point. It's rude, but still a good one. You're two for two today. I'm impressed. Thanks."

"You're welcome. Listen, you are Colton James Sutter, the baddest-ass older brother in the world. You got this."

"I got this," I repeated. Hoping like hell he was right.

CHAPTER 13

Madi

I needed to go straight to church on Sunday and confess my sins. Most of which were made up of impure thoughts thanks to the sight of the shirtless Cozy Creek Fire Brigade and one dark-haired, blue-eyed firefighter, whom I was about to take as many pictures of as was professionally appropriate.

"You're next, Cole!" Kenzie turned and shouted. He had gone up to his office to get some paperwork done.

"He won't hear you. He's all the way upstairs."

I sent him a text to let him know it was his turn.

She wiggled her fingers together beneath her chin and cackled at me. "Dude, your face is so red. Try to chill out, okay? Or he will figure out exactly how hard you're crushing on him."

"Shut up!" I hissed. "The guys will hear you. Dang, Kenzie."

"No, they won't. They're all back in their little firefighter garage, playing with their hoses. No one will hear me from all the way down here." She was sitting on the back of the old firetruck, swinging her legs and laughing at my nervous dismay as I fiddled with my camera equipment.

"You're too much. I should have had Gigi help me."

"Gigi's a bigger perv than I am." She scoffed. "Who's the one who thought this entire thing up?"

"Ugh, fine."

"Why did I save him for last?"

"So you can be alone with him." She flicked her wrist, checking her smartwatch with a smirk. "Oh no. Something suddenly came up," she deadpanned with a smirk. "I guess you'll have to take hottie Cole's picture all by yourself." She hopped off the truck and waved at me. "Ta ta, don't do anything I wouldn't do."

"Kenzie! What the hell? Where are you going?"

"Nowhere. Everywhere. Or maybe just back to Gigi's. I'll meet you at your place when you're done." She tossed me her keys. "I'll leave my car since you have all that camera crap. Later."

"This isn't cool! You are on my list," I hollered at her retreating back as she waved at me over her shoulder.

I shook my head. It didn't matter if she left. I was a professional. I could take Cole's photo *professionally* and not drool all over him. Probably.

Out of all of them, Cole seemed to be the most ill at ease. He had excused himself and practically ran to his office when I started. But to be fair, none of them had watched each other get their photos taken. They'd taken turns posing in front of the old truck, then gone back inside to do whatever they did in the station when they weren't out fighting fires and saving lives.

"Shit," I muttered as I waited for him to come down. "He's just a man. You've got this. You're a trained professional, and he is just a man. He is just the sexiest firefighting man in the entire world, damn it. I don't got this at all. I got nothing." I shrugged my shoulders up and down and did a little hop to pump myself up.

"You okay there, Madi? Are you cold?"

"Huh?" I spun to face him, nearly tripping over my feet as the heel of my boot got caught in a crack in the sidewalk. "No. I'm not cold. I'm totally professional—I mean fine. I'm totally fine." I caught myself and smiled at him.

"Okay." His lips tipped up at the corner. "I have an extra jacket in the station. If you need it, let me know."

"Thanks." Gah! How can he be so hot and sweet at the same time? It was not fair to us mere mortals.

"So, uh . . ." He fidgeted with the suspenders on his pants and looked at me questioningly. He was struggling with this. He was nervous, and my heart melted.

"Right. All the other guys posed right over there. By the truck. Does that work for you?"

"Yeah, sure."

I didn't want to make him even more uncomfortable by asking if he wanted to remove his shirt, so I didn't. It wasn't like he needed to anyway. He had changed into a blue Cozy Creek Fire Brigade branded T-shirt, and it was snug.

His biceps strained at the sleeves, and his pecs were pec-ing all over the place. Good lord, his chest was broad, like a freaking wall. My eyes were about to pop out of my head like one of those old-timey cartoons. I was in real danger of embarrassing myself over him.

I thought I had it bad when I saw him jogging all over town. That was nothing compared to how I felt right now.

I was face-to-face with his glorious pecs, abs, shoulders, and all the other gorgeous parts of his body. Seriously, the man was without flaw, and he rocked the crap out of that T-shirt.

Plus, I knew him better now. His personality, in combination with his looks, was lethal. He was super shy about having his picture taken, which was completely adorable.

I wanted to cuddle him.

In his lap.

Naked.

Damn it.

"How about you stand by the door." My voice came out squeaky, like a horny little mouse. "Maybe put your hand on the hood and lean in?"

"Sure, yeah." He did what I said, but it seemed like he forgot how to be human in the process.

He was rigid.

He was stiff and awkward.

He was also pink-cheeked and embarrassed, and I swear I fell a little bit in love with him.

I snapped a few pics as he squirmed and tried to smile.

"Hey, I might have a better idea. Give me a second." I dropped my hand, holding the camera to the side, and hitched my hip as I contemplated the truck, his body, and all the awkwardness, and tried to figure out if there was any way I could make him more comfortable with this whole thing.

He was the chief. He had to be in the calendar. It would be wrong to make it without him.

"Please do not ask me to keep standing here like this." He dropped his head back between his shoulder blades and threw his arms to the sides. "It's like I forgot how to work my face or something. Why is smiling so hard? I can't even lean against this truck right—"

"It's okay. Shh, I got this. Come on." I headed to the truck's rear, where Kenzie had been sitting, and patted the back. "Sit here."

"I don't know about this," he joked. "Sitting might be too complicated for me too."

At that moment, Evan and Natalie headed up the street, looking all windblown and adorable with their pink cheeks and messy hair. Sure, they were both in their teens, but that didn't mean they couldn't be cute.

"Hey, you two," I called. "Come help me take your dad's picture."

"Great," Cole muttered. "Now, I'll never hear the end of it. You're giving them ammo to tease me with, you know."

"Nope. I have an even better idea now, and you'll love it, I promise. Sit tight." I gestured to his arms. "May I adjust you?"

"Yeah." His eyebrows shot up. "Do whatever you need."

I stepped into him, taking his hands in mine to place them near his thighs at the edge of the truck. They were warm, his palms wide and strong. I managed to avoid tracing the fascinating trail of veins leading up his forearms, but it was hard.

"Hold on right there and just pretend you're at home on the couch relaxing instead of the middle of Main Street getting your picture taken while wearing a tight T-shirt." Our eyes met, and his crinkled at the corners in that swoony way that was quickly becoming an essential part of my days here in Cozy Creek. "You look hot, Cole," I added under my breath. "You're gonna raise a lot of money."

"If we do, it will be because of you." His voice was deep and husky. Hearing it felt like taking a shot of whiskey. It sent a thrill zipping through me, but I couldn't focus on that right now. His kids were here.

"Oh, it absolutely will; I know it," I answered with mock severity. "Natalie and Evan. Come over here and stand behind me."

They ran up, breathless and flushed from the chill in the air. "Is this for the calendar?" Natalie asked.

"Yup. And I'll take a few shots of you together when I finish."

Cole's eyes warmed on me. "Thanks," he murmured. "I'd like that."

I gave him what I told myself was a jaunty, non-flirtatious wink. "I promise at least one of them will be suitable for framing."

He chuckled. "This might take us all night then."

I shivered at the idea of doing anything all night with Cole.

Yum.

"Don't you worry about a thing. I've got skills. Hold on to the truck, lean forward, shoulders back, and flex every muscle you have. Don't think. Just react. Natalie and Evan, it's time to dance with me. We're going to shake our tail feathers."

I started shaking my booty and wiggling my body in a ridiculous, rhythmless display of nonsense.

Evan cracked up and started shaking his hips immediately.

"That's right, Evan. Shake that thang," I encouraged. "Who needs music? Not us."

Cole burst out laughing.

Click.

After Natalie caught on, we did our best to keep Cole laughing while I aimed my camera and clicked away as he cracked up at our antics.

Perfection.

I knew I had a ton of good shots of him. He was gorgeous, and once we got rid of the nerves, the camera reflected that.

"All right, kids. Go stand by your dad." They did what I asked, and I got a few more pictures for Cole to keep. "That's a wrap!" I declared, wishing so badly I could somehow get a picture of the two of us together.

I wanted to remember this moment when I was back in Colorado Springs or to have it as a memento of an early day in our relationship, but I shoved the thought out of my head. I was being ridiculous and fanciful—we had no relationship, not yet, anyway.

"You guys go wait for me inside, okay?" Cole hopped down and sent his kids into the station.

I watched them go, waving at them before putting my camera away.

"I don't know what to say, Madi."

He was so tall in front of me. He was so freaking beautiful and wholly focused on me. It was intoxicating. I tilted my head back and grinned up at him. "You don't have to say anything. I got some great shots."

"You made this so easy. I was nervous." He ran a hand through his hair and looked away. "I sometimes have a problem with being the center of attention."

"I get it; you can be shy, and that's okay." I poked him in the stomach, and my eyes widened at the hardness of his abs. "But I told you I was a pro, didn't I?" I teased.

"That you did, and I appreciate it, Madi. More than I can say."

"Well, I'm happy I could, uh—" I fought the urge to throw myself into his arms and hug the crap out of him. My stomach swirled, and my heart was turning somersaults in my chest. "I'm just happy," I finally said. It was the truth, after all. He made me happy every time I saw him. "It was fun being here with you. And your kids are amazing."

At first, I tried so hard not to objectify him when I took his picture. But after a few moments, it was easy; he was more than just a man with a devastatingly handsome face and an unbelievable body. He was also self-effacingly funny, humble, and brave. He was a good dad and a gentleman, and he deserved to have the pictures to show it. But I had to admit, he was still the most beautiful man I have ever seen in my entire life.

"Thank you. They like you a lot. Okay, well, I'll get going. I have to drive the kids to my ex's place." He was saying goodbye but lingering.

"Yeah, okay, bye, Cole." I zipped my camera into the case and grabbed the light while avoiding his eyes.

It felt like we should kiss or at least hug. Something was pulling us together, but for some reason, we ignored it—maybe because we were in public or because his kids were so close by.

"See you tomorrow night," he said as he stood on the sidewalk, looking at me with his gorgeous blue eyes.

"Yep." I breathed. "My brownies and I will be there at six."

"Can't wait." He turned and headed to the station's lobby entrance. Then stopped to turn back and wave at me.

Even though I didn't get a kiss, it felt like I was drifting on a cloud as I crossed the street to get into Kenzie's car and drive back to my place.

I found her waiting for me on one of the Confectionery's outside tables. She was sipping an iced tea and furiously texting someone on her phone.

"Let's go upstairs." She stood. "You're going to spill your guts, and I mean everything—all of it. The look on your face is telling a thousand tales. And at least half of them are dirty."

I unlocked the door, and we hurried up to my place.

"I'll never get over today, Kenzie."

The sight of the shirtless Cozy Creek Fire Brigade was most likely permanently burned into my retinas. No matter how hard I tried to force it out, it wouldn't get out of my brain.

And Cole? Gah! Was I falling for him? I was pretty sure it was happening. The crush was growing, and I was powerless against it.

She grabbed Kenny and flopped on my sofa. He curled up on her chest, purring his brains out while Sage perched on the chair above my shoulder. Victor was in his usual spot by the fireplace, silently judging us as we poked over the day's events.

"I get you." She shot me a grin. "I don't even like any of them that way, and I won't be over it any time soon either. And freaking Tate? Who knew he was hiding all that sexiness under his shirt? Did you?"

"I had no idea. I mean, we probably should have, though. They run all over town like they're being chased."

"He has an eight-pack. Eight, Madi, I mean damn. Oh, and let's not forget about Pace. And Mason, and freaking Jeff—his wife is so lucky. The rest of them started to blur together after a certain point. I think I stopped retaining new information, and the word 'hot' just *beep bop booped* inside my head as I tried not to drool. Do eyeballs feel happiness? Because I think mine are fucking overjoyed right now. And don't get me started on my ovaries. I feel like I need a cigarette."

"Right? I'll never be able to look any of them in the face at Gigi's ever again. Not when I know what they all look like shirtless. We have too much information now—that phrase is legit."

"How was it with Cole?"

"He's so sweet. I knew he was a nice guy, obviously. But he was shy, and it was adorable. And his kids are amazing."

"I told you. He's a good one. Gah! I love shy guys. It makes me want to climb them like a damn tree." Kenny hopped to the windowsill, and she flopped to her side on the couch. "Hey, aren't your sisters coming to see you tonight?"

"Yes." I heaved out a disgruntled sigh. "To talk about Ross. They have something to tell me. And Kenzie. I do not want to know."

"You're better off without him, don't forget that. I'll get out of your hair." She sat up and stretched before heading to the front door. "I should get back down to the bakery anyway. Those sugar cookies aren't going to decorate themselves."

"I'll see you tomorrow morning."

"Yeah, bright and early."

My text notification went off. Kenzie paused at the door. "Is it Cole already? That's a good sign."

> **Riley:** Meet us at Bookers. Thirty minutes. Abigail is already two margaritas deep. I'll wait until you get here to start. Shots!

"Damn, no. It's not Cole. It's Riley. She wants me to meet them at Bookers for dinner. Abigail is already drinking. This should be interesting."

She laughed. "I'll see you closer to lunchtime, then. Knowing those two, you'll be out late and wake up hungover."

CHAPTER 14

Madi

Bookers Pub was as crowded as it ever was. Okay, so I'd only heard how busy it could get from my sisters. This was my first time here.

"Over here!" Abigail stood on her chair, waving her arms above her head.

I watched Riley tug her down and whisper in her ear. Abigail threw her head back, laughing, and I knew I was about to have fun. Tipsy Abigail was hilarious.

The three of us were as different as could be, but that didn't mean I didn't enjoy their company. Riley was stylish and sleek, all about designer clothes and perfectly polished hair and makeup—she was immaculate. She wore designer jeans and a black blazer over a shiny white silk tank top tonight. Her pointy-toed, bright pink stilettos were her only pop of color.

Abigail was her opposite—picture a thirty-two-year-old version of Stevie Nicks with wild chocolate brown waves and boho clothes. According to Abigail, one could not have too many accessories; she was dripping in silver—a stack of bracelets on each wrist, a tangle of shimmery necklaces, and a ring on almost every finger.

My style fell somewhere in the middle. I had changed to a simple black sheath with long sleeves and a deep V-neck. Black patent leather stilettos were on my feet. I felt pretty. If I was about to get bad news, I had to look hot while I got it. Somehow, it made me feel better.

We were different in so many ways, but we always, *always* had each other's backs. I hoped like hell they weren't here to try to get me to take Ross back. Because *no*.

Riley stood, holding her arms out and wiggling her fingers as I approached. "Hugs!" she shouted as I walked into her arms. "I missed you, Mads." She kissed the top of my head and then pulled away with a grin. "This one is trying to choose a Fire Brigade member to hit on. Help me keep her under control." She eyed me sharply with a cat-eating-the-canary grin on her face. "We've heard Cole is off the market again. Is that true? Because I approve, one hundred percent. He's a great guy. I've always thought so."

"Um . . ." I slid into their booth, trying to decide what to tell them about Cole, if anything.

"Don't worry, I won't flirt with him ever again." Abigail passed me a tequila shot as she attempted to reassure me quietly. "Last time I was here in town, Gigi told me he was divorced, so—" She shrugged. "Look, he was single and hot and right there across the street. Convenient, right? But he wasn't interested in me, and I don't have feelings for him—at all. So now that he's yours, it won't be a thing. Don't worry."

"He's not exactly mine, and I'm not worried. I, uh—"

"That's not important now," Riley cut me off and covered my hand with hers. "We have news, and it's not great."

I sighed. "Just tell me. Is Ross going to try to get me back? Because that's never going to happen. It's over—"

"Not quite. He is—"

"Fuck!" Abigail pointed to the entrance. "He's right fucking there." She was aghast. "What the hell is he doing here? Oh my god, Riley?"

"What?" I hissed. "He's here? Are you trying to set me up—I thought—but you just said—" I was stammering in confusion because what the hell was going on?

"Hell, no." Abigail drew her head back on her neck, and her eyes widened. "Fuck that guy, and I mean that, Madi. Fuck. Him. Shit, shit, shit. Riley, he's coming this way with *her*."

"Her?" I twisted in my seat but couldn't see above the back of the booth. "What do you mean, *her*? What her? Who her?"

Ross was here? In Cozy Creek?

With another woman? Who?

I took a glance around the side of the booth.

"That's Hanna Hadley," I said through my teeth at Riley. "What is she doing with him?"

"We know who she is," she gritted back. "Her grandma is frenemies with Gigi, and her mother, Heather, is currently attempting to screw her way through the Fire Brigade—she's not having much luck, though. Ask Mom, they went to high school together, and Mom can't stand her. Those three Hadley ladies are trouble."

"What do you two know? Is this why we're here? Also, frenemies? I had no idea. Gigi never said a word to me about that."

"Well, you've never been to a poker game. That's probably why it never came up. The Hadley's are, uh, not great. Gigi is all about keeping your friends close and your frenemies closer. It's better to see shit coming, you know? She likes to keep an eye on them."

"What the fuck is he doing here?" Abigail was still fretting. But I needed answers.

"Riley, please. Tell me what's happening."

"He's nothing but a selfish prick, Madi." She took my other hand. "He promised to let us tell you first. He swore he'd stay out of Cozy Creek until you knew everything and had time to process."

"Process what? Does Gigi know what's going on?"

"No. Nobody knows anything as far as we can tell—including her family. He's dating Hanna Hadley, Madi. I'm so sorry. Abigail and I saw them coming out of his apartment when we went to pick up the rest of the things you left there."

"Wait a minute." My hand went to my chest. "Back up. Is he seeing someone else? Already? Are you sure?"

Ross wasn't a commitment phobe.

It was me. He didn't want to commit *to me*.

I didn't want him anymore. I didn't even miss him.

But this fucking *hurt*.

What was wrong with me? Why hadn't he wanted me? I would have made a great fucking wife, damn it.

I swallowed the lump in my throat, snatched a napkin from the table, and dabbed it beneath my eyes as I stared into the light above our table, trying to blink back the rapidly forming tears.

"You guys." I waved a hand to fan it in front of my face and bounced in my seat. "I think I'm going to cry. I don't want to cry. Tell me to knock it off."

"No. Stop. You are not crying over that asshole. Don't you dare. You're going to be fine," Riley all but growled. "I'll fucking make sure of that. Don't you worry about a thing, Madison. I got you. Do not look outside of this booth. They've stopped near the bar for a second. *Shh.*"

"He's a goddamn prick, and I never liked her," Abigail stated pointedly as she stabbed a fingertip at the top of the table. "Say the word, and I'll smack her around for you. Him too. He's tall, but I think I can take him. I'm pretty fucking pissed right now, and liquor gives me courage. No one fucks with family." I almost laughed. She sounded like a mafia guy.

"That's sweet of you, Abigail, but no thank you. The last thing we need is a scene. You guys, is he coming over here—with her? What the hell am I supposed to do?"

"Act like you don't care," Riley answered under her breath. "We'll get rid of him."

"I don't care. But also, I do. I have never had this feeling before—"

"Get rid of him? No way," Abigail protested. "There are three fucking drinks left on this table. He will be wearing at least one of them when he leaves. But don't worry, we can get more."

"No. Please," I begged her. "Don't start anything. I don't want that, then everybody will know something is going on. I just want to go home. Get me out of here. Do not cause a scene, Abigail."

"But I'm so good at it," she whined. "Let me do this for you, my little baby sister. You're too sweet to handle this properly. This needs to go down ugly, Madi. He doesn't deserve it any other way."

I burst out in a startled laugh. "Don't make me laugh when I'm—I don't even know how I feel about this."

"You don't care," Riley insisted again. "He's not worth it. *You* dumped *him*, and he deserved it. Do not forget that."

Tears filled my eyes again, but I managed to blink them back. "Yeah, but he's already moved on? What was wrong with me? It's barely been two months. He cried when I broke it off. I told you that, didn't I?"

They exchanged a look, and I grew alarmed.

"Nothing is wrong with you," Abigail slurred. "Not one fucking thing. You are not crying over that prick, not tonight. We got you. Try not to listen to anything he says. It'll all be a bunch of bullshit anyway."

The time was nigh. He was almost here at my table. As he approached, he looked at me like he felt sorry for me. *What the hell?*

"Madi. I heard you were in Cozy Creek." His eyes drifted to Riley and Abigail like they had planned this. Like they were expecting him to show up here tonight.

"Don't look at us like we're all still friends, dick. We didn't tell you she was here." Abigail huffed.

My eyes darted between them. The music here was loud, but I had a feeling Abigail would become louder.

"I told him," Hanna confessed. "I can't wait anymore. We need to clear the air before we announce our engagement. With you being Gigi's granddaughter and her being so prominent in town, I felt it was important to give you a heads-up. I didn't want this to cause a scandal—"

"Why would this cause a scandal?"

Ice ran through my veins when I saw a ring on her finger. *That* finger. A big round solitaire on a white gold band. I didn't want it, but it should have been mine.

Weird thoughts coursed through my mind as I put the pieces together.

They were engaged.

Already?

What the ever-loving hell?

"Um..." Ross looked to the ceiling, searching for words. It was a familiar quirk, but I no longer found it cute. Instead, I wanted to throttle him.

"Well, honestly, it shouldn't be scandalous at all," Hanna answered earnestly. She looked up at him with adoration and took his arm with both hands. She was all blond, bubbly, head-over-heels, and full of smiles for him. "Love rules all of us, doesn't it? I met Ross last Christmas at the coffee shop when he was here in town, and we fell in love. It was amazing, special, and almost at first sight, right, baby?"

He looked down at her and winked in answer.

"When you know, you know," she continued. "It's as simple and as complicated as that."

"Wait a second. Back up. Hold on." I shushed them. "Last Christmas? When he was here in town *with me*." I did the mental math. "Ten months ago."

Ross held his hands out placatingly. "About that. Let me explain—"

I held up a hand to quiet him. My mind was whirling with dates and numbers, and I realized that Ross would never have asked me to marry him when he had already been falling in love and planning his happily ever after with *someone else*.

"Hush. Shut up. Be quiet. Excuse me? Ten months. *Ten months.* TEN MONTHS. *We* were together ten months ago. You. And. Me. Together." I was getting louder and louder and couldn't stop it or find it in myself to care. Causing a scene was the last worry on my mind now. I was so angry.

"Wait for me outside, Hanna. I'll handle this."

"Handle?" Abigail screeched. "*This?* You mean the situation you caused by being a selfish motherfucking prick?"

Heads were turning in our direction.

Eyes were on me.

I decided to see what he had to say. I had to; grim curiosity was killing me, and I knew I'd regret it if I didn't know every detail. I required closure on all things. I needed it to survive. Not knowing something would be worse than walking away on the high ground.

She kissed his cheek. "Okay, sugar. I'll be in the car. You were the one to break up with him, Madi." Her eyes were harsh on me. "Don't forget that it was you who ended it. He was so upset."

"This bitch is delusional." Abigail got up to follow her out. I reached across the table to stop her, but she was too fast for me to catch.

"Riley!" I grabbed her hand in alarm. "Go after them."

She scooted to the edge of the bench seat and then hesitated.

"Damn it. I shouldn't have let her start drinking. We were going to break the news and show you a good time tonight. Make it go down easy, then distract you with some cheese fries and some fun sister time. I'm so sorry, Madi. This is—" She shook her head as if torn about which sister needed her more. "I should have known better. I don't want to leave you alone with him. Abigail will be okay."

"No, I'll be fine. I want to hear him out. It's—it is what it is. And none of this is your fault. Please don't let her get arrested. Oh my god."

"Okay, I'll be right back." She glared at Ross after she stood. "Watch yourself, do you hear me? You'll have me to deal with if you say anything stupid and upset her any more than she already is."

"I'm not here to upset her, Riley."

"You're a moron, Ross. The biggest idiot I've ever met. If I come back here and she's in tears, you are a dead man. Do you get me? You know I won't fuck around when it comes to making sure you get what you deserve."

"Yes. I got it, Jesus Christ, Riley. Just go and collect your sister, please, before she scares Hanna."

"I'll be okay. Get Abigail."

"I'm so sorry." She hauled ass to the door.

Ross grabbed my hand and squeezed it. "One last dance? We need this closure. That's why I came. To say I'm sorry. And to give you a proper goodbye."

"Get your hands off of me," I seethed. "Closure? Okay, sure. Consider this closed. Don't worry about me. My heart is closed up pretty tight right now. If you have something to say, then we can talk right here. Are you sure your fiancée won't mind if you sit with me?"

"Of course not. She trusts me." He slid across from me into the booth, giving a wary eye to the tequila shots on the table.

I popped an eyebrow up. Maybe he'd be wearing one before our talk ended.

"Was that meant to be ironic? I trusted you, Ross. Look where it got me. You made me feel guilty for breaking up with you. I actually felt bad, and you had been cheating on me for months."

His blond hair flopped over his forehead as he shook his head. "Oh no, no, no. I am not a cheater, Madi. We need to get that straight first. We weren't working, Madison. Our relationship had been on shaky ground for the last couple of years, and we both know that. You were right to end things. Hanna is not like you, though. She can't cook worth a damn, and she turned all my white clothes pink." He chuckled as if I would take it as a compliment that I was better at cooking and doing his laundry.

Thanks a fucking lot.

"You let me think you were going to propose to me when you'd been with someone else. You cried when I broke it off. But you were cheating on me—*for almost an entire year.* What the hell, Ross?" I was angry at myself for feeling embarrassed when he was the one who was in the wrong.

"It wasn't cheating on you," he reiterated in a whispered tone, eyes darting outside the booth. Yeah, plenty of people were listening. I knew I would eventually care, but I was just too upset to think clearly. "I would never do that. Hanna and I weren't sleeping together," he said under his breath. "We were just talking. A text here and there. That's all."

"Oh, gee," I answered loudly as I toyed with a shot glass, considering whether I should toss it in his stupid face or drink it. "That makes me feel so much better."

"Keep your voice down. People are watching us, Madi. I didn't think you'd cause a scene. You're too sweet to be this sarcastic. Come on now. It's time for both of us to move on. Should I have told you I was talking to Hanna? Probably. But I wasn't sure it would work out with her, and I didn't want to lose you, did I?"

"You are unbelievable," I managed to say, struggling for control. I was so angry that I didn't dare raise my voice again, or I would end up screaming my head off at him.

He tried to hold my hands across the table, but I yanked them back. "And you're wonderful, Madi. You were the best girlfriend I've ever had. But it worked with Hanna; now she's ready to move forward with me. We'll be spending a lot of time here in Cozy Creek while she plans the wedding with her mother."

"Oh, I see. I get it now. Having the specter of our former relationship hanging over your head doesn't work for your new fiancée if I'm not cool with it. Is that it?"

"Exactly. I knew you'd understand. I had to tell you myself, but Riley disagreed; she thought the news would be better coming from her. I had to come here. It was the honorable thing to do."

"Honorable?" I threw the word at him like I was about to throw this damn drink in my hand. "No. It would have been honorable if you had told me the second you met someone you were interested in. Have you heard of emotional cheating, Ross? That's what you did, and it's just as bad as if you were screwing her behind my back."

"I. Am. Not. A. Cheater. Why can't you see that?" He shook his head vehemently. "I would never do that to you or anyone."

"Fine. You're not a cheater, just a total fucking moron then. Why didn't I realize you were so selfish?"

His expression briefly clouded with anger. "I'll let that go—you're upset and not thinking clearly. This is not you. I'm sorry you feel this way. I was hoping we could end up as friends someday."

"That is not looking good." Blood pounded in my temples as I struggled to maintain what was left of my composure. "Did you want to do this publicly so I wouldn't lose my shit?" Anger was singing the edges of my control as I struggled to contain it. I had never been this mad before.

"The thought crossed my mind," he admitted. "I wanted you to listen to me. If we were alone, you'd probably storm off to pout like you sometimes do."

My lips thinned at his chiding tone. "I—"

"Listen," he cut me off. "You're upset, I can always tell, remember? Please try to understand this from my perspective. We'd been together for so long, we were, what? Four years into our relationship when I met Hanna. I didn't want to throw all that history away on a mere possibility. You and I were so good together for a long time. It just started unraveling toward the end, is all."

"You are seriously unbelievable." My embarrassment and anger had turned to raw fury.

I lifted the shot glass in my hand and tossed the tequila at his chest. I would have picked his face, but I was familiar with his suit. It was his favorite, and it was expensive. He loved that fucking suit, the tie too. I'd given it to him on his twenty-ninth birthday; it was also expensive. I grabbed the second shot and tossed that one at him too. But the third one was for me. I raised it in a silent toast, then tossed it back, smacking my lips at the tequila burn.

He drew back as if struck. "I thought I knew you, Madi. I can't believe you're reacting this way. I'm not a cheater—"

"No, you don't know me at all, and it's clear to me now that you never did. I have to get out of here." I climbed out of the booth, and he grabbed my arm and then stood at my side, towering over me with a determined look. I tried to pull away, but he held tight. "Let me go."

"No, I can't have you leaving this conversation thinking I'm a cheater. I have to make you understand first—"

"I do understand. One hundred percent." I tried to yank my arm away, but he wouldn't let go. "I understand that I never want to see you ever again. I understand that you chose to string me along for five years—for your convenience, never mind what I wanted or how it would make me feel to have you constantly avoiding discussions about our future together. That is your mistake. Not mine. You live with it. I don't forgive you. I'll have my peace but won't give you yours because I've given you enough."

"Madi, please! I'm sorry, okay? I can see that I hurt you, and it's not what I intended—"

"No, Ross. Let me go."

"I can't. Not like this. We meant too much to each other to let it become this ugly."

"I cannot believe you," I sputtered, staring up at him in astonishment. "Like, I think I'm in actual shock right now."

I didn't want him back, but I wondered what was so fundamentally wrong with me that he would spend five years making me think we had a future together and, worse, that I'd believed it.

How could he do this to me?

How could I have been so blind?

I would never be able to comprehend this kind of casual cruelty and selfishness. Maybe that's why I had believed in him for all those years.

Who could do such a thing and be able to live with it?

And why would he think a chat in a bar would provide closure? *Ridiculous.*

And his explanation? *It was laughable.*

And the thought that we could be friends after this? *Zero fucking chance of that.*

He had cheated on me, for fuck's sake. Emotional cheating was real. How could he not see how serious that was?

I stopped struggling and stood there stupidly as my mind raced through all the ways I had been so fucking gullible and dumb.

For five years.

I shook my arm out of his grasp. I mindlessly crossed the dance floor toward the exit, not tracking my surroundings as I stewed over everything I'd discovered until I saw Cole sitting at a table with a few Cozy Creek Fire Brigade crew members and his brothers. Concern flashed across his face, and I shut my eyes against it.

Ross caught up to me and grabbed me again, turning me forcefully to face him.

"Please, Madi. Will you just listen to reason?"

My breath caught in my throat.

Could this be any more humiliating?

Apparently.

"Do it," I heard Tate say.

"Get your girl," Quinn added.

CHAPTER 15

Madi

I opened my eyes and found Cole standing beside me with his hand on Ross' shoulder.

"I think this dance belongs to me." His voice was soft yet edged with steel. "Would you like to dance, Madi?"

"What?" Ross sputtered. "No, she would not. Madison and I are having a talk—"

"And now she's done talking to you. Right?"

"Yeah, we're finished." I blinked, focusing my gaze on Cole, thankful he was here. I knew I could handle myself, but I didn't want to make this night any worse if I could help it. "Absolutely. I'm one hundred percent finished, and I would love to dance with you. Let's go."

But Ross would not take the hint. He shook Cole's hand off his shoulder and turned to the side, pulling me closer to block me from walking away with Cole. "And you are?" The sneer in his voice shocked me—the nerve of this man.

"Who I am doesn't matter to you." The angry growl in Cole's voice was a surprise. I stood on my tiptoes to see him glaring at Ross with his face like stone. "Take your hand off my—my Madi, before I do it for you."

"Madi? Are you with this guy? I've met him before, haven't I?"

"Yes. This is Cole Sutter. He lives across the street from Gigi," I belatedly introduced them as I hurled myself out of his arms and glared at him. "I guess you aren't the only one with news tonight, Ross. We've been seeing each other."

Cole banded an arm around my waist and yanked me back into his chest. His other arm went across my upper chest, and his hand rested on my shoulder.

Ross took a step back, eyeing us derisively. "Fine. Well, I won't keep you then."

My mind whirled as Cole turned me into his arms, holding me close while guiding me to the darkest edge of the dance floor. He tucked me in tight against his big body like my shield.

One hand settled at my waist, and the other rested on the back of my head, his fingertips sifting gently into the strands of my hair. I buried my face against his broad chest and took a deep breath.

"You're saving me again," I murmured into his pec. "Thank you for getting me away from him." To my dismay, my voice broke slightly.

My heart raced as I took a deep breath, trying to relax and control the thoughts spinning rapidly through my mind.

"There is no place I'd rather be than here with you. Believe that. You deserve a man who will take care of you, respect you, and treat you like the amazing woman that you are. Not some dumb motherfucker who would try to humiliate you in a goddamn bar." His voice held a note of steel beneath the words. I followed, trembling in his arms, as he led me to the room's darkest corner of the bar. I looked up to meet his eyes. "You're okay, Madi. Take another breath for me."

He was angry with Ross, but he tempered it. He spoke to me in soothing whispers as his hand sifted through my hair.

He cared how I felt, and it was evident in every interaction we'd ever had together. Especially now, he was strung tight. I could feel the rigidity in his arms, the tension. He was pissed, and I had the feeling he was ready to fight Ross if he had to; he maybe even wanted to.

I shivered and snuggled closer. He was so tall, well over six feet, but I could see his face better in these heels, even in the dim light of the bar. He would protect me. I knew it.

"I'm glad you're here too," I murmured. "Whenever you're around, I feel better. About everything."

"You're amazing, Madi. Everyone in town thinks so. He wouldn't be here in this weak attempt to put you in your place if he didn't realize that. But he's not worthy of your time and does not deserve to flaunt his new life in front of you. That's just cruel, and I will not tolerate it."

"How do you know? Does everyone know? That fast?"

Sympathetic eyes met mine. "Unfortunately, yeah. That fast. None of you were quiet over there; this is a small town. Plus, Abigail is currently screaming at Hanna in the parking lot. Everybody in here knows at least some of what happened. I'm so sorry."

I turned my head toward the window. Riley was holding Abigail's arm as she yelled at a crying Hanna. "Oh, crap. Oh, no." Tears filled my eyes. "This is humiliating. I should have tried to be quiet but was too mad."

He placed his hands on the side of my neck and pulled me closer to the warm strength of his body, blocking my face from view with his big arms. With his back to the room and mine to the window, no one could see that I was slowly breaking down.

"Dry those eyes, Madi. Please don't give him the satisfaction. Don't let any of them know you're hurting."

"I'm not sure I can do that." I heard the tremble in my voice, and I hated it. I liked it better when I was pissed off, even if I had yelled at Ross, and even if everyone in this bar knew what happened because of it.

"No one can see you now. I'll take care of you. Take a deep breath. I'm here." He pulled me close again, and I rested my cheek against the broad wall of his chest as he stroked my hair and kept us swaying side to side, giving the illusion we were dancing rather than him holding me together while I tried to stop losing my mind.

"Okay." I took a deep breath like he said. "But how, Cole?"

He pulled back and wiped beneath my eyes with his thumbs. "I'm going to kiss you, that's how. Nobody will remember anything else if we kiss."

"Kiss?" God, I wanted that.

The thought of everyone in this bar knowing my business flew out of my mind when I thought about how it would feel to be kissed by Cole. I'd been imagining it since I first arrived in Cozy Creek.

"Say yes or no. Yes means we'll put on a show, so nobody in this bar will ever think you're hung up on that asshole. No means we'll just dance. But either choice you make will say that you are moving on. That he doesn't matter to you. You don't care."

"Kiss me, Cole." I had never felt like this. Not ever. "Please."

Asking him to kiss me had nothing to do with putting on a show for anyone.

It was for me.

I needed to feel his lips on mine like I needed my next breath.

Not only did I ache for him to kiss me, but the anger and misplaced heartache leftover from my conversation with Ross was gone.

I had better things to think about. I had been done with him when I got to Cozy Creek, and I wouldn't let him ruin any more of my time here.

The fact that he had cheated was moot when I had been the one who had decided to move on. If anything, it rid me of the guilt I had felt when I left him.

"Are you sure?" His voice was a whispered groan as he gently tugged my hair to tilt my head back, unwrapped his arm around my waist to cup my cheek, and raised my face to his as his eyes searched mine.

"Yes. I'm sure." I wanted to keep this feeling. Cole made me feel safe. Like, if I decided to trust him, it wouldn't come back to bite me someday.

I knew this was supposed to be fake. But it didn't feel that way as he dipped his face low and gazed into my eyes.

"Forget about him. Forget anything he said that made you feel like you were anything less than beautiful, Madi. You are sexy as hell right now in that black dress. I noticed you the second you walked through the door, and I had to force myself not to stare. It's not your problem that he didn't know what to do with you when he was lucky enough to have you."

I felt the whisper of his breath on my lips before he pressed his mouth against mine.

His lips were soft, but he kissed me hard like he'd been thinking about it for a long time, like he couldn't hold himself back anymore. My knees went weak, but he held me tight and kept me out of sight, blocking me from the room with his tall, muscular body, just like he'd promised me he would.

"More," I breathed out, and he gave it to me, backing me into the corner to push his leg between mine with a deep, growly groan. His hand slammed into the wall above my head right before his tongue slid into my mouth, and I matched his sexy groan with one of my own.

We were as close as two people could be, upright and fully

dressed. I threw my arms around his neck and held on. I didn't want him to stop kissing me.

It felt real.

It felt right, and I didn't want it to end.

"Damn, Madi. What are we doing?" His whispered voice tickled my lips, and I clutched at his big shoulders for support while wondering the same thing until he kissed me again, and I lost all ability to form a coherent thought.

His mouth opened on mine, and he ground himself against me, hard as steel. This was real. It had to be.

Slowly, I came to my senses and pulled back, trying to catch my breath. "I could ask you the same question."

He traced a fingertip down my nose, letting it drift across my lips as a soft smile slid over his mouth. "God, I love your freckles." Then his eyes darted from mine as he ran a hand over his chin in frustration, steadied me on my feet, and stepped back. "I'm sorry," he whispered. "I didn't mean to take it this far."

"Hey, it's okay," I soothed. "I was a willing participant. And you were right. No one will be talking about poor, pathetic, cheated-on Madi. They'll be discussing the hot kiss at Bookers and debating how serious this thing is with Gigi's granddaughter and the Cozy Creek Fire Brigade's chief. And I'd much prefer that."

"Come here." He pulled me in for a hug and whispered in my ear, "Do you want me to get you out of here? I can drive you home if you like."

"Yes, please. I can feel everyone's eyes on us. I've never been the center of attention like this before, and I don't think I like it too much."

"I have. But at least this time, it's for something I wanted."

CHAPTER 16

Cole

That kiss.

That fucking kiss was everything I knew it would be from the moment I first laid eyes on her.

But I should not have taken it that far. No matter what she said, it was not okay. No matter how much I wanted to do it again and again, I couldn't.

I wanted to be there for her like no one had been there for me the night I saw my wife and my best friend together as a couple for the first time and lost my mind.

My intention was pure, but I allowed myself to get carried away, and I owed Madi an apology.

"I should check on my sisters." She turned to the window where the scene in the parking lot seemed to have calmed down. They were talking by Riley's car, and Hanna and Ross were gone.

"I don't know what to think about any of this, what he did, and why he did it here. But you know what? It's over and done with, right?"

"Yes. You don't have to think about him ever again." I wished I could never think about Sherry again, but having kids with her made that impossible.

"I was finished with him when I got here, and I won't let him destroy my peace of mind. I want zero thoughts in my head, like when we were kissing. Let's get out of here. I can feel everyone watching me, and I can't stand it."

"Absolutely." Apologies could come later; now was not the time to make it about me. I took her hand and led her outside, where we met her sisters.

"I'm so sorry, Madi." Abigail threw herself into Madi's arms and burst into tears. "I never would have started drinking if I knew he was planning to show up tonight. I ruined everything."

Madi rubbed circles around Abigail's back as she soothed her. "Shh, I know you wouldn't have. Riley told me what you two had planned, and it would have been fun, okay? You were trying to make this easy for me. You didn't ruin anything, I swear."

"Really?" She sniffled and pulled out of Madi's arms.

"Are you the one who cheated on me? Are you a selfish, lying jackass? No, you aren't. That is who Ross is. I thought I had broken his heart. I felt terrible for leaving him, like I'd been asking too much of him or putting pressure on him to do something he wasn't ready for. Can you believe that?"

"He was good at pretending to be sweet," Abigail said. "We all loved him. Don't beat yourself up."

"Men are sneaky like that, and it sucks," Riley added.

"Of course, they weren't talking about you, Cole." Madi smiled reassuringly at me. "You've always been an open book with me, and Gigi loves you. Gigi is never wrong."

"Of course not." I chuckled. "I think there are people who cheat and people who would rather die than cause that kind of pain, and when they end up together, it always gets ugly before it blows up. Relationships are complicated because you never know what type you will get."

"The collateral damage is real and far-reaching, isn't it?" Riley's voice was sad as she agreed with me.

"Yup. Then the cheaters go on their merry way and leave the rest of us to clean up their messes." I knew Riley was divorced, but I hadn't realized we had this much in common.

"This is getting way too real for me," she stated. "I feel I need to go home and crawl into bed. I'm having flashbacks from my divorce."

"Go home, it's okay." Madi hugged her. "Take Abigail with you, and you two get some rest. I'll be fine."

"There is no way you are fine, my selfless sister." Riley kissed Madi's cheek and smiled at her in sympathy. "Tonight was horrific. We should start a club or a support group. Cheated On Anonymous or something."

"That's not a bad idea. But I really am fine, I promise you. I was holding on to some guilt for having so many expectations of Ross. He killed all those feelings tonight. I'm embarrassed about how it all came out. But I also feel free."

"You should feel free, I'm glad. I'm sorry we ever introduced you to him in the first place."

"I'm sorry too, Madi." Abigail had a hand on Riley's car for support. She looked queasy. "I also need to lie down with a barf bowl and maybe some crackers to soak up all the alcohol. What was I thinking?"

"It's Bookers." Riley laughed. "You always get drunk here."

"True. They have the best margaritas in the entire world. But I'm pissed we never got to eat dinner."

"Do you need a ride home?" Riley asked me. "We could drop you off."

"I'll walk. It's just around the corner. Maybe the fresh air will do me some good."

"My kids are with my ex tonight, so I don't have to rush home. I'll drive her," I volunteered. Cozy Creek was a pretty safe town. But it was getting late, and she was upset.

"Good. Thanks, Cole. We'll call you in the morning, Madi."

We waved goodbye. "Let's get you home."

I guided her to my truck, taking her hand to help her climb into the cab. She'd put on a good show for her sisters, but I could tell she was still shaken. I leaned over and helped her buckle up. "You'll be okay," I whispered.

Her eyes, shiny with unshed tears, met mine as she nodded. A feeling of rightness settled into my chest. I kissed her forehead and then closed the door.

The drive was short, just up the street. I pulled to a stop near the alley behind the Confectionery where the outdoor entrance to the apartments was.

"Thank you for driving me." She opened the door to get out, and I touched her shoulder to stop her.

"I have to apologize to you again."

She turned to face me. She was breathtaking in the moonlight.

"Are you sorry it happened?" she asked. Her gorgeous brown eyes shimmered, and her lips were still swollen from our kisses. She was more beautiful than any woman I'd ever seen in my life. "Or are you sorry because you think you took advantage of me in a weak moment?"

"I meant it to be a peck. A way for you to show everyone you'd moved on. I didn't mean to make out with you against the wall. I took advantage of you, and it was wrong. I let my feelings take over when I should have been taking care of you like I said I would."

"You didn't take advantage of me," she insisted. "I wanted it. I asked you for more, didn't I? I've been thinking about what it would be like to kiss you ever since I arrived in Cozy Creek. And I want to do it again. For real, this time. With nobody around. Can we?"

At a loss for words, I blinked and didn't answer.

She wanted me to kiss her?

She ducked her face, hiding from me behind the fall of her hair. "Um, unless you don't want to. Did I misread you, Cole?"

"Misread me? It's taken all I have in me not to kiss you every time I see you, Madi. So, no. You have not misread me."

"It felt real. In Bookers, I mean," she whispered.

"Because it was real. But I'm not going to kiss you again right now. I took advantage of the situation, and it was wrong."

"Oh." Her eyes drifted out the window, dejected.

"You kiss me this time. Do anything you want to me. Climb in my lap, shove me against the door, take what you need, go as far as you want—"

She grabbed my collar and yanked me close, bumping our noses together. "God, I'm so sorry," she whispered as she smoothed over the fabric of my collar with a dainty hand, then stroked down the bridge of my nose with a delicate fingertip. "I get clumsy when I'm nervous."

Damn, that tiny touch on my nose almost undid me. I felt it to the tips of my toes.

"You don't have to be nervous with me, and please don't be sorry, Madi. Just kiss me, and don't fucking stop. Please," I begged, pressing my hands to the seat at my sides. I didn't want to scare her off with my eagerness to be close to her. I was hers to take, and I silently vowed not to touch more than she offered me.

I would never take advantage of her again.

Her lush breasts pushed my upper body back against the door of my truck as she leaned across the seats and pressed herself close to me.

The tip of her tongue teased my upper lip as her hands slid up my chest and into my hair. I opened my mouth for her with a groan. She tasted like strawberry lip gloss and mint, with just a hint of tequila, and I was in so much trouble right now.

My hands itched to pull her close and feel her against me, like in the corner at Bookers. But the truck's console was in the way. Then, there was the fact that we were parked outside in a relatively public place.

Damn, I wanted more than what I could have right now. She fit me to perfection. Like she was made to be with me, and this was only one of the millions of kisses we had shared.

And who knew? Maybe in another lifetime, she was already mine. This was pure, beautiful torture. My dick ached, straining against the fly of my jeans. I was so hard for her that it hurt.

Then my stomach growled and ruined it all.

She broke the kiss with a giggle. "I'm hungry too. They promised me cheese fries at Bookers, and I didn't get them."

"We shouldn't go back there; the gossips are probably still out in force. Have you ever been to the Skytop Diner?"

"Yes, Gigi loves that place, and I may or may not have been addicted to their burgers for years."

"Perfect. I was thinking earlier. At the station, I mean. Before the calendar shoot, I decided to ask you for a date. Out to dinner or something."

"Maybe this could be a date? Right now? To the Skytop?" Her eyes bugged out, and her cheeks went up in flames. "Um—Sometimes I can't believe the things that come out of my mouth—"

I touched a fingertip to her lips.

"I love the things that come out of this gorgeous mouth. You said yes. No taking it back now. This is our first date. Even though we've already had our first kiss, it was fake." My lips tipped up at the corner.

"And in a bar. With an audience of eager gossiping spectators and your ex-boyfriend. Not to mention my brothers, your sisters, and all my coworkers..."

"Oh god. We'll probably be hearing about that for a while. But I wouldn't change a thing about it." Her soft sigh made me smile. "I think it still counts. Plus, it's our thing, remember?"

"Ahh, yes. Me coming to your rescue?"

"Exactly. And now you'll buy me dinner and save us both from our lack of proper nourishment."

I started up the truck and took her hand across the console. "The kids love the Skytop, but I've never taken a date there before."

"Oh, yeah? Where do you usually take a date?"

I grinned at her. "Somewhere without fluorescent lighting and greasy food. But I haven't asked a woman out in over two decades, so who knows?"

Her eyes bugged out, and her jaw dropped. "Huh?"

"I probably shouldn't have said that out loud, right?" The fact that I'd only ever been with Sherry was something best kept to myself. Yeah, I'd married the first girl I ever dated. A player, I was not.

Would it be a turn-off?

It would have been easy to figure it out if she really wanted to. Small-town life was not conducive to keeping secrets.

"Wait." Her hand fluttered in the air between us. "But you look—I mean, you're so freakin'... *look* at you. And you're so sweet and funny too. And a good dad. You're a total catch, Cole. I don't get this at all."

I shrugged self-deprecatingly. "I mean, I've had opportunities. But I've never been tempted to act on it until you."

I backed out and turned onto the road. Driving would give me something to focus on besides how pretty she was and how much stupid shit was coming out of my mouth.

"Oh, Cole. I'm honored to be the first. I haven't been on a date with anyone besides Ross in five years, so you're my first too. Maybe we can take baby steps together."

"I'll take you somewhere fancy for our second date." I froze.

I was doing this all wrong. Maybe I should have taken Evan and Natalie's advice about how to ask her out. I shut my eyes; I didn't want to see the look on her face. "I mean, if—"

"Yes." She reached out and stroked my shoulder as I turned onto the highway. "I would love to go out with you again. Don't worry, I'm already having a good time with you. The best."

I let out a relieved breath. "That's good. And listen, if the meeting at my house tomorrow feels too rushed or too intimate now, let me know. We can meet at my office or Gigi's instead, okay?"

"No, it's fine. I'd love nothing more than to spend time with you and your kids."

I took her hand across the console. "Good, they have been looking forward to it."

"I love that so much. They're so great. Do you know what I'm in the mood for tonight?"

I shifted my eyes to her briefly as I drove. "Tell me."

"Grilled cheese." She squeezed my hand. "Never underestimate the power of cheese, Cole. I'm looking forward to this. Fancy places make me nervous, anyway. Give me all the diner food, please."

"Well, a grilled cheese sandwich is something I'll never turn down. Or any kind of cheese in any kind of form, if I'm being honest," I confessed.

"Ha! Same. What else should we order when we get there?"

I shrugged as I turned into the Skytop's parking lot.

"Chicken nuggets? I maintain that they are not a kid's-only food."

I pulled into a space in front and cut the engine. "Sure, my kids love them, but can't a man enjoy a high-quality dinosaur-shaped nugget from time to time?"

"Absolutely. I totally agree." Her laughter rang through the truck, straight into my heart to warm me up from the inside. "We need a strategy. I'll order the grilled cheese. You get the chicken nuggets, and we'll share. Oh! We need an appetizer."

"Wait. Stop." With a mock-serious look, I turned her toward me, hands on her shoulders. "This is important. Should I get fries or tots with the nuggets? Or will you get wild on me and suggest onion rings?"

She smiled huge and leaned across the console, drifting her hands up my chest to my collar to straighten it with a sideways smile decorating her pretty face. "Onion rings belong with burgers. How about tots? You look like a Tater Tot kind of guy. I mean, you kind of remind me of a Tater Tot."

"Oh, yeah?" I was breathless, wanting to feel more of her touch, but I refrained from pulling her closer. I did not want to risk this moment by pushing for more since it was perfect as it was.

Her cheeks turned pink as she ducked her head to hide behind the fall of her gorgeous waves again. "You're smushy on the inside," she murmured.

My eyebrows shot up. "Don't stop now. You have to tell me more about how I'm smushy." I chuckled.

"Well, on the outside, you look, um, you know..." She patted my chest, then pulled back to wave her hand in front of me.

"Crunchy?" I teased. "Golden brown and sprinkled with salt, or possibly doused with ketchup?"

"No, you dork! Um, firm?" She rolled her eyes in exasperated amusement. "Obviously, you work out, Cole." She gulped as her gaze drifted up and down my torso. "I've seen you in your garage with all those weights. And with the other firefighters running all through town, okay? And let's not forget the entire calendar shoot experience. Yes, you kept your shirt on, but it was thin, Cole. And blue, tight, and—" Catching herself, she met my eyes and bit her lip. "You have to know what you look like. You're a beautiful man, hard as a rock and covered with glorious, mind-boggling muscles. But on the inside, where it matters, you're fluffy and warm—you're smushy."

My heart raced wildly in my chest at her words. "That might be the nicest compliment I've ever received." I swept a hand around the back of her neck, pulling her close to kiss the hell out of her. "Thank you."

"You're welcome." Her eyes burned brightly into mine. I've never held such a tight leash on myself as I did at this moment. Forget dinner; I wanted to drive her home and take her to bed. I was tempted to try and keep her forever.

She was beyond beautiful. She made my heart soar.

Pretty pink lips smiling shyly up at me.

Deep brown hair streaked with gold shining in the early evening light.

I wanted my hands in that hair. I wanted my mouth on those lips.

Freckles dotted her nose like little kisses from the sun. Fuck the sun. I wanted to be the one to kiss her. I didn't dare allow myself to look below her face, or I would get lost in exploring the curves of her body.

I wanted to drown in her, sink inside, and never come up for air.

Our kiss at Bookers had flipped a switch inside me. I wanted to be more than just her friend, and now that it was an actual possibility, I couldn't stop thinking about how it would feel to be with her.

Before I could get carried away, I suggested we go inside. "I'll get the door for you. Sit tight." I got out and went around to help her out of my truck.

The breeze blew her hair over her shoulder as she stepped down, and I tucked it behind her ear as if I'd been doing such things for her forever. As if I had a right to touch her with familiarity. Something had changed between us after we kissed, and I didn't want to return to how we were before.

Hope flooded my heart, shocking my system, and I took a deep breath to center myself. I hadn't felt like this in way too many years to count.

She took my arm, smiling up at me when I opened the diner's door for her to pass through. "Thank you," she murmured as we followed the hostess to a booth.

"I feel like there's an elephant in the room." She took my hand across the table after we'd ordered drinks. "I know you heard some things tonight. You had to, or you wouldn't have swooped in to save me like you did."

"I did. I heard how he spoke to you, and I didn't like it. You deserve better than that."

"I didn't like it either. I feel like I was in love with someone that didn't exist and that my life for the last five years was a lie. How do you get over something like that?"

"I wish I knew. Add a marriage, two kids, and a cheating scandal, and you're me. Sometimes I wonder if any of it was real."

"That reminds me—I have to tell you something, and I should have done it a lot sooner, but I didn't quite know how to bring it up."

"It's okay. Just say it. I'm all about honesty. Keeping things hidden is not healthy. For anyone. When something needs to be said—say it."

"Okay, good. I feel that way too. Sometimes, Natalie talks to me about her mother when we're out walking Basil. Not about your relationship with her or anything like that. Not with details. But she confides in me about how much she's hurting because of the divorce and the way her mother has changed."

I squeezed her hand. "I know she does. She told me the two of you have a lot in common. Except for her, it's her mom; for you, it's your dad. And the same, no detail, just feelings. I figured it would come up when it felt right."

"It feels right now."

"So much about tonight feels right, Madi. I almost don't believe *this* is real—me and you."

"It's weird how tonight started like a nightmare, but now I feel like I'm living in a dream."

"I feel it too."

We ordered, and our food arrived. We ate, and we chatted. It was natural and effortless. Once I got out of my head and stopped worrying whether she was judging me, the conversation flowed easily.

There had been many moments tonight when our chemistry would have led to us getting closer, to touch across the table, to kiss, or to say something sexy, and we'd let most of them pass us by. But oddly, I didn't feel like I was missing out by keeping things relatively chaste throughout dinner.

It was the opposite. I didn't just want to date her; I liked her too. She'd already felt like a friend—granted, she was the kind of friend I wanted to have all the benefits with someday—but now we were more, and I couldn't wait to find out how far we could go.

CHAPTER 17

Madi

He had dropped me off and walked me to my door, kissing me goodbye and holding me close like everything that happened tonight wasn't too good to be true, like it was real.

How could this be real?

Moonlight filtered through my window, casting shadows across the room as I tossed to my side, displacing Kenny, who had decided to fall asleep on my boobs. "Sorry," I whispered in the dark.

He meowed and cuddled into my chest, purring while I stroked his soft fur. Victor stared at me from his position at the foot of my bed while Sage had turned herself into a black cat loaf on the pillow next to mine to stare at me with her glowing golden eyes.

"Is it real, Sage?"

She closed her eyes, ignoring me as if it were a stupid question and I should know better and trust my instincts. Rude.

I tugged my quilt to my chin and hugged Kenny against me like a cat spoon. I was exhausted, but sleep did not come easily.

It felt real.

Why did having hope have to be so scary?

I shut my eyes, willing my racing thoughts to stop.

Hours later, I awoke to the dim light before sunrise filtering through the big bay window and three cats staring at me from atop my dresser, waiting to be fed.

"Fine, have it your way. I'll get up. Good morning."

I threw my quilt to the side and sat at the edge of the bed.

I needed more sleep.

My bed felt empty without him, even though he'd never been in it.

I also needed to think—to gather all these swirling thoughts I kept having and form them into something cohesive, a plan I could implement rather than a few random ideas about the direction I wanted my future to take.

Pinning hopes and dreams onto a man was foolish. Thanks to Ross, I'd already learned that lesson. But I wanted to stay in Cozy Creek. I wanted to work with Gigi, live in this apartment, and get to know Cole better.

We had dinner plans this evening to discuss the rest of the details for the fundraiser. His kids would be there, and I took it as a good sign that he was okay with me being around them even before we went on our accidental first date and had our accidental first kiss.

I could still see his eyes as he drew back in surprise. There was electricity between us. I had known it was there in theory, and I felt he did as well. But when his lips touched mine, it exploded like I'd always suspected would happen with him.

I couldn't wait to see him again.

I ran through my morning routine, choosing a skintight pair of deep pink leggings and matching hoodie to wear on my walk with Basil.

My phone pinged with an incoming text. It was probably Natalie asking if she could join me.

> **COLE:** Good morning, gorgeous. I woke up thinking about you.

My heart banged hard against my ribs as I read, then reread his message, then reread it again because, holy crap, it felt good to know he had been thinking about me. Especially since I hadn't stopped thinking about him all night. I'm pretty sure I even dreamed about him, but I was not about to tell him that.

Putting all your cards on the table was never a good idea—another lesson from Ross.

Why was retrospect the thing that had always made me learn?

From now on, I would keep my head out of the sand regarding love. I had to protect my heart.

> **MADI:** I thought about you too. You turned a bad night into something extraordinary.

> **COLE:** See you at dinner tonight. The kids can't wait to see you too—you and your brownies. ;)

I blushed. It's a wink emoji, not even a real wink.

Wow. I had it bad.

He called me gorgeous. A small squee may or may not have come out of my mouth.

I needed some perspective before my heart ran away with all my newly earned good sense.

We had shared a kiss and a date. We'd had a few great conversations and had chemistry that wouldn't quit.

But none of that made him *mine*. It was real, but there were no guarantees that I wouldn't get my heart broken.

Five years with Ross had never made him mine, no matter how

many lies I'd told myself about his intentions. He'd given me just enough hope to keep me hanging on, and whenever I doubted him, he gave me some more. I had been a fool, but those days were over. I would never think about Ross again. He didn't deserve it. He was out of my life.

Actions over words. That was the key.

Promises were too easy to break.

I made it to Gigi's right as the sun came up. The deep blue sky burst into pastel hues of pink and orange as the sun rose on the horizon. As I got out of my car to greet her, trees in silhouette defined themselves in the shimmering light to cast dappled shadows on the sidewalk. She was sitting sideways on one of her porch swings with her foot elevated. I loved how pretty it always was here, and selfishly, I was glad to see the boot still on her foot. I wasn't ready to go back home.

"Good morning, honey. There's coffee inside if you want to fix yourself a cup and sit with me on the porch for a spell."

"Hey, Gigi. I'd love to have coffee with you." Basil ran up to me with his tail wagging, excitedly barking because he knew what we'd be doing. "Hello there, boy. Who's ready to go for a walk?"

"He adores you. Look at him!" Gigi called.

"And I love him right back—"

"Whatever, Mother! It's not fair, and you know it!"

I jumped and almost fell on my ass as I spun on the lawn toward Cole's house and the sound of Natalie arguing with what had to be her mother. Where was Cole?

"That's Sherry's car in the driveway." Gigi tutted. "The two of them haven't been getting along lately. She's here to drop them off. They arrived a few minutes before you pulled up, and they argued all the way into the house."

It tore at my heart to hear it. I knew how much she had been hurting, feeling abandoned and unloved by her mother. I felt the same way from time to time about my dad. I'd yet to see my father, and I'd been here for ages.

"Did that used to happen a lot when they were together? The fighting?" I picked Basil up and set him next to Gigi as I joined her on the porch. "She's usually outside to meet me. I'll wait and make sure everything is okay before I leave. Sometimes, we talk when she walks Basil with me. I want to be here if she needs me."

"No. Never. Not until after the divorce. But Sherry always was a little self-centered. Cole didn't see it; he probably got used to it since they grew up together—he sees it now, though, no doubt about that. Her family used to live right there." She pointed to the house next to Cole's. "I've known them both all their lives. Her momma is just devastated by this entire situation."

"Oh, no." I hadn't thought much about Cole's history with his ex beyond the fact that he was divorced. I didn't want to speculate on his life or his feelings. I didn't want to know anything about him until he told me. He must be feeling awful.

"They dated all through high school and got married right after college. It's shameful what she did to him. And his best friend too. He and Todd had been thick as thieves since they were kids until she got between them. However, it takes two to tango. He's just as much at fault as she is. Terrible, the entire situation."

"Yeah, Natalie told me a few things. I feel horrible for her." My eyes drifted across the street to his house. "And he deserved better. No one deserves to be lied to that way."

"He sure did deserve better. He's always been a good boy. And now a good man. One of the best."

Cole's front door flew open so hard we could hear it slam into the drywall inside.

"What the hell is going on over there?" I went on alert.

Natalie stormed out of the house screaming, followed by a woman who looked like her older carbon copy.

"That's Sherry," Gigi whispered. "We were never that close, so you might not have met her while you were here. I don't remember."

"All my friends are allowed to have a date to the Fall Ball," Natalie shrieked. "Why can't I? You said I could before!"

"You're too young, that's why. I thought about it again and the answer is no. You're only fifteen—"

"So what?" She whirled on her mother. They were in the middle of the lawn now. "That's old enough."

"See?" Sherry's arms flew out to the side in exasperation. "Thank you for proving my point. You're screaming in the front yard at sunrise for all the neighbors to hear, Natalie. A fifteen-year-old should know better. It's early. You'll wake the people up."

"Oh, I get it," Natalie shot back. "Age is so important, right? You're thirty-eight years old, mother. Why didn't you know it was wrong to cheat on your husband with his best friend?"

"Oh god." I started to stand up but changed my mind and sat back down. "Should we go over there? Where's Cole?"

"Dad!" I heard Evan yell from inside their house.

The crack of Sherry's hand against Natalie's cheek echoed across the street. "Watch your mouth, young lady," she bit out.

Gigi let out a gasp. "Noooo." She breathed, clambering to her feet to put Basil in the house.

"I hate you!" Natalie shrieked. "I never want to see you ever again." Her sobs broke my heart.

Without thinking, I ran, meeting Natalie in the middle of the street and catching her in my arms as she collapsed against me.

"I'm so sorry, Nattie," Sherry cried when she caught up to her. "I didn't mean to—I would never—oh my god, please—"

"What's happening?" Cole came barreling through the front

door and into the street, dripping wet with a towel wrapped around his waist.

I pulled back to check on Natalie. Red bloomed across her cheek in the perfect print of her mother's hand.

"Did you hit her?" He gasped. His mouth hung open as he gaped at Sherry. "You hit her? Sherry, what the hell were you thinking?"

"Dad?" Evan's voice was small and scared as he stood in the doorway watching.

"Go back inside, bud."

"But—"

"Please, Ev," Cole repeated his request. "Go on inside. I'll be right there. It's okay."

Gigi rushed around me to take Evan into the house.

"It'll be okay, bud. Go inside with Gigi."

"No, it won't!" Natalie yelled. "Nothing will ever be okay ever again." She buried her face in my neck and held on to me.

"Oh, sweetheart." I held her tight, finding Cole's eyes over her shoulder.

"You should go, Sherry," he said. "Let me handle this."

"I—I swear I didn't mean to. It just happened. She said something terrible, and I reacted without thinking. I'm so sorry. Natalie, I'm sorry, honey. Please look at me."

Sherry hovered at my side, trying to get Natalie's attention.

Natalie clutched the fabric of my hoodie tight in her fists as she mumbled into my neck. "Make her leave me alone. I can't talk to her right now."

"Excuse me? *I'm* your mother; she has nothing to do with this." She glared at me. "Who even are you?"

"I'm Madison Winslow—"

She waved a hand in the air and cut me off. "Oh, okay." She dismissed me. "One of Gigi's girls."

"Now she's Dad's girl." Natalie pulled back, her eyes glinting angrily as she glared daggers at her mother. "She's coming over for dinner tonight, right, Daddy?"

Sherry's eyebrows shot up as she looked me over. "She is? Isn't she a bit young for you, Cole?"

"Sherry," Cole barked. "Leave. Go home. We'll talk later. You're making this worse."

He had obviously been in the shower. His hair was full of shampoo bubbles, and his smattering of chest hair was matted into his skin with soap swirls. He also had a few tattoos, but I couldn't tell what they were. They were obscured in all that lather.

I blinked the sight out of my mind and refocused on the scene at hand.

Damn.

"Okay, I—okay," Sherry stammered. "Natalie, baby, I'm sorry. I'll make this better. I promise you." To Cole, she said, "I didn't mean to hurt her. This has never happened before, you know that. You know me! Please make sure she understands that I would never—"

"I know. I'll get to the bottom of everything. I got this, Sherry. Go home."

"Okay. I—thanks." After one last glare aimed my way, she got into her car and left.

"Natalie," I whispered. "She's gone now, honey."

Her tear-filled eyes met mine when she pulled away. "I practically tackled you. Did I hurt you?"

"No. You didn't hurt me. I'm fine. Don't you worry about me." I cradled her red cheek in my cool palm.

"Natalie, sweetheart." Cole's gentle voice went straight to my heart, even though his words were not meant for me. Natalie was so lucky to have a father like him. "Let's go inside, yeah?"

"Okay, Daddy. Am I in trouble? I was really mean. I shouldn't have said what I did to her. It was terrible. I—"

His eyes softened on her. "No, you aren't. Not at all."

She turned to me. "Um, thank you, Madi. I was freaking out, and you were right there when I needed to get away from her—I don't know what I would have done if you weren't here. I probably would have just kept on running." She laughed as she wiped her cheeks with the sleeve of her sweater.

"Hey, you're welcome. I'm glad I was able to be here for you."

She hugged me and went inside, leaving Cole and me standing in the street.

"Madi," he said. "I can't thank you enough."

"Of course. I mean, anyone would have—"

"Oh, yeah? Her own mother didn't care enough not to hurt her."

"Oh god. I'm so sorry, Cole."

"It is what it is when it comes to her. The slap was new, though." He shook his head. "And now I'm in the middle of the street, covered in soap, wearing a towel. No one will be talking about the kiss in Bookers now."

"I wouldn't worry too much about that. You look hot." I brushed a lock of his shampoo-y hair back from his forehead with a smile. "Plus, I forgot to tell you I threw tequila all over Ross's favorite suit last night. Maybe that will eclipse your nudie booty towel stroll in the street."

A startled laugh escaped him as we exited the street to stand on the sidewalk in front of his house. "Jesus. Thanks for making me laugh. Maybe I should have knocked him around for you last night. I'm kind of known for that around here."

"We make quite the pair, don't we? So much scandal."

His eyes burned into mine. "Yes, we do. I better get in the house. Talk later? Yeah?"

"Absolutely." I took his hand to stop him. "Wait a minute. I'm just going to throw this out there. My mom used to let me skip school from time to time if I was going through something rough. I'll be at the Confectionery all day, baking brownies, among other things. Natalie and Evan are welcome to join me there. Baking with Gigi has always been therapeutic for me, ever since I was a little girl. It might take their minds off things until you can all talk it out together."

His eyes crinkled at the corners as he smiled at me. "I'll take you up on that. I'm on shift at the station, and I can't skip it. Can I drop them off later this morning?"

"Absolutely."

"I'll try to join you there after lunch. Is that okay?"

"Of course. Maybe I'll teach them the secret family brownie recipe."

He dropped a kiss on my forehead. "Thank you. You're an angel."

I headed back to the porch. Gigi joined me a couple of minutes later.

"What a mess," she muttered. "Cole has his hands full with that ex of his. I'm so disappointed in her. I can hardly believe what happened."

"It was—definitely shocking."

"Hopefully, she can turn it around. Nothing like that has ever happened before. Not that I'm aware of, at least. I used to babysit Natalie and Evan from time to time over the years if their daycare provider was sick or for a date night here and there. I would have sensed something off, don't you think?"

"You sense everything, Gigi. So, yeah, I think you would have noticed if something bad was going on with them. Cole would have too. And based on what I know of him, he'd never allow that kind of thing."

"Good point." She relaxed. "I hate the thought that I could have helped somehow. But you're right. He absolutely would not have allowed such things in his home. And Sherry is self-centered, but she loves her kids. She'll come around. Hopefully, this is just a phase, and once she's settled into her new life, things will calm down."

Did thirty-eight-year-old women have phases? I had my doubts about her but kept it to myself.

"I invited Natalie and Evan to bake brownies with me today. I hope that's okay."

"Of course it is. You're a good girl, Madi. You have a heart of gold. I hope you know that. Cole knows it. Doesn't he?" Her smirk was knowing.

"Maybe he does," I confessed. "But I got it from you. That, and the belief that while delicious baked goods may not solve your problems, they make them easier to think about."

"You got that right. Operation Cheer Up the Sutter Kids is the mission of the day. Let's make today a better memory for them."

CHAPTER 18

Cole

"Hey, Dad! Check this out." Natalie's smiling face behind the counter was the first thing I saw when I entered the Confectionery door. It was after lunch and before school let out, so it was slow. The dining area was practically empty.

She held two little jars, one in each hand, and shook them over her head.

"Whatcha doing, kiddo?"

Madi came through the swinging doors to join her with two jars of her own. "We're making small-batch compound butter to go with the fresh bread."

Evan trailed behind her. Somehow, while he was here, he had grown a faint chocolate-colored mustache. "Dad! You're here! We had a sprinkle fight in the kitchen. Sprinkles are everywhere. It was amazing. And this time, the brownies have frosting. You're going to love them. Madi let me frost them and add sprinkles!" He shook his head, and a few sprinkles flew out. "See? Some of them are tiny, like sugar."

"We're also dancing." Kenzie burst through the swinging doors, shaking her hips along with her jars in her hands. "Come on, kids," she said to Nat. "Don't leave me hanging. One woman conga lines are just sad. We have the whole place to ourselves. Let's do this! Oh, Ev, you got a little something on you. Frosting mustache! It happens to the best of us." She wiped his face with the hem of her apron and then handed him a jar. "Shake it like I showed you," she ordered.

The kids smiled as they followed Kenzie and Madi around the dining area, and my heart lightened. They were dancing, and they had smiles on their faces. Shaking butter jars and partying with Kenzie and Madi was not what I expected to find when I got here, and I couldn't be more relieved.

I also couldn't seem to take my eyes off Madi. Each time I saw her, I wanted to look at her longer. I wanted to get lost in her. I wondered if there would ever come a day when I didn't have to look away.

"When you get Madi and Kenzie together, you get nothing but trouble and fun. You're guaranteed to laugh, that's for sure." Gigi raised an eyebrow at me from her table in the corner. "Come and sit with me a spell. Do you have time?"

"I do, in fact." I joined her, smiling in thanks when she poured me a cup of tea. "How's the ankle doing?"

She looked at Madi across the room, dancing with my children. "My doctor says it's almost healed." Her somber eyes shifted to mine. "But I don't have to tell her that yet, do I?"

No. Please don't.

But instead of telling her what I wanted, I answered with what was right. "I wish I could agree with you. But lying never leads to anything good. Even the little white ones."

"I know." She patted my hand and sighed with a sad little smile dancing across her face. "You always were a good boy, Cole. You always make the right choices."

I squeezed lemon into my tea and stirred. "The kids' moods are polar opposite from this morning. You work miracles in here, Gigi." I had to change the subject before she delved further into my growing feelings for Madi. I wasn't ready to talk about that with anyone yet.

"Well, I can't take all the credit. Kenzie heard the words 'sad kids,' took one look at their faces when they showed up, and then turned her personality to the high setting. They've been laughing nonstop since they got here. And by now, you know how Madi is, don't you?"

"I do. She's an angel. I wish she didn't have to go home. I wish—never mind. What I want is irrelevant. I wish she could stay, and I shouldn't."

"I do too, my darling. More than anything. She belongs here." Her shrewd eyes met mine. "What are you going to do about it?"

"I shouldn't do anything. I should let her go. My life is a disaster."

"Nonsense."

"It's not nonsense." A hot ache grew in my throat as I watched Madi across the room. "The last thing she needs is to get involved with a guy like me. Take this morning in the street with Sherry, for example. And Bookers, when I knocked Todd out. And you know Sherry won't let up until she forces Nat to forgive her. What am I going to do about that?"

"Things have a way of sorting themselves out when you care as deeply as you do. You're a good father and a good man. You're their anchor amid all this upheaval. They will be okay as long as they have you. Believe in yourself, Cole."

"I wish I could. We have an appointment with a family therapist next week. That's what's really going to get us through."

"See? That's excellent. You're already making the right decisions."

"Thanks, I—"

"I'm pooped." Madi sat in the chair across the table, and I let the subject drop.

"Are you too tired for dinner tonight?" I asked. "This morning was a lot."

"I'm okay. Don't worry about me."

"Why don't you two head upstairs and have your meeting now," Gigi suggested. "The fundraiser is coming up fast. You can't fall behind on the planning. Order takeout and get to work. Kenzie and I can take the kids home to my place and rustle up some dinner. Right, Kenzie?"

My pulse kicked up. The idea of having alone time with Madi took over my thoughts. The possibility of being able to talk to her, laugh with her, and kiss her again uninterrupted was a heady thing.

"Absolutely. After we close up here, we can grab a pizza and eat at Gigi's place. Sound good?"

"Yes! Please, Dad." Evan put his hands together like he was begging. "I want to play with Basil in the backyard."

"I don't see why not. As long as you're both doing all right, Nat?"

"I'm feeling so much better. Today was fun. We can talk about everything later. I don't want to think about any of it tonight."

"Okay then." I stood and held out my hand to Madi. "Shall we?"

She took my hand and stood. "Can we order sushi?"

"You got it."

"Yay! And sake."

I grinned at her. "You got that too."

"Oh! And a Diet Coke."

"Whatever you want." I chuckled.

"Make him buy you a dragon roll," Evan suggested. "The one they light on fire. He hates that."

"Fire should not be used for fun," Natalie singsonged my frequent rant as she sat across from Gigi.

People didn't take fire as seriously as they should. What kind of fire chief would I be if I didn't talk about fire safety whenever I could casually sneak it into a conversation?

"All right now. Come on, guys." My lips twitched in amusement. I'd save the repeated lecture for another day.

"I want a dragon roll," Madi teased, smacking Evan's outstretched hand in a high-five.

"Not you too? Ahh, Madi." I shook my head in mock disappointment. "And I was telling Gigi I thought you were an angel."

"Okay, I want a dragon roll. Hold the fire," she amended her request, barely able to keep the laughter out of her voice.

"Attagirl." I winked at her. "Being good can be fun. You'll see."

Her eyes heated on mine. I watched the emotions play across her face from amusement to hot and couldn't wait to get her alone.

"Why don't you two go to Madi's place right now?" Gigi suggested. "We have it under control down here. Don't we?"

"We sure do," Kenzie agreed. "Right, kids? Sweeping up all the sprinkles in the kitchen will be so much fun."

"Go ahead." Natalie waved. "We're okay. We had an awesome day. I promise."

"Later, Dad." Evan waggled his eyebrows up and down at me.

"Watch it, bud." I grinned at him.

I guess I was dating Gigi's hot granddaughter, just like he'd predicted.

I tried to recall what time I had any game in my past, but then I grew dismayed when I realized it was back in high school when I first got with Sherry.

It didn't matter. Thinking about Madi brought out something primal in me. Our chemistry just existed; I didn't have to try when it came to her.

It was only when I got stuck in my head that I doubted myself.

She had freed something in me, and I should get out of my own way and let it happen. I deserved to be happy as much as anyone else did.

CHAPTER 19
Madi

We finally reached my apartment, and I could barely contain myself.

His hand was on my waist.

His eyes roved over my body.

The thought of kissing him again.

All of it made me want to run straight up the stairs so we could be alone. It was electric.

I was wrapped up in him in a way I never was with anyone else in my life—ever.

My head swam with the overwhelming, palpable chemistry sparking between us. I wanted him more than anything.

He backed me against my door, put his hand on the frame above me, and buried his face in the crook of my neck, breathing me in as he peppered kisses up the length of my throat.

His lips seared a path across my jaw to nibble on my earlobe, then whispered, "My god, you're stunning. I love how pretty you look when I make you blush."

"Cole..."

His hands went to my waist, and my knees weakened when his

mouth met mine. Then I trembled as he kissed the tip of my nose, forehead, and each cheek.

"Is this our second date, or are we sticking to fundraiser business?" His whispered question had a hint of a dare in it.

"I can't even think right now, Cole. About anything other than how you're making me feel."

He pulled back, and I sighed and dropped my cheek against his chest.

"I've never felt anything like this." The racing beat of his heart confirmed his confession as he locked his arms around me. "Not in my entire life."

"Let's go in." I came to my senses and dug in my pocket for my keys.

Once we crossed the threshold, Victor glared at us with sleepy eyes from the wing chair by the fireplace as if we had woken him up. Sage and Kenny were asleep, curled up in the window seat.

"Would you like a drink? Or something to eat. Or anything?" I asked inanely. All I could think about was kissing him again.

"No, thank you. All I want is you. How about we update last year's fundraiser theme, call it done, and you let me kiss you some more?"

"This idea has a lot of merit." I ran my hands up his chest, then threw my arms around his neck. "What was the theme?"

His lips tipped up at the corner. "A harvest dinner and a non-ironic bonfire, which I was completely against, but I got outvoted."

"Unbelievable. You allowed a bonfire? *You?* Mr. Fires Are Not for Fun, Cole Sutter."

"They're not for fun. I'm against it one hundred percent. But I figured we'd be okay with the entire Cozy Creek Fire Brigade in attendance. Just that once."

"Well, I love it. Bonfire for the win—we can roast marshmallows, and I know a perfect recipe for a s'mores cocktail. We'll have dinner, dancing, and the bachelor auction. And we can serve steak Diane—"

"Steak Diane?" He stared at me, then burst out laughing. "Funny, Madi. No."

"A veto for steak Diane? How about chicken brochettes flambé? Lobster à l'Américaine? Coq au vin?"

"Oh, you're fucking hilarious, aren't you?"

"Baked Alaska for dessert." I waved a finger in the air. "Or maybe bananas Foster. Don't say no."

"Do you want to mess with me, or do you want me to kiss you? And a side note: I didn't realize you were such a foodie, or maybe you're an undercover firebug? But we have time to discuss that later. Now, what'll it be? Kiss or keep messing with me? Or should we order the sushi and have dinner?"

"I want you to kiss me. But you should know that messing with you is an unexpected pleasure. You get this adorable little smirk, and it makes me want to kiss you right here."

I placed my lips near the corner of his mouth, where, when he was clean-shaven, I could see the cutest little dimple. I touched the tip of my tongue to it so he'd know exactly what I was referring to.

"I first spotted it during our Tres Chicas lunch meeting, but I managed to hold myself back."

He grabbed my waist and hauled me against his chest. "I wanted to kiss you then too."

"Why didn't you?" I breathed.

"So many reasons that aren't important right now." He hesitated, eyes on mine as he bit his lip. Doubt briefly replaced his smoldering look. "Just look at you. You're so damn beautiful, Madi."

My only response was the rapid thud of my pulse. As if he heard it, he lowered his face to mine and kissed me again.

His palm went to my throat as our lips met, wrapping around to hold me still as he gently stroked my jaw with his thumb.

My hands went to his waist to hold myself up because what had started as a brief touch of our lips quickly deepened and went wild.

"I want you," he whispered, his breath hot against my cheek. "So much."

"I want you too, Cole. Let's go to the couch. Sushi can wait. Everything can wait. I need you."

He swept me, weightless, into his arms to carry me through the living room. He sat on the couch and settled me on his lap with my knees bent on either side of his thighs.

His hands explored the length of my back, my hips, then up to my breasts. My nipples hardened beneath his touch, and I let out a gasp.

"Is this okay?"

"Yes. It's my favorite."

His eyes shot to mine in the dim light. "Yeah?"

Using his thumbs, he stroked me softly and then gave my nipples a little pinch.

"Mm-hmm..." Involuntarily, my back arched, and I ground myself down on his lap.

"You're sensitive here," he observed. He then tested that theory by pinching a bit harder.

Mindlessly, I nodded as he cupped my breasts and rubbed circles around my nipples.

"You could make me come just like this," I whispered, lips parted, eyes at half-mast as I drifted along in the waves of pleasure he was giving me.

"I want to see. Arms up." His hands went down to the hem of my sweater, tugging lightly as his eyes met mine.

My eyes burned into his as he lifted the sweater over my head and tossed it to the coffee table. "You too, Cole. I want to see you."

He leaned forward and tugged his shirt over his head with his hand behind his neck, letting it fall somewhere behind the back of the couch.

"Oh! Your tattoos!" I not quite shouted. "Let me see."

With a chuckle, he raised his arm to let it rest on the couch and leaned back. On the left side of his ribcage were two tattoos—a mountain range on top and a line of spiky pine trees below.

"The kids drew them. The Rockies are Natalie's, and the trees are Evan's. They're from our backyard along the fence line. You'll see whenever you come over."

"Oh, Cole." My heart fluttered as I traced a fingertip along the craggy outlined form of the Rocky Mountains, smiling when a trail of goose bumps followed the path of my finger.

"Enough of my tattoos. It's my turn now. Come here." His hands touched my waist, warming my skin as he kissed a trail down my chest. "What's this?" He dropped a kiss between my breasts as he unhooked my bra.

A few sprinkles scattered from the cups and landed between us.

"Oh, that." I looked down at my chest and let out a small giggle. Beneath my bra, my chest was streaked with melted food dye from sprinkles and colored sugar, like a swirly faded rainbow tattoo. "We had a sprinkle fight. What turned into a couple of handfuls of sprinkles and dyed sugar crystals tossed around in the kitchen ended up as a bucketful being dumped over my head. I guess some went down my sweater."

"Damn. Why is this so sexy?" He licked up the underside of my breast, taking my nipple into his mouth with a hard pull.

I drew in a sharp breath. "Cole. Yes..."

"You taste like candy." He sucked harder. My core clenched as I rocked against his hardness. "So fucking sweet."

"Don't stop. Please..."

"More?"

"Yes. More. Harder." He sucked harder while pinching and rolling the other nipple between his finger and thumb. It was debatable which felt better.

With a pop, he pulled away. "You have the prettiest breasts I've ever seen."

"Are you a boob man, Cole?" I panted, grinding my hips against his now hard cock and wishing we were naked. I wanted to feel him inside me.

"No, I'm your man, Madi. And you are beautiful. Everywhere." His eyes were hazy with pleasure as he looked up at me.

My heart unfurled its broken wings and flew around in my rib cage before settling back into place with a shuddering boom.

"Let's go to my bedroom. I can't do this with the cats watching us."

"Anything you want."

He slipped his hands beneath my thighs and stood.

"Over there." I gestured to the door down the hall on the left as I wrapped my legs around his waist.

He walked us to my room, threw the door open, and let me slide down his body before gently pushing the door shut.

CHAPTER 20

Cole

I slammed my lips to hers and let my palms drift down to finally grab hold of that gorgeous heart-shaped ass of hers I'd been dying to get my hands on. "You feel so good," I whispered against her lips. "Is this okay? Are you sure?"

"Yes." Her voice was a breathy moan. "I want this. I want you so much. Come to bed with me. Victor was judging us out there, I could tell."

I pulled away to take her hand, smiling as she tugged me toward her bed.

Seizing her face between my palms, I kissed her again.

Her hands drifted down my sides to follow my belt line around to the buckle, where she gave a little tug before undoing it.

My abs clenched, and hot desire shot to the base of my spine, making me hard. I was already burning for her, but the touch of her hands so close to my cock nearly drove me insane.

Not wanting this to be over so fast, I took her wrists in my hands, moving them behind her back as I kissed her again. Her touch drove me to the brink, and I wanted to focus on her.

"Fuck. I knew it would be like this with you," I groaned against her lips.

"Like what? Tell me."

"It's almost too much, having your hands on me. Don't talk. Shh." Slamming my eyes shut, I inhaled a deep breath. "I need a minute, or this will only last a minute."

I lowered my head, encouraging her to lean back over my arms so I could slide my mouth lower, trailing kisses over her neck and along her collarbone, then back up the delicate column of her gorgeous neck.

Her soft giggle was like music. "That tickles, but please don't stop."

"God. Damn. You have no idea how much I want to get inside of you right now, do you?"

Freeing a hand, she palmed my erection. "Is this a hint?" she teased with a giggling grin.

Struck by a sudden jolt of vulnerability, I took a step back. "Don't play with me. Please, Madi . . ."

Her expression softened. "I'm not playing." She stepped forward and slid her leggings down before kicking them off to leave her in only a lacy red pair of panties. "I want you as much as you want me, I promise. Touch me and find out for yourself."

"Are you sure about this?"

Reaching out, she took my hand to guide it between her legs. She was hot and already wet for me. I could feel it through her panties.

She brushed her lips against mine, whispering, "How does this feel?"

"It feels like you need me." Our eyes met, and something unspoken passed between us, putting me at ease again. "I've thought of this. A lot."

"Take these off." She tugged at my belt buckle. "Come to bed with me."

We quickly removed the rest of our clothes and slid under her covers.

She was beautiful, with dark waves of hair trailing over her shoulder and gorgeous brown eyes watching me.

"Listen, Sherry cheated, as you've probably heard around town. I've been tested. I'm safe—"

"I'm safe too. I got tested after I broke up with Ross. At the time, I wondered what compelled me to do it, but now I'm glad I did. I have condoms in the bedside drawer too."

"Good. We're set. Come here. Enough about them. It's all us now..." I leaned into her, banding an arm around her waist to pull her into my chest, tipping her face back so I could kiss her lips. "I love how you feel against me. So fucking soft. So perfect."

I had to take this slow, or it would be over before it began. I drew her leg over my hip and slipped a finger inside her. I needed to know how she felt before I knew her for real, just a little hint of what would come before I lost my mind entirely.

She was slick, wet perfection. She was everything I'd ever dreamed of.

I swirled my thumb over her clit, grinning when her eyes lit up in pleasure.

"Cole, please..." Her hands tugged insistently at my hair as she panted against my neck, kissing and nipping at my collarbone, my jaw, my earlobe. "I need you now."

"I've wanted this for so fucking long, but I never let my imagination get this far. You have me so worked up that I don't trust myself not to explode the second I get inside of you. I have to make sure you come first. Get on your back, beautiful Madi. Let me get a taste of you."

"Oh god, yes. I want that." She flipped to her back, kicking the covers down, smiling as I rose to my knees at her side. "Look at you, Cole. You're the gorgeous one." She took my cock in her hand and squeezed it as her eyes roved appreciatively over my body.

The weight of her gaze landed on me like a touch, and I shivered. I'd never been this hard or wanted a woman this much. It was almost too much. Pulses of pleasure shot through me; my cock jerked in her hand as she stroked her thumb over the tip, and I had to look away.

It had grown foggy outside; the haze against her huge window was otherworldly. It was all just streaks and bursts of early evening light from outside reflecting off the glass.

Reality ceased to exist as I willed my heart to stop racing. I forced myself to lose focus in the darkness of her room and let my thoughts spin out of my head until *she* became my reality, and my focus turned solely back on her.

"You're like heaven, Madi. I swear you're better than a dream," I whispered as I straddled her body and bent to take the stiff pink peak of one of her nipples into my mouth.

Her breasts were full and round, far more than a handful, and more beautiful than I had pictured when I would lie alone in my bed with only the hope of having her beneath me like this to fuel my fantasies.

She was soft in all the best ways, and I knew I would never get enough of her. I slid my cock down the slippery wet perfection of her pussy, rubbing it up and down as I sucked on her nipple hard like I knew she would like.

I let out a groan as she shoved her hands into my hair to pull me closer. "That feels so good." Her breath ruffled my hair as I kissed and licked my way to her other breast, my mouth too full of her to answer her.

I moved lower, between her candy-coated breasts, dotting kisses and soft nipping bites over the cute, slightly rounded curve of her belly and down to press a kiss right above her clit. "Open for me, Madi. Let me in."

She spread her legs, lifting her knees high one by one as I moved to my stomach to lie between them. Rosy and wet, her glistening skin was like silk beneath my tongue as I licked a path from her opening to her clit, swirling around it in a circle before sucking it gently into my mouth with pulsing little pulls. I could spend a lifetime here, between her trembling thighs, feeling her hips undulate beneath my hands, with her body writhing against my face and the salty, sweet taste of her in my mouth.

I wrapped an arm around her hip from beneath and rubbed her clit as I entered her with my tongue.

"God, Cole," she panted as the soft squeeze of her thighs against my ears muffled her words, and her driving hips shoved my face away from where I was determined to stay.

"You're close, aren't you?" My lips quirked in a sideways smile as my eyes drifted up the lush curves of her body to meet hers.

I pressed a hand against her lower stomach and bit her inner thigh. "Be still like a good girl, and I'll make you come." She was up on her elbows, watching me, so I smiled at her, chuckling as her head dropped between her shoulder blades and her back arched before she collapsed against the pillows.

Her gorgeous thighs shook as she spread them wide and attempted to hold still for me. "Oh god, I can't be still. Please, oh please..." She was desperate, eyes pleading, mouth opened on a silent moan as I slowly inserted two fingers inside, seeking that spot that would drive her over the edge.

I could feel her need to come. Her pussy was like a fluttering, pulsating vice around my fingers; she was so tight. Ever so lightly, I bit her clit, then licked it with the flat of my tongue. I wanted her to need me. I wanted her to beg, to make demands, to plead for me to make her come so I could give it to her, give her everything I had.

Her lips parted, and then she smiled as she came against my mouth and reached for me. "Your turn," she murmured. "Get up here. Condoms are in the side table drawer."

Rising to my knees, I slipped on a condom, then pressed the head of my cock to her opening. Finally, god, fucking finally.

I gripped her hips like they were made for me to hold on to, digging my fingers into the soft curves of her flesh as I thrust inside of her with one hard stroke.

Every muscle in my body grew taut as I fought against coming. "You're a fucking goddess, you are. Look at you. Look at us. Fuck, Madi. Fuck," I repeated as I drove into her.

Her breath hitched as she took hold of my forearms that I'd planted at her sides, nails digging in as she moaned and looked down her body to where we were joined.

"Nothing has ever felt as right as this," she said on a gasp. And she was right. We were perfect together.

Every drive inside made her gorgeous breasts bounce; she was more than beautiful; she was ethereal, an angel, a fucking temptress beneath me; just the sight of her alone almost undid me.

I shut my eyes, throwing my head back as I fucked into her. Her legs wrapped around my hips, holding me tight as I slammed inside of her slick, wet heat. Over and over and over, grunting in crazed pleasure each time I bottomed out, grinding myself against her clit before pulling out to do it again.

"Madi," I growled. "Get there again. Come with me."

Opening my eyes, I saw her—head arched back, eyes shut tight, arms over her head, holding on to the slats of her headboard with her teeth sunk into the flesh of her inner arm.

Jesus Christ, I'd never seen a sight as beautiful as she was right now, spread wide for me with my cock moving in and out of her.

"Don't stop," she mewled. Her eyes opened and locked on mine.

"I've never—I've never come like this. Please, Cole. Please don't stop." Her voice was a breathy moan, and it went straight to my dick.

All the words in the world wouldn't be enough to describe how good it felt to be buried inside of her like this. I was finally where I'd wanted to be ever since I met her.

"I fucking knew it would feel like this to be with you. Fucking knew it."

"You feel incredible," she confirmed as she bit her lip and came in rippling waves around my cock, sending me spiraling inside of her in an orgasm so intense I collapsed forward, mindlessly giving her my weight for a moment before turning to the side and gathering her close to hold her against my heaving chest.

My heart hurt. It beat out of control both from my orgasm and the thoughts that kept coming unbidden into my mind.

Was this too soon? Was I ready to feel like this?

There were no assurances that I wouldn't get hurt again.

Was throwing my heart into the ring like this so soon after the divorce a good idea?

"Come here." I pulled her closer, placing a kiss on the top of her head. I shoved the doubts out of my mind. I shouldn't be thinking this way right now. Not when she felt this good in my arms. Not when it felt this right to be with her.

She tilted her head back to look at me. "I know you can't stay the night with me. But I wish that you could."

"Me too." I kissed her upturned lips. "But you're right. I have to get home to the kids."

I wondered how this would work with her when I knew she wouldn't be staying in Cozy Creek.

I couldn't exactly pack up and move to be with her. I had two kids going to school here. Was I supposed to uproot them for a woman, even one as amazing as Madi?

I had my job, the one I'd dreamed of since I was a little kid. I couldn't be the Cozy Creek Fire Brigade chief somewhere else.

My entire family and my house were here. My mother would freak out if I told her I wanted to move. Dad would tell me that my home was here, that Sutters had been living in Cozy Creek since before it was even called Cozy Creek.

Everything I loved was right here in this town, except Madi. Who, as soon as Gigi's boot came off, would be gone back to her regular life—without me.

What the fuck had I just done?

CHAPTER 21

Madi

I woke up alone. Well, not alone. I woke up with three cats in bed and no Cole—but I still felt him. I loved how he held me close after we made love and told me how much he wished he could stay with me all night. But Gigi and Kenzie were with his kids, and he had to get them.

I rolled to my side, holding my pillow against my naked body as I squinted into the early morning sunlight shining through my window. I'd slept late. I was usually up before dawn to walk Basil and get a head start in the Confectionery.

The text notification went off on my phone with an incoming text message. But it was muffled because Kenny was sitting on it. "Kenny! Move your fluffy booty." Sage was on the pillow next to me. Watching as I flailed to the edge of the bed to reach for my phone while Victor was in his usual spot at the bottom, keeping my feet warm. "You guys, give me a break. What if it's Cole? We like Cole. We like him a lot. Too much."

Kenny hopped to the bed with a meow, and I snatched the phone, almost fumbling it in my haste to see who'd sent me a text. It was Cole. Yes!

> **COLE:** Good morning, beautiful. I wish I could have woken up with you.

Tingles shot through my body. Head to toe. Oh my god.

> **MADI:** Me too. I miss you. I started missing you the second you left.

> **COLE:** I'll see you later today.

I hugged the phone to my chest as if it were him that I was holding so close.

Damn it. I was falling for him. There was no *what if* about it now. I was invested. My heart was no longer entirely my own, and I knew it for a fact.

And not only was he amazing, but his kids were too.

I shoved thoughts of Cole out of my mind. I got up to shower and get the day started. I couldn't think straight, not when every thought I had involved his hands on my body and his mouth on mine.

I had things to figure out.

I turned the water on and stepped into the shower, running through my routine by rote as endless thoughts tortured my mind.

I was here for two reasons: to get over my breakup and take care of Gigi. I was over my breakup—that was dead, buried, and gone. Now, all that was left was Gigi. She was the only reason I was here now. She had an appointment with her doctor this week, and let's face it, her ankle was almost healed. Soon enough, I would have no excuse to stay.

I didn't want to leave Cozy Creek. But I had responsibilities in Colorado Springs. I wrapped myself in a robe and padded out of the bathroom.

Ugh. Frustrated thoughts tortured me as I fed the cats and made coffee. Basil would have to be content with the backyard today. I had things to do.

I should call Kenzie. Although she was sometimes a bit out there, she was usually the most impartial if I asked her for advice.

The trouble was, I didn't know quite what to ask.

Maybe I shouldn't talk to her. She was firmly in the Madi should move to Cozy Creek camp, just like Gigi was. Who was I kidding? She could be impartial when it came to Cole—maybe. But not when it came to where I should live.

I needed to get out of this apartment. I couldn't think in here, not when it was the best place I'd ever lived.

I threw on a purple legging and hoodie combo and some running shoes, styled my hair into a wet braid, and got the hell out of there to go for a walk. Or a pouty stomp. Or a stress-pacing session in the park. Whatever, I'd see how I felt when I got outside.

After locking it behind me, I stopped on the sidewalk outside my door and looked down the street. The weather was nothing but ideal autumn perfection today—because, of course, it was. Actual leaves were blowing in the perfectly crisp breeze—scarlet, gold, and orange.

What the heck was I doing?

This entire damn town was the best place I'd ever lived.

Freaking *look* at it. It was like the set decorator for *Gilmore Girls* had stopped by and did her thing. It was an ode to fall in all its glory, dang it.

"Ugh, damn, stupid, gorgeous town," I muttered as I stomped toward the park—it looked like it would be a pouty stomp for the win! I directed my gaze to the sidewalk in front of me and kept on trucking. Stress pacing was up next, and I didn't want to waste another minute. I had a lot of thinking to do.

"Hey. Madi, hey!"

I stopped as if someone had grabbed the back of my hoodie and given it a yank.

A quick spin around showed me that Cole was calling out my name. Tate, Pace, and Noah ran ahead, razzing Cole and wishing me a good morning after they spotted me.

He wore his favorite loose tank, shorts, and tight pants combo, with all the usual muscles on full display. But this time, I knew what they felt like beneath my hands, mouth, and all the other pertinent body parts. I knew what they could *do*—seeing him hit differently now. I bit my lip and tried not to moan out loud.

"Hi." Should I hug him? Kiss him? Jump his bones right here? I mean, I wanted to do all three.

We'd had a bunch of sex last night, but that didn't mean I was any less awkward. I would always be a weirdo. Awkward was my middle name. Okay, so it was Nicole, whatever.

"Baby, come here," his sexy voice floated over the air toward me in the form of a low growl.

I went. "Are you headed to the park for a run?" I asked inanely as I stopped in front of him.

"Forget the park. Kiss me hello."

"'Mmkay..."

I tilted my head back, waiting to see what he would do.

For a man who said he didn't like being the center of attention, he sure hadn't greeted me that way. I decided to let him take the lead.

Big arms wrapped around my waist as he placed a kiss right below my ear.

"You smell good," he murmured and tightened his arms so he could dig his hands into my hips and haul me up against the tall, broad strength of his body. "I woke up thinking about you."

His low, gravelly voice in my ear sent delicious awareness surging throughout my body. Blood raced straight from my heart to pound inside my brain, making my knees weak.

"I never stopped thinking about you," I confessed, throwing my arms around his neck to hold on.

"Good." His lips captured mine. Demanding, claiming, and hard, he forced my lips open with his thrusting tongue, and I loved every single moment of it.

I let him in and returned his kiss with reckless abandon.

This was a surprise, and I reveled in it. No one could mistake that he was into me, and I didn't know how badly I needed him to show it—how badly I needed to feel wanted, special, and adored.

He broke the kiss. "Good morning."

I stared at him, my lips still tingling, my heart racing out of control, and my mind a chaotic swirl of feelings. "It is now," I finally said.

And it was. Somehow, he'd fixed the mood I had been drowning in when I left the apartment.

His eyes crinkled at the corners, and he smiled at me, soft and sweet. He drew the back of his hand down the side of my face, letting his palm rest on my neck. "Bad news. I'm on nights the rest of the week."

"Oh."

"I won't be able to spend as much time with you as I want."

My eyebrows raised as I perked up. "You want to spend more time with me?" I knew I was staring at him like a swooning, lovestruck freak, but I couldn't stop or even care. I wore my feelings all over my face, and I always had.

He huffed a laugh, smiling at me like he thought I was cute, and shook his head lightly as he traced a fingertip down my nose before dropping a kiss there. "Yeah, baby. I wish I could spend all my time with you. Is that okay?"

"Yes. I love that you feel that way. Because I do too."

"Good," he repeated and kissed me again. "I'm done with my run. I was headed back to the station. Are you going for a walk? Where's Basil?"

"Yeah, um, he's at Gigi's. I got off to a late start today. I needed to clear my head. I—never mind."

His eyebrows dropped in concern, and he pulled me close to whisper, "Are you okay? With you and me and last night? Please tell me if you aren't, and we'll talk it through, okay?"

"Oh, no. That isn't it. I'm fine. Last night was amazing. It's just, um, work stuff. That's all." It was some of the truth. He didn't need to know *all* my feelings. Not yet, anyway.

"Okay. But if that changes, talk to me." He flicked his wrist to check his watch. "I have to get to the station. I'll text you whenever I can."

"I'd like that."

After one last kiss, he ran off up the street toward the station, and I shamelessly watched him until he was out of sight before continuing on my way to the park, no longer pouty stomping but floating along on a cloud of unprecedented feels.

CHAPTER 22

Cole

I missed Madi.

It had been days since I'd last kissed her. We texted as much as we could and sometimes talked on the phone. It was better than nothing, but I wanted to touch her. I wanted to feel her against me again. I craved the way her body felt beneath my hands. I didn't get enough on our night together and wondered if I ever would.

I also missed my kids. They were with my parents tonight but would spend the rest of the week with Sherry, and I was worried. With the help of our new therapist, things had thawed between her and Natalie. Nat had forgiven her, and she said she understood. Sherry had promised that it would never happen again. But that didn't mean things weren't still tense between them, and it didn't make my concerns disappear.

Night shifts were the worst. It felt like being trapped in a different world sometimes.

The sound of my feet hitting the pavement pounded along with the incessant thrumming of the thoughts racing through my mind.

Cozy Creek was quiet at night. The street lights shimmered in the darkness and reflected off the windows of the businesses lining the street.

Tate was oddly quiet too. Maybe he sensed my mood, and instead of trying to make me laugh my way out of it, he understood I needed this time to think things through. Or maybe he was in the same mood I was.

Night runs with Tate used to bring me peace. They had always cleared my mind, but not anymore.

I spent the last week avoiding having any sort of real conversation with Madi about our future together or even thinking about whether or not *she* was expecting the topic to arise.

It was probably not a good idea to talk about things like the future, feelings, and doubts through text or phone calls anyway.

But what did I know?

The last time I saw her, I kissed her like I had a right to, as if she were mine. But she wasn't. And even worse, I'd done it in the middle of the sidewalk on Main Street where anyone could see and feel free to draw their own conclusions.

I didn't know how to navigate any of this. I married my high school girlfriend straight after college, and look how that turned out. I was so afraid of messing up whatever this beautiful, precious thing with Madi was that I remained fixed in place rather than risk everything in taking a step forward with her.

Running into burning buildings, I could do.

Laying my heart on the line with Madi? Not a fucking chance.

"I have no idea what I'm doing."

"Huh?"

I stopped. Ironically, we were near the exact spot where I'd last seen Madi and kissed the hell out of her.

"With Madi. I don't know what I'm doing with her."

He looked at me from the corner of his eye as he caught his breath. "Are you fucking her?"

"Tate!" It was dark. We were downtown, and the sidewalks were empty since it was so late in the evening, but I still looked around as if someone could overhear.

"You are. So, what is it? What's the problem?"

"I have no idea what she sees in me. I can't stop thinking someone her age would be better for her. That I'm just wasting her time like that asshole she used to be with did."

"Well, are you? Is she just a piece of ass to you, Cole?"

"No. She's not just a piece of ass," I barked. "But that doesn't mean I'm not wasting her time. Both things can be true."

"Sherry really did a number on you."

"I'm fine. That's over. I'm over her."

"You can be over her and still not be over the way she made you feel when she cheated. As you said, both things can be true, Cole."

I ran my hands into my hair, digging my palms into my eyes. "Fuck."

"You took a hit to your self-esteem. She played you for months with your best friend, who you never talk about—"

"Why would I talk about that motherfucker? He's dead to me now."

"And I get that. But look, I know how divorce feels. Your marriage ended. Your best friend since childhood betrayed you. Your life is completely different now. And you don't just get over it that easily. It hasn't been that long since the divorce. That sort of shit causes damage, Cole. It changes you. Trust doesn't come so easily anymore."

"Who wouldn't trust Madi?" I argued. "She might be a literal angel."

And that was the problem. She was too young, too sweet, entirely too beautiful, which made her something I couldn't resist. I was a selfish prick for pursuing her.

"You can trust Madi and still not trust yourself. They aren't mutually exclusive; you realize that, right? You can want her more than anything but still be afraid to get hurt again."

"When did you get so fucking smart, Tate?"

"Who recommended your therapist to you?"

I huffed a laugh. "Point made."

"This shit takes time. I've had months of practice sorting my shit out. You're going to be okay. Have faith in yourself, okay? You deserve a fucking break for once in your life."

"Am I self-sabotaging? Putting the brakes on something that could improve my life?"

"You might be. But there's nothing wrong with slowing down. You don't have to get down on a knee and propose to her. You don't even have to tell her you're falling for her. You're allowed to go at your own pace."

"Yeah, true. I don't want to go through it again. And I don't want to hurt her. Plus, I have a lot going on between Sherry, the kids, and the job. Is that too much to bring to the table?"

"Lean on your family. Let us help. You don't have to do it alone, Cole. We're all here for you—"

I froze as the all-too-familiar sounds of a fire hit my ears. Crackles, pops, and whispered rumbling hisses floated across the night air, but I couldn't tell where they came from.

"Shh." I held up a hand to quiet him. "Did you hear that?"

"Yeah, I hear it." Immediately, he went on alert. "And now I can smell it too. Smoke."

We followed the scent until we could see the smoke coming out of one of the dumpsters down the alley next to the Enchanted Greenery, the garden supply store. There were a bunch of cigarette butts strewn throughout the alley. One or more of them had probably ended up inside.

"If this isn't a sign, I don't know what is," I joked.

"This is not a sign, dumbass. We need to move that dumpster before the fire gets any bigger."

Despite my mood, I laughed. "My life is the dumpster fire. Every part of it is out of my control. And after this run, I probably smell like one too."

He rolled his eyes as he pulled out his cell to call the fire into the station.

The fire crackled as it ate through the dumpster's contents. If we didn't contain it immediately, it would spread and potentially put the entire block at risk. Most of these old buildings were connected.

The alleyway was too narrow just to pull it away from the wall. I had to get it to the street.

Putting my shoulder to the side, I shoved it to get it going.

It was heavy as fuck and hot. I grit my teeth, breathing heavily through the sting of it, trying to ignore the intense throbbing pain in my arm and shoulder as I braced my feet and finally got it to move.

Tate finished the call and found some cardboard to place against the side as we pushed it, but it was too late. I had burned myself, and I felt like an idiot. I knew better. And not only that, I trained people to fucking know better.

I was twisted up in knots, losing my damn mind, and I couldn't take it anymore. All it would take is one more thing to push me over the edge.

Sirens wailed in the distance as we made it to the street.

"Fuck!"

"Shit, Cole. That's a bad burn." His eyes darted up the street where one of our trucks, followed by an ambulance, had just turned the corner.

"I don't need a fucking ambulance," I ground out. My upper arm throbbed. "God damn it."

"You're welcome, jackass. Don't make me carry you to it. Do you fucking hear me?"

I gritted my teeth against the pain and looked away. "Yeah. I hear you."

"I doubt it's more than second-degree. I know it hurts, but now that we're under the streetlight and can see it better, I think you'll be okay."

"Fucking great. Thank you."

"You're welcome. Looks like you owe me a beer for saving your ass and calling for an ambulance too."

"I don't need any of this right now. It's too much."

"Hey, listen to me. All this shit, Cole? It's going to be okay."

I nodded. I couldn't answer him; I was hanging on by a rapidly unraveling thread.

I watched as Pace and some other guys put out the fire. They checked the alleyway and the other dumpsters to ensure everything was safe.

I held back on giving orders. Tate was on it, and I was a fucking mess as I sat at the edge of the ambulance, surprised when Amber, Tate's ex-wife, popped around to assist.

After a cursory glance at my arm, she stared her partner down until he returned to the back of the ambulance.

"We're taking you to the hospital. Get inside, Cole. The spot at the top of your shoulder looks bad. The rest will be okay. I'm not risking your arm to infection or—"

I shook my head, jaw tense with pain, interrupting her warnings. "No, I'm fine—"

"Do not argue with me, Cole. It's not worth the risk. Think about what you would tell any of the guys on your crew, repeat it to yourself, and let me do my damn job."

"Fine. Let's go." I got up, went inside, and sat at the gurney's edge.

Tate hopped in with me before she could shut the door. "I'm coming with."

"Tate. Good to see you."

"Amber. Yeah, you too." Belying her words, she shot him a glare before slamming the doors shut and hustling around to the cab.

"Well, this isn't awkward at all." Her partner's head tilted side-eye told the tale. "Take it easy, Cole. I got you." He applied more cold water to my arm, and I sighed in relief, already feeling slightly better.

I leaned back on the gurney and closed my eyes. I felt terrible that I didn't have it in me to comfort Tate right now. The two of them hadn't seen each other in months.

"I'm fine. It's fine. Rest," he said as if he could read my mind. And who knew? He probably fucking could.

"I'm sorry, man."

"I know you are." He smirked. "It's almost like I've known you my entire life."

He touched my knee as Amber sped toward the hospital with the sirens blaring.

CHAPTER 23
Cole

I opened my eyes to the bright lights of the ambulance bay at the back of the hospital.

Amber opened the doors, and I sat up. "I am not being wheeled in there. I can fucking walk."

She grinned. "I wasn't even going to ask. Let's go."

Tate avoided her eyes and got out before me to head through the doors toward the waiting room.

I followed her through the white halls and straight into a curtained-off space in the emergency room.

"It must be a slow night," I observed. The place was practically empty.

"I called Dr. Taylor to meet you here. I heard—I know you've been having a hard time lately, Cole. Your mom and I still talk sometimes, and I uh—I'm sorry, I didn't mean to make this awkward—"

"It's okay, thank you. I appreciate it, and I'm sorry for acting like a dick—"

"No apologies, I get it. You're in pain. You're frustrated. No worries, Cole. Take care of yourself." She hugged me quickly and then took off.

I sat at the edge of the bed to wait for the doctor. A few minutes later, Tate popped his head in.

"Is the coast clear?"

"Yeah, she left. Someday, you'll have to let me know what happened between you because I do not understand this one bit. She still talks to Mom. Did you know that?"

"Yeah, I know. But today is not *someday,* and I don't want to discuss it."

"Fair enough. I'm not pushy like you, so I'll let it go. But I am here for you whenever you want to unload."

"Touché, man. I hear you, and I know you'll be here for me. So, what are we supposed to do, fucking sit here and wait without talking?"

He flipped his phone to check his messages after the notification went off. "Actually—"

"Cole! Oh my god." It was Madi.

Her cheeks were streaked with tears. She was wearing slippers on her feet and purple and white polka-dotted pajamas. I could hear her taking in deep breaths, trying to stop crying, as she powerwalked her way toward me with her hair flopping around in a lopsided bun on top of her head.

She was fucking gorgeous. Everything flew out of my head the second I saw her. But she looked so worried, and I hated that I was the cause of it.

"Yeah, so, I texted her from the ambulance," Tate whispered. "I thought it was the right thing to do. She wouldn't be happy if she found out tomorrow. Don't you think?"

I shot him a glare. The last thing I needed was to make her worry about me—the fewer people who know about this, the better.

"Madi, I'm okay. I promise. It's just a little burn." I shifted to the side so she could see my arm. "See? No big deal."

"It looks awful!" she cried. "It's so red. How bad does it hurt? What can I do to help? Where are the kids?"

"They're at my parents' place. They do a grandkid sleepover once or twice a month. They're okay."

"That's good. Can I hug you? Will it hurt?"

"No, it won't hurt me. Come here." I held my good arm out, reaching for her. I pulled her close when she stepped into me.

"I'm sorry I'm crying. I was worried all the way here."

"I'll let you two be alone," Tate said. He got up and swiped the curtains closed.

"I promise I'm okay. Shh. Please, baby, don't cry over me. I'll be fine. This is just precautionary. I should have gone home. I know how to treat a burn myself—"

"Oh god." She burst into fresh tears. "You shouldn't have to take care of something like this alone. And ignore my crying. I'm not a drama queen. I don't want you to think I'm making this about me. Big feelings make me cry, that's it. I'm in control, I swear. Can I do anything for you?"

"Come here. Just let me hold you. That's all I need." I pulled her into my chest and rubbed circles over her back as I kissed the top of her head to the side of the bun. "Were you asleep when Tate texted?"

"Yeah. I rushed over here without thinking." She took a step back and shook her head. "Oh no, I'm still in my pajamas." Her lip trembled, and she bit it to gain control.

I looked her up and down. "Yeah, and you're fucking adorable."

She let out a startled giggle. "No, I'm—a mess. I mean, I didn't think of this—you getting hurt." Big brown eyes met mine and held. As she spoke, I cupped her cheeks and brushed her tears away with my thumbs. "I know you're a firefighter, in theory. And in practice too, I guess. From in the tree with Kenny. I didn't think of what it would be like to worry about you like this. Have you ever been injured before?"

"Yeah," I murmured. "But nothing too serious. Nothing to be afraid of." My hands drifted to her waist, and she shivered. I hugged her close, and she rubbed my back, soothing me even though I had intended to be the one to soothe her.

"Okay, that's good to know." Her words were muffled in my chest. "Will the doctor be here soon?"

"He's supposed to be."

She lifted her face with her chin on my chest. "I missed you." Her voice was like a wisp of air between us. Soft. Sweet.

I touched my forehead to hers. I fucking missed her too. So much.

But I didn't say it.

I should have said it.

I kissed her instead, touching my lips to that gorgeous mouth of hers, groaning when her lips parted beneath mine. Her arms wrapped around my sides as she drifted her hands up and down my back, and I went out of my head. The pain in my arm was almost forgotten as I got lost in her.

I tried to ground myself on what was real, to find all the reasons why this couldn't be, why I couldn't have her, shouldn't want her. But at this moment, I couldn't think of a single one.

She broke the kiss. "Do you need anything? A coffee? Coke? I want to go splash water on my face, and I kinda have to pee." She grinned at me sheepishly and traced a finger down the center of my chest. "I could bring something back for you if you like. There is a vending machine right by the restrooms. I passed it on my way back here."

"I'd love a Coke. Caffeine sounds amazing, but coffee sounds too hot. I've been up for too many hours to count by now."

"You got it." She kissed me quickly and caressed my cheek with a smile. "I'll be right back."

I watched her walk away, her slippers slapping adorably on the floor and her bun wobbling until she crossed through the big double doors leading out of the emergency room. Then I swiped the curtains shut again. I didn't want to talk to anyone else.

My arm throbbed lightly; it was annoying but tolerable. Which I knew was a good sign. If it didn't hurt at all, I'd be in trouble.

With a sigh, I reclined back on the bed, fluffing the pillow behind my head and closing my eyes against the bright white glare of the overhead light. This had been a long fucking day.

All I wanted was to go home and crawl into bed with a few ibuprofen and a cold water bottle for my arm. And maybe I wanted Madi to crawl in with me so I could hold her as I slept. Was that so bad? To want her?

Didn't I deserve to be happy too?

I sat up, startled, as the curtain opened. One of the little hooks popped off from how hard it was pulled.

It was Sherry. Once she caught sight of me in the bed, she drew them closed with a dramatic flourish.

"What happened?" She eyed me up and down derisively. "You look fine to me."

"What are you doing here, Sherry?"

"The hospital called me. I'm still on all the emergency contact forms from the station."

I heaved out a sigh. "Yeah, sorry about that. I'll have to take care of it when I return to work."

"No worries. It's fine. Where are the kids? Are they with *her*?"

"*Her*? If you're referring to Madi, then no, they're at my parents' place. You should know that. They do it every month, remember?"

"Yeah, whatever. Okay, good. I want to talk to her if you decide to get serious. Or are you already serious about her?"

"*Good*? What is that supposed to mean? We're not serious. We're just starting, seeing where things go. What I do and who I do it with is none of your business. Are you out of your mind?"

Her eyebrows raised to her hairline as she studied my face, waiting for my reaction. "She's a bit on the young side, don't you think? I don't know how I feel about them being with her."

"How *you* feel? Oh, that's rich coming from you. You didn't bother to consult me when you started screwing Todd behind my back, in our bed, for that matter. And neither of you bothered to think about how the kids would feel after you ran off and got married."

"Please. Give me a break. Todd isn't some twenty-something little thing like she is. He's already a father. He knows how to be a parent—"

"And you're both doing so well with the whole parenting thing, right? Todd won't stop putting his kids in front of ours so you can spend some time fixing your relationship with Nat and Ev. How many brunches have you canceled with them? Our kids matter too, Sherry. They need you."

"That's low, Cole. I'm doing my best to try and balance—"

"No. Stop it. And for the record, Madi is thirty. And don't worry, with the way my life is going right now, I'll never get fucking married again. It's not worth the pain-in-the-ass heartache when it all goes to hell. Can you please leave? This is the last thing I need right now. I'll get your name off the forms as soon as I'm done here."

"Now that I know you're okay, I'll go. I'm sorry. I didn't come here to fight with you."

"And yet that's all we seem to do—"

"Cole. How are we feeling tonight?" With perfect timing, Dr. Taylor drew the curtains aside, fixing the hook that had popped off as he stepped through with Madi and Tate directly behind him.

Fucking great. How much had she heard?

"Always a pleasure, Sherry." Tate beamed at her as she walked around them to leave.

"Whatever you say, Tate," she muttered.

Madi's eyes were wide with alarm. "Are you okay?" she mouthed. I nodded as Dr. Taylor examined my arm.

"I'll just leave this here." She passed a can of Coke to Tate. "I'll, um, get out of your hair so you can talk to the doctor. Text me if you need anything." I didn't miss the tears shimmering in her eyes, but there wasn't anything I could do now. "Bye, Cole."

"I'll call you when I'm home." She didn't answer. She was already halfway to the exit. "Madi—" I shouted. "I'll call you."

She waved over her shoulder, and I couldn't make out her answer.

Dr. Taylor excused himself to grab some supplies that he needed. I wasn't paying attention and, at this point, didn't give a shit about my arm, so I had no idea what he was getting.

"Should I call her now?" I asked Tate.

"She was standing outside the curtain listening to you and Sherry. Dr. Taylor and I got here at the same time. What were you talking about with her? Was it anything that would set Madi off? Or upset her somehow?"

"I said something about not getting married ever again, I think? I don't remember. Sherry was pushing all the usual buttons. She inferred that Madi was too young for me, and she was worried about the kids being around her."

"Jesus. She has a lot of nerve. Okay, that doesn't seem like a big deal. If she heard everything, she's bound to understand you were frustrated. Call her tomorrow. You need to get that arm taken care of. And you need to go home and crash."

"Okay. Good thinking. I'm exhausted. Talking would be pointless now, anyway. I'll probably end up saying something stupid."

He smacked my good shoulder. "I'll take you home when you're done. I got a couple of the guys to drive my car over."

"Thanks, man."

"It's gonna be okay."

"I hope so. But I don't have any energy left to think about it right now."

CHAPTER 24
Madi

The drive across town back to the Confectionery went by in a haze of starlight and tears, peppered by the occasional glare of a streetlight. If the roads had been busy, I would have pulled over to cry it out, but lucky for me, I had a clear shot home.

But now that I was home, I didn't want to go inside.

I cut the engine and tapped a restless beat on the steering wheel as I sat stewing on what I'd heard in the hospital.

I couldn't seem to acknowledge the significance of Cole's words, even though they had been repeating on a loop ever since I'd heard them. I tried to brush them aside and think positively, but it wasn't working.

"We're not serious. We're just starting out. Seeing where things go."

"I'll never get fucking married again."

I didn't want to hear it when I was standing outside that hospital curtain, eavesdropping like a little freak, and I didn't want to think about it now. I had wanted to cover my ears like a child and pretend he wanted to be with me as much as I wanted to be with him.

It's not like we had a commitment. We hadn't made any promises to each other. But at that moment, my heart didn't want to be logical. It hurt.

This thing with Cole came on fast. It was all at once. It was everything. I didn't want to lose it, so I grasped at every straw I could think of that would make it make sense.

He was scared to move on.

He was afraid to be in a new relationship. That's probably all it was. *That had to be it.*

I couldn't conceive of him feeling any other way. He was so good to me. He was too good of a person to string me along. He wouldn't do that.

Plus, I had to admit that if I had an ex like Sherry, I would be scared too.

I broke up with Ross and as far as I was concerned, even if he moved in next door to me, I never had to speak to him ever again.

Cole didn't have that luxury. Like it or not, he had to deal with Sherry. They were bound together forever because of Natalie and Evan. And if I somehow ended up with him, I would have to deal with her too. I'm not sure how I felt about that. But there was no need to put the cart before the horse at this point.

I glanced at the dashboard clock. It was after midnight. I hadn't realized how late it was when I left. Tate had called, and I spared no thought about anything other than getting to the hospital to be with Cole. It was as simple as that. That was a massive clue that my feelings for him were far more profound than I had allowed myself to contemplate.

After I got out, I heard a rustling sound in the alley. Momentary panic flooded my senses, and I almost jumped back into the car before I heard the distinct sound of Kenzie muttering to herself.

I shuffled around the corner and found her huddled next to the dumpster, leaving a voice note for someone on her phone.

"Kenzie! What the hell are you doing out here? Do you know what time it is?"

She let out a whispered shriek and fumbled her phone into her lap. "Shit, Madi. You scared the hell out of me."

I stood next to her in the shadow of the dumpster. "I scared you? I just got back from the hospital. It's the middle of the night. The last thing I need is to hear whispering in the dang alley. And why are you out here? Are you okay?"

"Yeah, I'm fine. Kind of. I mean, I'm alive, I guess. But back up a second. Hospital? Is everything okay with you?"

"It's not me. Cole got burned. He's going to be fine."

"Okay, that's good. I'm glad to hear it. But you don't look fine. At all."

"I overheard some things, but I'm refusing to freak out until I know more. I have to talk to him about stuff. Madison 2.0 does not bury her feelings and let things fester until they explode. But she can also read a room. Timing is everything."

She patted the cement next to her, and I sat.

"That's good. I overheard a whole bunch of shit too, and I've totally lost my mind. Cut to me sitting in an alley waiting for the midnight baker to come out so I can jump his bones. I need to get over Drew. Immediately. Like, right now. I have got to get him out of my mind."

I nudged her shoulder with mine. "Ah, the whole get under someone new to get over another someone old thing. Is that it?" I kept it light. Kenzie would spill her guts to me if, and only if, she was ready. It was best to let her tell me whatever had happened to set her off tonight on her own time.

"Exactly. You get me. Now, get lost. I can't seduce him if you're here."

I side-eyed her. "I wouldn't count on seducing him out here. Dumpsters are not sexy. But at least this one isn't on fire."

"You're right. I'm miserable. I don't know what to do."

"Do nothing. Hang with me. Neither one of us needs to do anything tonight." I leaned into her side. "I'm pretty miserable right now too. I'm falling in love with Cole. I know it for sure now. It's happening."

Her eyes shot to mine. "And that's a bad thing? I don't see how. Cole is awesome. I've basically been telling you this since you got here."

"It's a potentially bad thing when tonight I overheard him say that we are not serious, and he is never getting fucking married ever again."

"Oh shit. And that's all you want to do since forever ago. Playing Barbies with you was like being stuck in the nineteen fifties. Damn, that sucks."

"Hey." I nudged her shoulder with a laugh. "I'm not that bad."

"Okay, fine. If the nineteen fifties included bank accounts for women, property ownership, and freedom—whatever. I know you were into Astronaut Barbie too, but that's not my point. Don't pretend you don't understand what I'm saying. You're no trad-wife wannabe, but you want to have a family, Madi. And we both know why."

"Yeah. I do. I want that—more than anything. I want to create everything I never got to have growing up. I want to be like Gigi. Is that a bad thing?"

"No, there's nothing wrong with it. Everyone should be able to choose what they want."

"And you still want Drew. Right?"

"Yeah, but I can't have Drew. I'm not that woman. Nobody cheats on me."

"I know. Everything is stupid and frustrating right now. Let's cry, maybe stomp around, or throw things. We can solve our problems like grown adult women tomorrow."

She gestured to my tear-streaked face. "Cry? You mean keep crying, right?"

Taking note of her own puffy eyes and tear-streaked cheeks, I whispered softly, "Yeah, something like that."

"Who says grown adult women aren't allowed to be frustrated and cry?" She leaned her head on my shoulder.

"You're right. We're allowed to be upset."

We sat, hugging each other, crying and shivering against the cold brick wall of the Confectionery.

There was a sourness sitting in the pit of my stomach that wouldn't go away. I felt wretched about tonight. I shouldn't have left him there. I should have been the one to drive him home and take care of him.

"I'm freezing my ass off out here. Maybe we should go up to your apartment." Kenzie broke the silence in a strained tone. "Can I crash with you? I don't want to be alone, and I don't think you should be either."

"Yeah, of course. I'm always here for you, Kenz. We'll be okay in the morning. Or not. I don't fucking know."

Her burst of laughter lacked her usual humor. "I feel so comforted right now."

The kitchen door flew open, letting out the smell of delicious fresh-baked bread, along with Gigi, with who could only have been the midnight baker standing in the shadows behind her.

My blood ran cold when I noticed the boot was gone. I knew she had an appointment with her doctor today. One of her friends had taken her. I also knew her ankle was getting better and that she had been milking her injury for as long as she could, which was another thing I had shoved out of my mind to think about later.

It seemed like all my *laters* were catching up to me.

I had no reason to be in Cozy Creek now unless I made an active choice and decided to stay.

"Drew?" Kenzie's jaw dropped as she quickly scrubbed her hands down her cheeks to get rid of her tears.

I looked past Gigi as she stepped into the alley. Drew was behind her. They were taking out the trash, each holding a bag.

He didn't answer. He gritted his teeth, his jaw ticking in dismay. He frowned and handed Gigi the trash bag he was carrying, and then he turned around to go back inside without a word.

But the look of defeat on his face could not be mistaken.

"Let me take that." I took the bags from her and tossed them into the dumpster.

"Drew is the midnight baker?" Kenzie deduced in a trembling voice. "I've been making an ass of myself over him all this time. Imagining who he was is what kept me from thinking about Drew so much; it was a distraction. Why am I like this? Why didn't you tell me?"

"I'm so sorry." Gigi's face radiated sympathy and guilt. "I wanted to tell you, but I couldn't. He didn't want me to. He wanted to give you space. And I think you know why."

"Because we broke up." She flattened her lips and looked away. "Damn it. He needs this job, and it's perfect for him. He deserves to have a place like this to spend his time. He needs to feel safe and secure after all he's been through. I'd never try to take this away from him. You're a good person, Gigi. Better than me."

"You're hurting right now, Kenzie. I'm not better than you. I was just trying to keep two people I care very much about happy. I'm sorry if I mucked it up by keeping this a secret."

I looked between the two of them, waiting for an explanation.

"Drew was a Marine," Kenzie explained. "He's seen some shit. He said he needed to figure out how to, like—live again, I guess. He needed peace. I mean, what was he doing with me, right?"

I hugged her against my side. "Kenzie, stop it. You could cheer anyone up. Do not sell yourself short. I won't let you."

"Madi is right. And I'm not trying to get in the middle of the two of you, Kenzie. But I couldn't fire him. I just couldn't. He's doing so much better now. He's in therapy, and we talk almost every night—"

"No, I'm okay. I get it, Gigi. Totally. And I don't want you to let him go. His job here has nothing to do with me. I'm no petty bitch."

She waved her hand. "Oh, honey, I know that. Under all that smartassery, you're just a giant tender heart full of love. But I think the two of you need to talk," she added gently. "For real, without all the anger and fighting getting in the way. But that's not up to me to decide."

"When he can give me a real explanation for what he did, then maybe I'll listen. Maybe we can, like, be friends or something—someday. When we're senior citizens, and I don't want to jump his bones all the damn time."

"Hey." Gigi was offended. "Just because you're old doesn't mean you don't still need to get your freak on from time to time."

I stood there blinking, choosing not to process what she said.

Kenzie stuck her hand out for a high five. "I take that back. Go, Gigi. Get yours. It's Mr. Nightingale, am I right? I see how he looks at you when he comes in for his green tea and banana bread. And how he always brings you all the zucchini and tomatoes from his garden."

"Perhaps." Her lips tilted up in a secretive grin. "But that's not what we need to discuss right now. What we need to address is why you two girls are crying in my alley in the middle of the night. What's going on? Are you okay?"

"Not at the moment. But we will be," I answered. "We were about to go upstairs to crash. Can we talk tomorrow? Maybe we can all have breakfast together."

"Yes, my loves. I have to get back inside with Drew. He's probably so worried about losing his job right now."

"Wait." Kenzie put a hand on Gigi's shoulder to stop her from opening the door. "Does he ever talk about me?" she whispered. I could tell it killed her to ask. "Is he over everything?"

Gigi looked her in the eye. "Yes, he talks about you, and no, he's not over anything. But if you want to know how he feels, you need to let him tell you about it himself. Listen to him, Kenzie, and if you don't like what he has to say, what you do about it is up to you. You are the most stubborn person I've ever met. Though I can hardly blame you for it."

She hid her face in her hands. "I'm an entire mess. I know."

"My darling, you are not a mess. But you have guarded your heart so completely that nothing gets to it anymore. Drew got in there, and it terrified you. And that was before the mystery of the back seat thong happened."

"Oh god, you know about that?"

"Kenzie," I said gently. "Everyone knows about that. You weren't exactly quiet the last time he came into the Confectionery."

"Right. Great. Okay, maybe I will move to Colorado Springs with you," she muttered. "When I get mad, I get loud. It's like I just start yelling no matter who is around."

Gigi held up a hand. "No one is moving anywhere. Not until we have a long talk." She looked at both of us in turn. "I mean it. If I find out you have packed up and moved overnight, I'm going to hunt you down and drag you back."

"I would never do that," I promised. "No matter what is going on. I'll always talk to you first."

"Deep down, I know it. But it had to be said. Also, is something happening I should know about? What are you doing out here?"

"Cole got hurt tonight." I exchanged a glance with Kenzie, warning her without words not to bring up the love stuff.

Her hand flew to her chest. "Oh my god!"

"He's okay. He'll be totally fine. I just came from the hospital.

From what Tate said, he was in there more for precautionary measures. He might even be home now."

"I'll go over there tomorrow and bring him a chicken pot pie. He loves those."

"Hey." I grinned at her. "I love those. Bring me one too," I teased.

"Come over tomorrow, and we'll make it together and bring it to Cole."

"You're always planning something, aren't you?" I said as I hugged her goodbye.

"I can't seem to help myself. I do it because I love you and want you to be happy. Get upstairs, girls, and get some good sleep. Good night."

"We love you too, Gigi."

We said our goodbyes to Gigi and went upstairs to sleep for the rest of the night.

CHAPTER 25

Cole

Thanks to the painkillers, I woke up okay. My burn throbbed with a dull ache, but it was bearable.

I was alone but otherwise fine. Lonely, but I'd live through it, like usual.

Sherry was scheduled to pick up the kids from my parents' place, so due to my injury, I had an unexpected day off from the station.

Maybe I'd stay in bed all day. I punched the pillow behind me and flicked on the TV. I was mindlessly watching whatever was on the screen as thoughts rattled around in my brain like ghosts to haunt me.

My arm, the burn, and how stupidly distracted I'd been last night when I knew better.

Sherry's harsh words about who I had chosen to spend my time with. Yeah, Madi was younger than me. But thirty wasn't *young*. I had no idea why she took issue with it, and it pissed me off.

The hurt look on Madi's face when she left the hospital last night, rushing through the emergency room like she couldn't wait to get away from me. She heard everything, which had to be the cause, and I had no idea what, if anything, I could say to make her feel better. I couldn't control Sherry or her opinions.

I should check on her. But I had no idea what to say when I had no idea what I wanted—other than to be with her as much as I could before she returned to Colorado Springs.

I was not in a place in my life to make any promises. Finding love had not been on my radar, but how else could I explain all these feelings I had for Madi? I was falling for her, and I had to stop it.

I didn't want her to go home, but asking her to stay in Cozy Creek would be wrong. Part of me wanted to lay down my heart and beg her to be mine. But the adult part, the part that wasn't selfish, needy, and desperate for her, knew she could do so much better than me.

I was the guy who'd married his high school sweetheart, a woman I had known forever, and still couldn't make her happy.

Getting to know Madi made me question everything I thought I knew about love, and I realized I knew nothing.

Maybe I am fucked up.

Maybe Tate was right, and Sherry messed me up more than I was willing to admit.

Enough.

Staying cooped up in my bedroom and torturing myself was useless. With a toss bordering on violent, I threw my quilt to the side and stalked to the shower.

I had to check on her.

I had to explain—myself. Or at least talk to her until we could come to an understanding. We needed to be on the same page. I had to find out what she had heard last night and how much it had upset her. The thought that she'd walked away from me hurting last night didn't sit right with me.

After hurrying through my shower, I dressed quickly in jeans and a T-shirt, then headed to the Confectionery, hoping to figure out what to say to her when I got there.

It was early. At this time of day, customers pick up their orders to take with them to work rather than sit down to enjoy their treats.

Instead of finding Madi behind the counter, Gigi was standing there. There was a pensive gleam in her eyes. She didn't seem like her usual cheerful self. She was worried about something. And she was not wearing her boot.

As I waited in line, my heart's last spark of hope for a future with Madi diminished. Logically, I knew I was overreacting, but I couldn't stop the negative thoughts from forming. They popped up faster than I could shoot them down. Logic was not my friend today. By the time I reached the counter, my mood was bleak, and a cold knot of tension roiled around in my gut. I took a deep breath and tried to relax.

"Good morning, sweetheart," she greeted me.

"Good morning. Your ankle is better. I'm glad to see it." As casually as I could manage, I asked, "Does Madi know yet?"

"She knows." Her voice was calm, her gaze steady, as if she could read my mood. "We were supposed to have breakfast and discuss it, but she wasn't feeling well this morning. She's upstairs. I let her be since she had a late night. Poor thing is just tired."

"Oh." I nodded. "Okay." A familiar flash of loneliness struck me, and misery, like a weight, settled into my chest.

Would she be packing?

Getting ready to go home?

Was I too late? *For what?* What was I going to do?

She wasn't here right now, and it threw me off. She was always here when I arrived. I had grown accustomed to seeing her smiling face in the morning, whether behind the counter or at Gigi's when she met Natalie to walk Basil.

Insecurities I had thought I had gotten over flooded into my thoughts. I couldn't make Sherry happy, and I'd known her since we were children. How in the hell would I ever be able to make someone as unforgettable as Madi want to be with me?

"You should go up and talk to her," Gigi suggested.

"Yeah, that's why I came—"

"Oh! Your arm. How is it? I should have asked you first thing. I'm so sorry. I'm a bit unsettled this morning. Too much is going on."

"No, it's okay. I'm fine. It wasn't a serious burn. How's the ankle feeling now that the boot is off?"

"Better. I'm fine too, damn it." She bit her lip and looked away. "I don't want her to go, Cole," she whispered.

"I know . . ." I shut my eyes for a moment, feeling completely miserable. "I'll go up and talk to her."

"Good. I'll be here if you need me."

If I needed her?

Why would I need her? This didn't bode well for me. Or was it just an innocuous statement? I drove myself crazy, stewing over the possibilities while walking up the stairs. My heart thumped madly as I stabbed the doorbell and pounded on the door. Each knock felt like a bad omen.

I should leave.

Would it be better to leave whatever this thing was between us as it was? Would trying to define it ruin it?

Her footsteps across the wood floor had me holding my breath. I released it to clear my head.

All I had to do was be honest with her. If she couldn't understand my trepidations, she wouldn't be the person I thought she was.

She flung the door open and smiled at me, and for a brief moment, I felt relief. Then her smile shook, and she stepped aside to wave me in after her.

"Good morning, Cole." She was formal. And while she wasn't cold, she wasn't the Madi I had grown accustomed to. "How are you feeling?"

"Much better, and you?"

"Fine. Just sleepy. I was up late with Kenzie."

"Ahh, I see."

"We should talk."

"We need to talk."

We spoke at the same time. But I could tell she was as nervous as I was when neither of us laughed.

"Would you like some coffee?" she offered. "I just made a pot."

"Sure." I accepted, even though caffeine was the last thing I needed. My heart was about to race out of my chest and run a lap through Cozy Creek.

"Sit down, and I'll bring it out."

I found my way to the couch. All three cats sat glaring at me from the windowsill, telling me with their eyes not to fuck this up.

"I can't make any guarantees, okay?" I mumbled. "I'm probably going to put my foot in my mouth." I was talking to cats. Clearly, I had lost it. At least I wasn't expecting them to answer.

"Did you say something?" she called from the kitchen.

"Uh, no."

She came back carrying two mugs. "I remembered you said you like my coffee creamer too. I hope this is okay."

I took a sip. "It's perfect. Thank you."

She sat on the chair adjacent to the couch where I was. "So, Gigi got her boot off and I—"

"You're going back to Colorado Springs?"

"Um." Uneasiness snuck into her voice as she continued. "I was thinking about staying here, actually."

"Not for me, though. Right?" Awkwardly, I cleared my throat.

What was I saying?

Everything I had wanted to express to her was getting twisted through the disastrous labyrinth of my insecurities before it came out of my mouth. I was already fucking this up, and we'd barely gotten started.

Her face turned red. "Um—I. Wow. Okay. I don't quite know what to say to that . . ." she stammered, bewildered.

"That came out wrong. I didn't mean it that way."

"How else could that come out, Cole?" We locked eyes briefly before she looked away, biting her lip nervously. "I thought we had something together. I thought that maybe we had a future. Or at least something special."

"We did. I mean, we do. I just don't want you to leave your home and your life behind for me and my mess. What kind of selfish bastard would I be if I let you do that, Madi? You deserve more. You deserve better."

A warning bell rang in my head. I was going about this the wrong way. This is not what I had intended to express to her.

"Better?" Her face darkened with unreadable emotion, and I braced myself as I waited for her to continue. "Is this because you're older than me? Because you're divorced? Is it because you have kids and I don't? You think I can't handle it. Is that it?"

"I—no, that isn't it. I have a lot of baggage. I have a lot going on and I need to straighten my life out before I can—"

But she didn't let me finish. She was incensed, and I couldn't blame her.

"You listen to me, Cole Sutter." Her face had turned a vivid crimson while the double whammy of hurt feelings and longing lay naked in her eyes.

I shut my mouth, afraid to say anything more. The way I had expressed myself was terrible.

Maybe it was because I was exhausted. Or perhaps it was because, deep down, I was scared of getting hurt again, so I was subconsciously screwing everything up so I wouldn't have to tell her my real feelings and put myself at risk.

I was a coward, and even though I was ashamed, I couldn't stop it.

"Your kids are awesome, and anyone lucky enough to be with you gets to be with them too. And that is a gift. Not a burden, Cole. Any woman who sees them as baggage is someone who doesn't deserve to be with you, okay?"

"No, that isn't it," I bit out. "It's not you, and it's not the kids. It's me. My life is a mess, Madi. And it wouldn't be fair of me to—"

"What exactly about your life is so messy, Cole?" Her eyes drilled into mine while my chest felt like it would burst from holding back the words I knew I should be saying. "You have an ex-wife, and she's a pain in the ass. So what? Your kids are amazing, and they will make anything she has to say worth it. *You* will make it worth it too. You are not a mess."

"No, that's only part of it. I'm not ready for something like this, and maybe you aren't either. We both just went through huge breakups. I think we need time."

"You don't know what I'm ready for." Sudden anger lit up her eyes. "Don't try to make decisions for me or put words into my mouth."

"You're an angel, Madi, and I'm—"

"You're a hero, Cole. Why can't you see what everyone else sees? This whole town adores you. Gigi can't say enough good things about you. Why don't you see it?"

"I just don't, okay?" I shrugged, resigned. "I can't. My mind doesn't work that way. Look, maybe we can be together whenever you're in Cozy Creek to visit Gigi. When you're here, you can be mine, and I'll be yours. No strings until we figure out what we want. I won't be with anyone else, just you. I don't want anyone else."

"I'm okay with a slow burn, Cole." Her eyes gentled. "I'm okay with taking our time, moving slow. But I'm not okay with denying my feelings. I need strings. I'm not okay with not calling this what it is. If you can't admit you have feelings for me, then I'm going back to Colorado Springs, and I don't know if I'll be back at all. I won't be some kind of glorified booty call for you."

"That's not what I want." I shuddered inwardly at the thought of it. "That's not what I meant at all."

"Well, what do you want then? Tell me how you feel. Say it."

"I can't because I don't know—"

"That's fine. Let's stop right here." She set her coffee down and stood. I stood too; it was evident to me our talk was coming to an end.

"Madi, I'm sorry, I—"

She held out a hand, warding off my apology like the words physically hurt her. "Don't apologize. This really isn't anyone's fault. I want too much, and you don't know what you want, and that's okay. But one thing I'm never going to do again is beg for attention. For tiny scraps of what I deserve. Never again, Cole." Her chin lifted defiantly. "I deserve it all. And you do too. I wish you could see that." Her voice trembled as, for a brief second, she wavered. "Unless I've been mistaken about how you feel this entire time—maybe I was delusional. I have been accused of seeing what I want, what isn't there."

I took a step toward her, then froze when she stepped away. "Stop, Madi, no. You aren't mistaken." I dragged a hand through my hair. "I hate this, okay? I'm frustrated with myself because I'm out of control again. I feel desperate, like I'm holding on too tight. You make me feel things she never did. Things I never knew I was capable of. I'm not ready for any of this, and I'm afraid if I put pressure on it, I'll fuck it all up."

"You won't fuck anything up unless you refuse to try." Her throat constricted as she swallowed. Her eyes were glassy with unshed tears.

"I can't. Please understand. I can't do this right now."

"Okay, I get it. I should have known better than to push you, and I'm sorry about that. Pushing is wrong too. Please forgive me."

"No, don't be sorry. Please, I—"

I reached out to take her hand, but she drew it back before I could touch her.

"No. I don't need any more memories of how it feels to have your hands on me. I spent five years with Ross, but you obliterated those memories in less than three months. I'll remember you and me forever."

"Wait." Anguish, like water to drown in, filled my heart. "What do you mean, you'll remember you and me? This doesn't have to be over between us, we can—"

"But it is over." She was resigned. "It has to be, at least for the time being. You said it yourself: you can't do this right now, and that's okay. I even understand why, and I'm not angry with you. But since it's all I want, I have to protect my heart."

Stay.

The word was right there. Waiting for me to say it, but I couldn't. I didn't.

I turned and let myself out.

And I let her go.

CHAPTER 26

Cole

I sat with my feet kicked up on the railing of my porch, rambling on about what an idiot I had been to Tate and Quinn as we split a six-pack of beer and kept an eye on the neighborhood.

I hated how I left Madi. All I wanted to do was go back and make sure she was okay. But how could I when I was the one to hurt her?

"Colton James Sutter, I have a bone to pick with you."

"Shit," I muttered and sat straight.

Gigi came stomping across the street with Basil, his leash in one hand and a covered casserole dish in the other.

She'd spoken to Madi. That much was obvious.

"You're in for it now." Tate took a swig of his beer and watched me from the corner of his eye. "You've pissed her off."

Quinn shook his head, eyebrows raised as he passed me another beer. "You're probably gonna need this."

"Thanks, man." I took it, used the edge of my chair to pop off the cap, and took a healthy slug.

Whatever Gigi had to say, I deserved it and was ready to listen.

The sun had just started to set behind the Rocky Mountains in the distance, and usually, the sight of this familiar view was a comfort. But tonight, it felt wrong. My home didn't quite feel like home anymore. I had the nagging sensation that I'd destroyed everything when I let Madi get away from me.

She glared at me pointedly as she let Basil take a dump in the middle of my lawn. I didn't have it in me to protest.

Her glare turned into a hearty sigh of disappointment before her face softened, and she smiled at me. "I made you a chicken pot pie because I love you. But I'm letting Basil poo in your yard because you have made me mad. I decided to be passive-aggressive about this because I don't want to yell at you. I understand what you're going through, even if I don't like it."

"I—thank you?" I stood to grab the dish and help her out with Basil, but she shook her head.

"Sit back down." Her voice rang with command. She was back to being mad at me. "We're going to talk. Or rather, I will talk, and you'll listen to what I have to say."

Tate set his beer on the porch rail, eyes wide in alarm. Throughout our lives, we'd rarely seen Gigi get angry. "I don't know if I should stay or go," he whispered.

"You keep your behind in that chair, Tatum Jefferson Sutter. Do not even think of leaving that porch. You too Quinn. Don't even think about it."

"No worries, I wasn't planning on thinking, Gigi," Quinn assured her as he sent her a shit-eating grin.

"No sassing me either, Quinton. I'm in no mood for any funny business. Do not try to make me laugh."

"Yes, ma'am. I'm sorry." His smile slid to the side as he apologized.

"Okay, Miss Gigi," Tate said, reverting to what we used to call her. "What exactly did we do?"

"Nothing. I might need backup with this one. And I'm frustrated. Sorry for stirring up a fuss." She jerked her head toward me as her hands were still full.

"You got it, Gigi. Understandable, Cole can do that to a person." Tate sat back and put his feet on the railing. "We've been trying to talk some sense into this knucklehead since we arrived."

Basil finished his business and happily pranced to the porch to sit at Gigi's side.

"What in the heck were you thinking?" she demanded, plopping the casserole dish on the table near the front door and then taking the chair at the edge of the porch.

Basil hopped into her lap and curled against her, ready to relax after desecrating my lawn.

"I'm not completely sure," I answered. "I didn't intend to break up with her. I mean, I don't think I did. It wasn't clear what we had—"

"He keeps saying he doesn't know what he wants," Tate interjected. "Which is total bullshit."

"That's what I thought. Listen to me, Cole, this won't get easier, but you will get stronger. You've been hurt."

"Being strong has nothing to do with this," I argued. "Madi deserves more. That's the bottom line."

Tate threw up his hands in frustration. "I see we have gotten nowhere."

"No. She saw you for who you are, Cole."

I shook my head. "No. I don't know what she saw, but it wasn't me."

"She saw you, the real you. I see you. Tate sees you. Quinn sees you. This whole damn town sees you. You lost sight of yourself. That's your problem."

"She's right. What Sherry did messed you up. Hell, it would shake anyone's confidence. Give yourself a break for once in your life."

"I've become a fuckup since Sherry left. Fighting in public, getting into stupid accidents." I gestured to my injured arm. "I should have never started anything with Madi, at least not until I was better. I'm a mess, and she deserves the world, not some small-town, divorced single fool who resorts to picking bar fights to get his anger out."

"There it is!" Gigi clapped her hands together. "None of that is *you*. Do you think anyone thinks badly of you for knocking Todd's stupid ass out?"

My mouth dropped open. I had no answer for that.

"He deserved it," Quinn chimed in. "In fact, he deserved way more, and so did Sherry. I mean, it's good you didn't knock her out. That's not what I was getting at. But you've been far too kind to those two, considering the level of betrayal they perpetrated on you."

"But I hit someone, Quinn. I resorted to violence. I tell my kids not to get into fights. That makes me a hypocrite—"

Tate stopped me. "No one in Bookers that night judged you; I can promise you that. Before you got there to meet us at the Fire Brigade table, the whispers going around were about how *they* should be the ones to leave, not you. I tried telling you that—"

Gigi held up a hand. "You're not a hypocrite, honey. You're supposed to tell your kids not to solve their problems with their fists; it has to be in the proverbial parenting rule book somewhere, right? But sometimes you just have to lay an asshole out, Cole. Hit first and ask questions later. It's the only way. Todd had it coming." The words were matter-of-fact and spoken with her usual sweet voice. It was shocking coming from someone I'd always seen as a proper grandmother, an authority figure.

"Are you saying—? Do you think I'm being too hard on myself?"

"Jesus Christ," Tate burst out. "Yes!"

"Yes, honey, that's exactly what I'm saying. You've been through a lot, none of which was your fault. And you've always been too hard on yourself since you were a little boy. You've handled all of this better than most people would. Please, give yourself some credit."

I felt absolved. I'd been carrying around the humiliating shame of my actions for so long that I'd let what happened define me.

"Prove to Madi that she wasn't wrong about you," she continued. "You deserve to be loved, and my granddaughter deserves the best. And in case you're not hearing me and your brothers. The best is *you*. You are perfect for each other."

"But I . . . but she . . . I think I broke things off with her. I don't exactly remember all that I said, to be honest."

"You have some work to do, bro," Quinn muttered.

I flicked my wrist to check the time. "It's late."

"That it is," Gigi confirmed. "She'll be back in Colorado Springs by now. She packed a bag and took off."

"I'll go down there tomorrow." I decided. "First thing in the morning. I'll sit outside of her place and wait if I have to. We can talk it out, and I'll make everything okay again."

"Tomorrow is the fundraiser," Quinn reminded me.

"Shit, I can't miss that. I promised her I'd be in that auction. Plus, we spent all that time planning it. Missing it would let her down. Do you think she's still coming?"

"I have no idea," Gigi answered. "But I know she is not one to back out of her responsibilities, so she'll probably be there."

"Okay. I have time. It's not like she will move on in the next twenty-four hours, right? She won't forget about me."

I pulled out my phone to send her a text. I didn't want to upset her by calling. Or maybe I should call her. I had no idea what to do.

> **COLE:** I'm sorry. Can we talk about this?

"She's not going to answer me." I shoved the phone back into my pocket. "Not like this. Texting is a weak move. But I don't want to make things worse by not reaching out."

"Give her the night to calm down and get her head together," Gigi said. "Let her be. She'll read the text when she's ready; at least she'll know you tried to get in touch. That counts for a lot, Cole."

"Okay. You're right. I'll get started fixing this tomorrow."

I glanced over at Tate. He popped an eyebrow. "Send her flowers, at least."

"And don't cheap out," Quinn added. "Get roses. Red ones."

"Oh no," Gigi protested with a sly grin. "Get her peonies. Baby pink peonies."

Tate grinned. "You heard the lady."

I got the strangest sense of déjà vu when the word peonies came out of her mouth.

Years ago, my mother used to grow peonies in the backyard. Maybe that was why.

"Peonies it is. I'm going to get her back. I can't believe I let her go in the first place."

"I have all the faith in the world in you, Cole." Gigi smiled.

CHAPTER 27

Madi

The elevator ride up to my apartment in Colorado Springs felt all wrong. It was like blasting off in a slow rocket ship to another planet. Or a time machine to the past. I didn't belong here anymore, and I don't think I ever did.

I didn't want to leave Cozy Creek when I finally felt like I had a real home there. But how could I stay if I couldn't have Cole?

I unlocked the door and stepped inside. After looking around, I was struck by the fact that my memory of being here with Ross had faded into insignificance. He meant nothing to me now that I tasted actual heartbreak. It would devastate me if I couldn't work things out with Cole.

I set my purse on the console table by the door and dropped my hastily packed overnight bag on the floor. It felt weird not to be greeted by a chorus of *"Where have you been?"* meows, but thankfully, Kenzie would drive the cats to my place tomorrow after the fundraiser—which I still hadn't decided if I would attend.

Luckily, Monica had always approved the décor and food and took care of the final run-through of the venue on the day of the fundraiser, so I had completed my part of the planning. I also had no excuse to show up other than my desire to be there.

With a groan, I found my way to my boring beige leather couch, which had no cute stripes or colorful toss pillows, and plopped down, kicking my feet up on my perfectly adequate coffee table.

This sucked. I felt wretched and couldn't escape thinking I'd made a colossal mistake.

Had I pushed him too hard?

With everything that happened with Ross and how I'd never managed to stand up for myself where he was concerned, I was worried that I'd overcorrected when it came to Cole and jumped the gun by insisting we talk about our future.

Oh well. It was too late now.

My stomach growled, and I burst into tears because it reminded me of the night of our first kiss, his grumbly tummy, and our dinner together at the Skytop Diner.

He was my smushy Tater Tot. Damn it.

I got up to grab my purse to find my phone to order takeout, wiping away tears and frowning when it wasn't there.

My mind raced to retrace my steps. I knew it wasn't in my car...

Crap, I'd left it on the counter in the kitchen back in Cozy Creek. I'd set it down when I grabbed a can of Diet Coke from the refrigerator for the road trip. Whatever, I'd get it tomorrow or get ahold of my mom in the morning and have her call Kenzie to bring it with her when she picked up the cats.

But I wanted takeout, dang it. If there was anything left in my fridge here, I didn't want to know about it—I mean, yuck. But I always had emergency mac and cheese in my freezer and Cool Ranch Doritos in the pantry. It was time to stress eat and comfort rewatch *Gilmore Girls* for the millionth time. I needed to get my mind off of everything and get some perspective.

I headed into the kitchen.

No more thinking. Only relaxing.

Or maybe I should think.

Maybe I should do *all* the thinking tonight and finally make some damn decisions. Decisions for myself and what I want out of my life. Everyone else and their opinions could screw off. I was back in Colorado Springs. I was supposed to be Madison 2.0 right now, taking charge and being in control.

It's funny how I'd gone to Cozy Creek to escape my life here, and now I was doing the same thing in reverse. It was time to handle my shit.

I nuked my macaroni while mindlessly munching on the Doritos. I decided to risk opening the fridge because I really needed a Diet Coke and was pretty sure I'd left a few in there. Yes! I had an entire twelve-pack.

Things were looking better; I would be okay. The little things in life always cheered me up, at least temporarily.

Ding. Ding. Ding.

My good thoughts flew away at the sound of my doorbell repeatedly ringing.

I wasn't expecting anyone.

I grabbed my big marble rolling pin from my baking rack and crept to the door.

I looked through the peephole and saw my mother standing there, furiously texting on her cell phone and pacing back and forth. I stepped back—shit. I was not in the mood to talk to her, or anyone, right now.

I jumped a foot when she started pounding on the door.

"Holy crap, Mother!" I set the rolling pin on the table and threw the door open. "You scared the hell out of me!"

"Oh my god! You're okay." She yanked me into a hug. "I've been calling and calling and—" She pushed me back, hands on my shoulders. "Why haven't you answered your phone, young lady?

Always answer the phone when your mother calls. That's the freakin' rule!"

"I'm sorry." I waved her inside and shut and locked the door. "I left it in Cozy Creek. And I'm thirty. Can we please drop the young lady thing?"

"You drove all the way up here with no phone? Madison Nicole Winslow! What were you thinking?"

"Well, I'm sorry. I wasn't thinking since I forgot it."

"Did you drive the bug? Please tell me you took Gigi's car or even Kenzie's."

"I drove the bug. But Quinn fixed it. It probably runs better than when it was yours."

"Oh. Well, good. Okay then." She took a deep breath, letting it out slowly as she looked me up and down, ensuring I was okay. "I totally freaked out." Her eyes shifted to the side as she smiled sheepishly. "You're fine."

"You think?" I laughed. "And, yeah, I'm fine. Alive and in one piece, at least."

"Oh, honey. I was worried about you. I knew from Gigi that you were upset, and then you didn't answer your phone when I called you. And it's dark outside. I'm sorry."

"It's okay. I get it, promise. I'd be the same way if I had kids of my own. But really, it's barely even dinner time. It's hardly late."

"Oh, honey."

"Stop it. You've got to quit '*oh honey*'-ing me; you're going to make me cry. I've cried enough today."

"Baby girl," she whispered, holding her arms out. "Come here."

I went. I burst into fresh tears and let her hug me. It felt good to get it all out.

"I'm such an idiot." I sobbed into her shoulder. "I think I ruined everything."

"You did not. That's impossible. Tell me all about it, and we'll make a plan to fix it."

I pulled back to study her face. "Haven't you heard most of the gory details from Riley and Abigail? Or Gigi?"

"No. They keep your secrets, honey. And before you ask, Gigi didn't tell me anything other than you were upset and I should come over here to check on you."

"Oh. That's nice to know." I followed her to the couch, and we sat down.

"However, I do know about your fondness for Cole. She didn't tell me on purpose. It's the way she talks about him, and I know you were planning the fundraiser together, and, well, I can put two and two together; let's just put it that way, okay? Am I right?"

"Yeah, you're right, and apparently, he wasn't ready for all this." I waved a hand up and down in front of myself. "And how do you know so much? You couldn't have figured it all out on your own. Please."

"I'm your mother. I know everything, don't you know that by now?" She tsked. "And even if I didn't, I have eyes and the power of observation. Ever since you were a little girl, you've always thought Cole was cute. Plus, the gossip from Cozy Creek has spread all the way to my office, thanks to my temporary event planner. Your itty-bitty crush is more now, yes?"

"Itty-bitty crush?" My voice rose in surprise. "I used to think he was cute? I don't remember any of that."

"Oh, yes." She brushed my hair over my shoulder and smiled. "You used to cry when Riley and Abigail played tag with the Sutter boys in the street. But you were too little to join, so Cole would always bring you a peony from his mother's garden whenever they were done. Those lovely pink ones in the backyard, all fluffy and soft. I wonder if they're still there."

I sat there blinking and wracking my brain, trying to remember. "How could I have forgotten that? I mean, maybe I remembered bits and pieces. I've always loved peonies. Maybe that's why?"

"I bet it is." She eyed me knowingly. "You were a toddler, and he probably doesn't even remember doing it. He was very young too, and being kind was second nature to him; he was such a sweet little boy. But I thought it was the cutest thing. Gigi and I used to swear the two of you would grow up and get married someday—after you graduated from college, followed your dreams, and grew up to be a fully evolved woman, of course."

I laughed. "Obviously."

"But then, your dad and I divorced, and we moved to Colorado Springs. Then that little Sherry girl from next door caught his eye, and that was that."

"Well. Holy shit." I loved the idea of having a history with Cole, even a minor thing such as this.

"I know, right? It's kind of like fate has stepped in, isn't it?"

"Well, I'm afraid I blew it."

"Well." She stuck her tongue out at me teasingly. "According to Gigi, he hung the moon. So most likely, he'll be removing his head from his ass at some point, and then he'll come crawling back, begging to be with you."

"Doubtful. And it's too late for that." I blew a disgruntled breath. "I'm hurt and also embarrassed. And a tiny bit mad at him too. I don't care if I have a right to feel this way. I just do. I put myself out there. I wish I could take it back."

"Gotcha. I'd probably be feeling the same thing. Love is a bunch of bullshit, isn't it?"

"It is. Total freaking bullshit."

"He's not that hot anyway. You could do better."

"He's totally hot, Mother. Are you blind? He's a firefighter. He literally saves lives for a living. He's a hero and a good dad too, by the way."

"Meh, whatever. Dads are overrated. Moms are where it's at. Take me, for example. I am here for you and ready to listen. I give the best hugs. Not to mention, I have the DoorDash app pulled up, and I'm ready to order all the takeout you want. I bet you're hungry. Aren't you?" She held up her phone.

"Oh, I'm starved. You'll just have to trust me; he's a good dad, and his kids are awesome. I want pizza. Get extra pepperoni and a huge Diet Coke."

"On it. Pizza sounds perfect. And you got me there. I've heard nothing but good things about those kids from Gigi. They're always polite every time I see them at her place."

"Oh yeah? Well, that's good to hear."

"He needs to work on his yard, though," she muttered as she tapped on her phone to order the food. "His front lawn has been looking a little lackluster. The last time I was at Gigi's, I noticed it was a bit overgrown. Maybe he needs a new mower."

"His yard is fine. He has gorgeous roses on the side of his house, and maybe you need glasses because he always does those straight mowing lines—it's actually perfect. I haven't been in the back, though. I have no idea if the peonies are still there."

She burst out laughing.

"God, I can't believe I fell for this. I know what you're doing."

"I'm not doing anything."

"Whatever. You're trying to remind me why I like him so much. You're always so sneaky."

"Sometimes, it's the only way to get you girls to talk to me."

"Ugh. I've said too much. Now you're going to be on Gigi's side."

She looked me dead in the eyes. "I'm always on your side, Madison. Always. Even if you're wrong, I will have your back."

"I love you, Mom."

"I love you too. In fact, I love you so much that I'm going to that fundraiser with you tomorrow night. Me, you, and your sisters. Picture it: the four of us, dressed to kill. We can take a family photo to put on my mantel. Me and my girls."

"What? You? In Cozy Creek somewhere other than Gigi's? In public? You'll go with me?"

"Yeah. Me. In Cozy Creek. It's time. If my baby is going to be living there, then I'll have to get used to the place again, right? Plus, I've missed the Skytop and their epic tots."

"Living there? I'm not at that point yet, if at all. But what if you run into Dad? Who knows when he'll be back in town."

"I know you haven't seen him since you've been there, Gigi told me. Sometimes, I wish I had picked a better father for you, but I was stupid in love back then, and I made so many bad decisions where he was concerned. But I can't regret any time I spent with him because now I have my girls. If I run into him, I'll deal with it. I'll do anything for you."

"I—I don't know what to say. Thank you." She pulled me into her arms for a hug, and I snuggled close. "This means everything to me."

"Of course. Now tell me what happened with Cole. Don't spare a detail."

"I was pushy. And I was demanding. I wouldn't blame him for never speaking to me again. He said he wasn't ready, and I didn't accept it."

She stroked my hair and pulled me tighter, reminding me of how I felt with her as a little kid. She worked a lot, but somehow, she was always there for me. I felt bad for losing sight of that.

"There is a line between standing up for yourself and being pushy. There is no way you crossed it. Okay? You're a sensitive girl. You've always known how to read a room."

I told her everything we had said to each other—all of it.

"So, he expressed the honest thought that he wasn't ready. He admitted he has feelings for you. He explained himself thoroughly and didn't want to end things with you. He just wanted to slow down? Is that it?"

I shifted out of her arms to sit cross-legged in the corner of the couch.

"When you put it that way, I sound like a freakin' psycho, Mother."

"You're not a psycho. Not at all. That's not where I was going with this. You are lucky to have a sense of clarity that he doesn't. You moved on from Ross. He can't entirely move on from his ex. Gigi told me about her and what she did to him. She's a piece of work, that one is. He probably doesn't want to put you through all the drama she'll inevitably cause. And he's hurting. I know you are too, and I don't want to compare your pain to his. But his situation is a lot more complicated with the kids and all that goes along with that."

"I totally get that. You're right, and I hope she gets better. For their sake."

"Think of it this way: he has to deal with her for the rest of his life. Ask me how I know what that feels like."

"So, you're an expert witness for the defense, is that it?"

"No, Madi. The two of you sound like you're on the same side. Take a breath, think about it, and you'll see it too."

"Okay. You're right. That's probably why I'm not completely devastated right now."

"Good. Now flip what I said. Did you tell him what you need?"

I nodded.

"Were you honest?"

"Yes..."

"Clear about what you want?"

"Yeah. I mean, I think so."

"Good. Always be forthright. If someone can't handle it, they don't belong in your life."

"You're right. I didn't mess anything up. Not being honest with him would have led to resentment."

"You are a fighter, Madi. I raised all of you girls to go after what you want. But you are also my sweetest girl. You are a people pleaser. You want everyone to be happy, and I love that about you. But you need to start pleasing yourself first. You matter."

"Okay, I matter. And I'll try to please myself first," I repeated, not sure where she was going with this.

Deep in my heart, I had always been afraid to let anyone down. A crazy mix of hope and fear shot through my body, leaving me breathless as I contemplated the life changes I was about to make.

"Slight change of subject. I don't want you to try to make me happy anymore. I don't want you to return to Cozy Creek and chase after Cole either. If he doesn't come around, then fuck him." I gasped. "I mean it. I want you to live your dreams. I want you to live your life on your terms, and if that means moving to Cozy Creek and taking over the Confectionery from Gigi someday, then that's what you need to do."

"Are you serious right now? What about the company?"

"If you don't want your job back, Jenny wants it. And even if she didn't, I can find someone else. You need to do what you want. This is your life, and I want you to live it."

"I think I want to live in Cozy Creek."

"I had a feeling about that, sweetheart, and you have my blessing. Not that you need it. But I want you to feel good. I don't want any guilt or confusion between us. Be forthright, always. Got it?"

"Got it, okay. Wow! I'm moving to Cozy Creek."

"I'm happy for—"

A knock at the door cut her off.

"That must be the pizza. Hold that thought."

I got up to answer it.

It was not the pizza.

It was a delivery person from the florist shop down the road carrying an armful of pink peonies wrapped in brown paper and tied with white lace and twine. The card attached said they were from Cole.

I shut the door and faced my mother, who was smiling ear to ear.

"Oh, honey. Maybe there is a little bit of fate happening right now. Or maybe it's Gigi."

CHAPTER 28
Cole

"I'm not sure about this. Do we really have to wear tuxedos? I'd rather be casual. Why did I let her talk me into this?" I glanced over Tate's shoulder in my hallway mirror, scowling at my reflection as I entered the living room.

My burn itched beneath my shirt and jacket. I wanted to take it off and put the ripped-up T-shirt I'd been wearing while I was healing back on.

"Fuck that. We look amazing." He adjusted his bow tie.

"I can't believe you two are going to be auctioned off," Quinn, wearing a standard suit and tie, teased us from the couch. "Remember when I was in FFA back in high school, and I auctioned off that pig? Ahh, memories. You two are bringing it all back for me."

"Shut the fuck up," we said in unison.

Natalie came out of her room, wearing the dress Sherry had bought her last week when it was her turn with the kids. "I think you both look nice. You too, Uncle Quinn."

"You look beautiful, Nat," I told her. "Purple suits you."

"Thanks, Dad."

Tate took her hand and twirled her underneath his arm. "You'll knock 'em dead tonight, kid. That little what's-his-name you've been crushing on won't know what hit him when you show up."

She blushed furiously. "Uncle Tate!"

"What did I say?" He looked at her with confusion etched across his face. "Didn't you go with some little turd to the Fall Ball?" His eyes shifted to me. "Didn't she?"

"Quit while you're ahead, man," I told him. Decoding teenage girls was not for the faint of heart. "Ev! Get a move on. We'll be late."

He opened his door but stood there with a sour look. "Do I have to go? I look stupid." He was wearing a suit and tie like Quinn.

"You look great," Tate told him. "Totally sharp."

"But Uncle Quinn said—"

"You look awesome, dude," Quinn clicked off the TV and reassured him. "I was just razzing my brothers. It's kind of my job to give them shit."

"I didn't razz Natalie yet. Should I?"

"Hell, no," Quinn answered. "You don't razz sisters, especially if they're older than you and stunningly beautiful like our Natalie is. Sisters have a different set of rules."

"That's what I thought. You look real pretty, Nat," he said.

My heart warmed. I loved it when my kids got along, especially when they were being sweet to each other. It made me feel like I was doing something right.

She burst out laughing. "Thanks, Ev. I can't wait to see what Madi is wearing. She's still going, right, Dad? Let's get out of here. I don't want to be late."

I hoped she'd be there. I still hadn't heard from her. My text from last night haunted me. I'd lost count of how many times I'd checked to see if she'd seen it. But it remained unread on my phone. I was worried that I'd completely blown it with her. I'd let my fears and insecurities get the best of me and regretted it. However, I did get confirmation that she'd received the flowers, which left me with a minuscule glimmer of hope.

Monica texted earlier to let me know everything was perfect. The decorations and food were good to go; all I had to do was show up.

Finally, we were all ready to go. We piled into my truck and Tate's Suburban and drove to Veterans Hall downtown.

The parking lot was half-full when we arrived, but we were early, so I wasn't worried. We filled this place every year, and I knew this one would not be the exception. Madi and I had worked hard to get the word out.

The McCreedy Ranch had donated pumpkins as they did every year. Since Halloween had passed, each had been hollowed out, and instead of spooky Jack-O-Lantern faces, leaves of various shapes and sizes had been carved into them. Flameless candles glowed inside, lighting the path leading up to the entrance.

Natalie grabbed my hand. "It's so pretty already, and we aren't even inside yet. I love the garlands; they match the ones at the fire station."

"Thanks, sweetheart. Madi is amazing. All of this was her idea."

"It's all pretty and stuff, but all I care about is the chocolate fountain she told me about," Evan said. "I'm going to camp out there all night."

"Chocolate fountain?" Quinn perked up. "You got yourself a partner, dude." He held his hand out, and Evan smacked it.

I laughed as they hustled to the door, leaving us behind.

Natalie swung my hand as we walked. "I'm going to sit with Dexter and his family. Is that okay? I know they're here. I saw their car. His mom said it was okay." She held her phone out, showing me the text from Dexter's mother, giving her permission, and telling me she would drive her home when the fundraiser was over.

"It's fine with me. As long as you stay with his family at their table the entire time."

"I will, I promise. His mom wouldn't let us go anywhere anyway. She's just like you. Strict but still cool."

"All right then." I chuckled, relieved. "Go ahead."

"Thank you, Dad." She took off, looking far too grown up for my liking. It was so much easier when she was a little girl, and I didn't have to worry about things like dating and all the potential heartache that came with it.

"Where did the years go?" Tate chuckled. "They grew up too fast, man."

"Don't I know it?"

After the slap, Sherry attended several sessions with Natalie. Things have been looking up with them since we began therapy.

We had agreed to let her go to the Fall Ball with Dexter last month, and now they were dating. I'd known his parents forever, which helped me feel okay about it. He was a good kid. I was also relieved that Sherry had committed to prioritizing our kids again. They needed her.

I stood on the walkway. I didn't want to go in without Madi. We'd spent so much time planning this it felt wrong to see it without her.

"She'll show up. There's no way she'd miss this. Have faith."

"I hope you're right. I hope I didn't fuck everything up."

"Let's get inside."

I followed him in and was greeted by a breathless Monica.

"Catch you later." Tate took off into the room.

"So? What do you think?" She held her arm out with a smile. I took it all in.

The tables were covered with white fabric and topped with bouquets of mums, marigolds, and roses dyed in autumnal shades. Buffett stations had been set up along the walls on three sides of the space, while a platform intended for the bachelor auction was on the fourth.

I gulped and fought the temptation to turn tail and run. I was not looking forward to this. At all.

"It's beautiful. Thanks for supervising the setup. It's flawless."

"Of course. This is always my favorite day of the Fire Brigade year."

"I wish I could say the same," I muttered, suddenly nauseous for reasons other than Madi. "I am not looking forward to standing on that platform." My stomach roiled. "In front of everyone. With people watching me—"

"Take a deep breath, Cole. It will go fast. I promise." Monica was always the de facto hostess of the fundraiser, while I was like the grumpy dad who said hi at a holiday get-together and then disappeared—not tonight, though. "I'll go easy on you. I won't make jokes or anything. I'll save that for Tate. He can take it."

"I appreciate it."

"I got you. I promise. Go get a cold drink and sit down. Maybe grab a plate too. You're looking a little green around the gills. Eat something."

"I—okay."

I trudged toward one of the buffets and grabbed a glass. The food looked delicious, but I couldn't eat. I filled my glass with chilled apple cider from the punch bowl and found a table in the corner.

"Hey." Tate slid into the seat across from mine. "Monica said you weren't doing too good. You look like crap. Take a deep breath or something. Do not puke."

I let out a sardonic laugh. "I'm nervous and can't stop wondering where Madi is. She still hasn't returned my text."

"I'll do the welcome speech thing if you want," he offered. "You can stay right here."

"Thanks. I don't have the capacity for any of this shit tonight."

"I got you. I'll just say you have a headache or something. Or your arm is still bothering you from when we saved the town from that burning dumpster."

I shook my head as I laughed. "Perfect."

"Stay here. Get something to eat. Quit thinking. I'll grab you when it's time to get on stage."

"Great. Thanks. I can't fucking wait." I was attempting sarcasm, but the blood pounding in my temples as I inhaled deeply gave me away, and Tate softened his expression.

"Hey, it's okay," he said. "You got this."

"I really don't," I muttered. "I feel like an extra in a weird-ass rom-com."

"If this is a rom-com, you'll get the girl at the end because you're no extra. You're the star attraction tonight, Chief Sutter."

"Oh god."

He laughed and darted toward the bidding platform for the auction to talk to Monica. It was not quite a stage, but that didn't make it any less intimidating.

"Hello there, Cole." I looked up. Heather Hadley had sidled to my table to run her hand up my arm.

I flinched. It was my injured arm.

Her mother and daughter were at a table near the platform, but luckily, Ross was nowhere to be seen.

"I got, um, I have an injury. I burned my arm. Sorry."

Why was I apologizing to her when I didn't want her touching me?

"Oh, you poor baby." She clicked her tongue. "Is there anything I can do to help you feel better?"

"No thanks, I'll be okay. Tate is waiting for me. I have to go. Have a fun night. Thank you for coming out."

"I wouldn't miss it." She bit her lip and fluttered her eyelashes.

Subtlety was lost on her. "I hear you're up for grabs tonight. I have plenty of money to spend."

I turned back around to face her. "It's not really a date. You know that right? Nothing romantic is intended. It's for charity. For fun. Tomorrow night. Dinner at the station. That's all it is." I spelled it out. Clear. Concise. To the point.

"I know how to have fun, sugar. Don't you worry about that. I'll show you a real good time."

Damn it.

My father had drilled it into me and my brothers since we were boys to always be gentlemen. But Heather Hadley was making it complicated. I couldn't deal with her like I'd done with Todd—no parking lot fisticuffs would be able to work this problem out.

I had to get away from her. Avoidance was the only way.

"I have to go."

"But I—"

"Bye, Mrs. Hadley."

"It's Heather, honey. Remember?"

I ignored her and all but ran across the space to hide out in the restroom, like a fucking adult or a man who was loath to be harsh with a woman.

I splashed cold water on my face at the sink and stared at my reflection. I had to get it together.

A few deep breaths later, I was back in the main room, heading toward the stage as if in a trance.

I made it up there with no time to spare. Monica shot me an encouraging smile as I tried not to vomit.

"We'll start the bidding for each bachelor at fifty dollars. First up is Cole Sutter, the Cozy Creek Fire Brigade chief. Let's have a round of applause for Cole! What a good sport you are. Do we have fifty dollars?"

Immediately, Heather Hadley stood up from her table and raised her hand. "Fifty dollars, right here." She sent a dirty wink my way and licked her lips.

I looked at the ceiling and tried to find a happy place to go to.

"Sixty dollars." My eyes snapped to the crowd. Abigail had bid on me.

She was at a table with Riley.

Where were Gigi and Madi? And Kenzie?

Or anyone else I could send rescue signals to with my eyeballs. Someone else had to bid on me. Literally anyone else would be better than these two.

What the hell was going on?

Shit. Shit. Shit.

Was Abigail interested in me again? I looked at the floor. Maybe if I stared hard enough, it would swallow me up. Getting sucked down to hell would be better than being in this event room right now.

"Seventy dollars." It was Handsy Hadley again.

There was no good option for me here. "What the fuck, Tate," I seethed at him.

"You'll be fine."

"The hell I will." I grabbed Tate to whisper in his ear. "You're up last. Sneak off and find Nat. Give her a couple hundred bucks and tell her to bid on me. Or Riley. Or find Kenzie. Or even Quinn. I don't fucking care. Help me."

He burst out laughing.

"This is not fucking funny," I rasped from the corner of my mouth. "This is my literal nightmare. I'm pretty sure I've woken up in a cold sweat from something like this at least once."

"You're right." He cupped his hand over his mouth to whisper back, "It's not funny—at all. I'm sorry. I have no idea how to help you though. Maybe we can get Mom to kick her ass? Too bad we don't have an older sister."

I choked on a laugh. "It's all good. I'll handle it somehow." He might not have a solution, but he could always lighten my mood.

"One hundred dollars," Abigail shouted, glaring at Mrs. Hadley. "Sit down, lady. I've got money to spare and zero compunctions about taking you out to the parking lot to work this out old-school style." She slapped her fist into the palm of her opposite hand for emphasis. "I need Cole, and I'm going to get him. You can bid on someone else. They're all the same to you, right?"

Riley was sitting at their table. I tried to catch her eye, but she was busy texting on her phone and didn't notice my desperate but silent cry for help.

"Two hundred dollars." Handsy Hadley flipped Abigail the bird and then blew me a kiss.

"Oh god," I mumbled. Would it be wrong to run out the back door and hide out at home until the fundraiser was over?

"Two hundred and fifty!" Abigail stuck her tongue out. "Watch it, Hadley."

"Five hundred dollars." A breathless Madi entered the room, followed by her mother and Gigi.

CHAPTER 29

Cole

"Oh, thank god." Relief flooded my veins, and it was twofold.

One, Madi was here, and she was okay. Two, she bid on me, which had to mean she still cared. Maybe I still had a chance with her after all.

Okay, my reasons were threefold. She was stunning tonight. I stared at her without words, my heart beating straight out of my chest. She was gorgeous in a russet-colored dress, with her beautiful chestnut hair flowing in waves over one shoulder. The dress hugged her curvy hips, and the strapless sweetheart neckline revealed just enough of her cleavage to make me lose what was left of my mind.

Nervously, she bit her lip and ran straight to the platform—to me, where Abigail and Riley quickly joined her.

"Thank you," I mouthed, smiling when she gave a subtle nod.

"Would anyone else like to place a bid?" Monica asked.

I squinted into the lights, scowling into the crowd with a silent warning to let it go.

"Do not even think about it," Abigail warned Mrs. Hadley, who glared at her as she shrugged, picking up her glass and sipping it with deliberate nonchalance.

Maybe she was over her preoccupation with me now that Madi

was here, and she would be risking the embarrassment of being shot down in public. One could only hope.

"Going once, twice, Cole Sutter is sold to Madison Winslow for five hundred dollars! We'll see you two tomorrow night at dinner."

I hopped off the platform, and we all hustled over to the side of the room.

Monica moved on to start the bidding on Pace. Lucky for me, he was a handsome motherfucker because no one except for the town's hardcore gossips paid me any mind when I left the platform.

"Don't worry, Madi." Abigail pulled her in for a hug. "I wasn't buying him for myself. Riley said to get him for you no matter what it cost. We were thinking of him as an early Christmas present. For once, we knew what you wanted."

"You're a nut." Madi laughed. "But I appreciate it."

"Oh, good lord, Abigail," Riley burst out, shaking her head.

"What? I couldn't let that old cougar get him either," she muttered under her breath. "I've seen her in action at Bookers. She doesn't understand the word *no* and can't keep her hands to herself. It's not okay for women to be that way either, you know. Everyone deserves to have boundaries."

"Thanks, Abigail." I smiled at her. "You had me worried for a minute there."

"Sorry about that. I mean, yeah, I flirted with you that one time"—she aimed a glare toward the Hadleys at their table before turning back to me—"but unlike some people, I know how to take a damn hint. Friends?" She held her hand out to me, and I shook it with a grin.

"Of course."

"Let me know if you need help with that old horndog."

"I hope I won't have to take you up on it. I only have eyes for one woman in this town."

"Aww! I love this." She waved her hand between Madi and me. "It would be my pleasure. All it will cost you is a margarita at Bookers and you making my baby sister smile again."

"Abigail! Jeez," Madi muttered.

"Okay, okay," Riley interrupted. "The Winslow sisters have your back, Cole. And, Mom, it took you guys long enough to get here. I thought Abigail would end up having to actually buy him."

"Traffic was terrible," her mother answered. "And parking was ridiculous. We should have had plenty of time. I'm glad to see you, Cole."

"You as well. Thank you for coming."

"Okay, okay." Gigi clapped her hands, taking control of the situation. "Come on, girls. Let's go to your table and leave these two alone."

I stopped her to ask, "Gigi, can you ask Quinn to drive the kids home and watch them for me? Evan is with him, and Nat is with Dexter's family at their table. I have to talk to Madi."

She grinned hugely. "Absolutely, and if he can't, I will. Go. Take as long as you need."

They went back to their table.

Madi was mine. We were meant for each other, and it was time to tell her exactly how I felt about her.

I pulled her into a dark corner. "It looks like you were the one to rescue me tonight." When our eyes met, I knew everything would be okay. "Thank you."

She broke into a slow, sweet smile. "You're welcome."

I was hers, heart and soul. No doubts were left in my mind.

"Will you forgive me for last night?"

"Yes, of course I will." Her eyes brimmed with tenderness as she ran her hands up my chest to rest on my neck. "And I'm sorry too—for pushing you. I shouldn't have done that. You weren't ready."

"No, it's okay. You told me what you needed, and I should have taken a breath and done the same. I was just stuck in my head and convinced I couldn't give it to you. A lot has hit me in the last few months, and I was overwhelmed. I should have been honest with you about what was happening instead of letting it build up in my mind."

"I understand. And I know what we have is new. But I've never felt this much for someone this fast. It was like I met you, then all at once, I had these out-of-control feelings building up, and I didn't know how to handle it either."

"You said you wouldn't beg for scraps of what you deserve. I want you to know you'll never have to—not with me."

"I love that." Her expression grew serious. "And I want to be that person for you too, Cole."

"I never should have let you go. I'll burn my entire life down before I let you leave it again." I pulled her into my arms, whispering into her ear, "I'm falling in love with you, Madi."

She tilted her head back to meet my eyes. "I want you, Cole Sutter. I want to be with you more than anything, and I'm falling for you too. Can we get out of here?"

I grabbed her hand and led her through the tables to the exit.

CHAPTER 30

Madi

We made it to my apartment in a glorious haze of held hands and whispered promises, with the streets of Cozy Creek fading into the distance as we drove through them into our future.

"You got my flowers," he said after we'd entered my front door. I'd stopped at home to drop them off before going to the fundraiser. I couldn't leave the peonies behind in Colorado Springs or let them wilt in my mother's car.

"They're gorgeous. Peonies have always been my favorite. For as long as I can remember. Thank you."

His mouth fell open as he stared at me, perplexed. "Say 'peony' but like this, 'peenie.' I know it's weird, but—"

A quiver surged through my veins, he remembered. "It's not weird, and I'll tell you why. As a toddler, I used to sit on Gigi's porch and watch you and your brothers play with my sisters, pouting because I was too little to join you. Sometimes, you would bring me a peony to cheer me up. My mother told me the story last night. I don't remember that at all."

"I don't either, other than a hazy image of you on Gigi's porch saying, 'peenie.'" He chuckled. "But it sounds like something I would do." He traced a finger down my nose and then kissed it. "I never knew I could feel this much so fast for somebody. My heart is full of you, Madi, and I don't want this feeling ever to stop."

"I don't want to lose this. Not ever," I murmured as I slid his jacket down over his arms.

"I want you. I need you. I'm so fucking happy right now I don't know what to do with it," he growled against my mouth.

"Take me to bed," I murmured.

He backed me into the door. His lips hit mine again, tongue pushing into my mouth, hands roaming everywhere, before tugging at the zipper of my dress until it loosened, then fell to the floor at my feet.

His hands dropped from my face to my waist, sliding lower, gripping my hips, and gliding down to grab me where my ass met my thighs. He lifted me, and I wrapped my legs around his waist with my back against the door.

His lips trailed up my neck, and I shivered when he nipped at my ear and kissed my jaw. "How about I fuck you against this door right now?" His voice was like gravel, low, deep, and needy.

He shifted my body to press his hard cock against my center. There was no denying he wanted me, not when I could feel the overwhelming evidence of it, not when he was kissing me like this and touching me as if he'd die if I turned him away.

My body melted against his as he held me. The only word I could manage to say was "Yes."

His lips touched mine like a whisper. "God, you're so fucking beautiful. You have to know what you're doing to me. I know you can feel it." He ground himself against me through his slacks. "Tell me what you're doing to me, Madi. Tell me what you feel."

My eyes met his. "Cole. Please." I was desperate to feel him inside me again.

"I'm right here and never letting you go again. I want you so much. Tell me what you want, and I'll do anything. Say it."

"I want—" I ducked my head, too shy to tell him.

He kissed my forehead, letting out a dark chuckle as his lips pressed against my temple, then slid down to my ear.

"Say it," he ground out. "Say anything, and I'll do it. I'm yours, Madi. You own me. You steal the breath straight out of my body every time I'm lucky enough to get my hands on you."

"I want you to take me right here." Our eyes locked. "Right here, right now, Cole. I need you."

My heels hit the floor, and he spun me around to kiss my nape. He kissed a meandering trail down my body, unhooking my bra on the way. The garment fell to the side and landed on the floor as he knelt at my feet.

"When I first saw you waving at me with your gorgeous hair blowing in the breeze, I knew." His words, murmured hotly against my skin, left goose bumps on my spine. "I knew you would destroy me, consume me, be the end of the life I had known. It scared me, but I held on. Because somehow, I knew if I got lucky, you would put me back together again."

"Oh god, don't stop talking."

"Tell me what you want to hear."

I didn't answer. I couldn't find the words, and why would I try when everything he came up with on his own was about to melt me into a puddle right here at his feet?

He chuckled against my right hip; then he bit me. My knees went weak, and I shivered as his big hands dug into my hips to hold me up. "Don't give out on me now. I just got started."

I twisted, reaching down to run a hand into his hair. "Get up here, Cole." He stood, burying his face in my neck while his fingertips slid into the waistband of my panties.

"I need you naked right now," he said as his insistent hands cupped my ass to shove them over my hips. I kicked them aside with a groan.

"God, yes."

"I want to make you feel as good as I do." He reached low, bringing my leg up to wrap around his waist before slipping a finger inside me. "You're so wet. You want me. You really want me." His voice broke with vulnerability. "This is real, isn't it?"

"It's real." I cupped his cheeks in my palms. "I'll always want you, Cole."

"I love you." He drew back, slipping his finger into his mouth with a dirty smirk.

"You—" An involuntary moan escaped before I could gather my thoughts enough to speak. "God, the cats are watching us. Let's go to my room."

He took my hand and pulled me after him.

I shut the door behind us with a decisive slam.

"Okay. Time to get naked," I demanded.

"Condom?"

"I'm safe—I'm on the pill. Get inside me, Cole. I need to feel you again."

"Anything you want . . ." He stood and quickly stripped off the rest of his clothes before slipping his hands beneath my ass to lift me against the door.

He entered me with one hard thrust, and I sighed against his neck as he pressed his chest against mine.

"It feels like coming home whenever I'm inside of you," he growled into my ear, ruffling my hair with his breath. "I've never felt like this."

I wound my arms around his shoulders as he drove into me. "I feel it too." I was powerless in his arms as he made love to me, unable to move save for the rippling pulse of my impending orgasm. "I need more. I want to touch you too. Let's go to bed."

"Hold on to me." I held him tight as he walked us across the room, put me down near the window, and spun me to face it.

"I've been fantasizing about seeing you like this. With me." His big arm banded around my waist, hand digging into the flesh of my hip.

I twisted back to look at him. "Yes, anything." I breathed.

He held my chin and took my mouth in a hard kiss. "This window is perfect. Look at us."

I turned and saw us in the glass. A riot of lights from the street below dotted our reflection, and I gasped as his hand snaked around to cup my breast.

"Now you can see for yourself how much I want you. How fucking beautiful you are. And how I'll never let you go again."

He stood at my back, and I watched, rapt, as the hand at my hip caressed a path down my body over the soft curve of my belly to cup me between my legs while the other continued to play with my nipple. "Look at us, Madi. You belong with me."

"Show me more." The warmth of his body against my back was intoxicating. He surrounded me, and I was enraptured—so in love with him that I was drunk with it.

His chin dropped to my shoulder as he slid inside me again, pushing me forward with his chest against my back until my hands came to rest on the bench. His palm wrapped around my jaw, keeping my head up so I could see everything he was doing.

In and out, he drove into me until we were both out of control and panting. Our gasping groans fogged up the glass, leaving us in our own little world up here as we fell apart to shatter into shimmering starlight together.

He swept me up and carried me to bed. We stared at each other as he wrapped me tight in his arms. The light filtering through the window glowed against our bare skin while the shadows from the wooden panes tied us together in shadowy vines.

"I love you, Madi," he murmured, pulling me closer to kiss the top of my head.

"I love you too. You've shown me nothing but kindness, love, and understanding every day since I met you, and I love you more than I can ever say."

This was a new beginning, one I hoped would never end. I glanced down at his body as he settled beside me, and I finally felt completely at home here.

Home.

How could I leave Cozy Creek? I knew I'd found everything I could ever want with him.

I couldn't.

I wouldn't.

He was my home now.

I drifted off to sleep in his arms.

Everything else would sort itself out over time as long as we had each other.

EPILOGUE
Madi

I woke up to sunlight on my face and joy in my heart. Cole couldn't spend the entire night with me. He had to get back to his kids. But we'd fallen asleep together, and now I knew what it felt like to wake up in his arms. It was dark when he had to go, but that didn't take away from the contentment I'd felt when I saw his sleepy eyes crinkle at the corners as he smiled at me before he got up.

After he left, I looked around my room and at the cats and thought about all the things currently making me feel like I was floating on a cloud. I was *home*, and I was never going to leave.

My phone pinged with an incoming text, and a smile burst across my face. It had to be him.

COLE: Good morning, gorgeous. I'm counting the days until we can wake up together every day.

MADI: I can't wait. See you at dinner tonight.

COLE: Sooner if I can get away.

He planned to tell his kids about us at breakfast so we could all go to the bachelor auction dinner together. I knew they liked me, but I was still a bit nervous.

Being friends with Gigi's granddaughter from across the street was much different than liking the woman your dad was dating.

I sat at the edge of the bed, slipped into my robe, and grabbed the closest cat for a snuggle. Kenny purred against my neck, then butted his head against my chin. "I know. I'm happy for me too," I whispered into his soft fur.

Another text came through.

> **NATALIE:** Madi!! I'm so happy right now! Dad said we're going with you tonight for dinner. Ev is happy too.

> **MADI:** I'm so glad you guys are okay with this! I'll see you all later. Talk soon.

I reread Nat's message, not quite believing that this could be real.

Relief shot through my body as I entered the bathroom to prepare for the day. I felt like twirling or squeeing or getting back into bed so I could kick my feet in the air. I was happy for a change, and it felt freaking great.

I wasn't going to Gigi's to walk Basil first thing today like usual. Instead, Kenzie was coming over to join me for breakfast to discuss life, love, and the fact that I was about to become a permanent employee of The Cozy Creek Confectionery and a full-time resident of Cozy Creek. I was beyond thrilled.

There was a very real possibility that I would explode from happiness. Of course, I'd experienced joy before, but not like this. Never had this many aspects of my life lined up to be awesome all at once. This was unprecedented.

I ran through my getting-ready routine, then paced in front of the doorway, waiting for Kenzie to arrive. Kenny, Sage, and Victor watched me like I had lost my marbles, their little heads bobbing side to side as I walked the length of the apartment. Then, I almost jumped out of my skin when she knocked.

I threw open the door. She stood there with takeout coffee and a bag of chocolate croissants from Cozy Coffee, the shop down the street.

"I've heard things." She beamed at me. "Good things. Gigi called me last night and told me everything. I'm so happy for you."

"Let's go sit."

She followed me to the couch, placing our breakfast on the coffee table before sitting. Crossing one leg beneath the other, she settled in to listen.

"Hey, what is this?" She slid her hand between the couch cushions to unearth a black scrap of silk. "Underwear? Go Madi! You're getting adventurous, aren't you? Doing it with that huge window right there where anyone in town can look up from the sidewalk to watch you bang Cole. I'm ten percent shocked, twenty percent scandalized, and seventy percent impressed. Look at me doing math. So what's going on? Thong in the couch? You?"

"No, ew." I tried to grab it, but she held it over her head and laughed. "We don't do it in here. The cats would see. Gross, Kenzie."

She brandished the thong, waving it around like it was exhibit A that showed I was a freak in the sheets—or a freak in my living room, as the case may be.

I shook my head. "Kenny gets into my clean laundry and steals my underwear, okay? He likes to sleep on them, probably because they're silky. Then he makes his biscuits, and they get wedged between the couch cushions. Don't worry, they're clean."

She threw her head back and laughed. "Only you. You're so freaking wholesome. It's unbelievable."

She tossed me the thong, and I caught it.

"Whatever. I'm going to get him his own undies. I'm sick of having to clean my fine delicates twice. Hand washing is a pain in the ass."

"What a little weirdo."

"Yeah, I know. Abigail stayed here a couple of weeks before I got here, and he stole one of her thongs too. We still haven't found it." My eyes got big. "Oh, Kenzie."

She froze, with her coffee cup halfway to her mouth. "He's gotten out a few times, hasn't he? Like that time in the tree. Gigi said he's a little escape artist. It was worse before you got here."

"Yes! Oh my god, Kenzie. Oh. My. God. Drew leaves his car window open. I know he does because I sometimes see it when I leave to walk Basil. And I'm not gonna lie; I judge him for it. Who does that in this day and age? I mean, really. Safety first. Always. Come on!"

"Focus, Madi. Does she wear La Perla? That fancy, expensive stuff?"

"Yes! She does. She gave me some for my birthday. She told me once my vag got a taste of the good stuff, I'd never go back. Like, she has a point."

"Yeah, yeah, yeah. I'm putting a pin in that to tease you with later. But Madi, what if Drew didn't cheat on me? What if this little orange menace put Abigail's thong in the Corolla? What if he isn't a jackass cheater, and I'm just a stubborn jerk who wouldn't listen?"

"Stubborn, yes." I winced. "I'm sorry, but it's true. But you're not a jerk. And to be fair, you did listen to him. And so did I. He said he didn't know how it got there. Which would be hard for anyone to believe."

"Yeah—I have to go. I'm sorry about breakfast. Help yourself to the croissants."

"Don't apologize. I'll be in town forever now. We can talk anytime."

"Yeah, you will!" She pulled me in for a hug. "God, I'm so happy about this. So listen." Her hands went to my shoulders as she pep-talked me. "You're going to look beautiful tonight. His kids will love you as much as he and everyone else in this town does, and you will live happily ever after. Do not be nervous. It's all happening, and it's all good. Hopefully, for the both of us."

"Happy. That is the word of the day around here. Go on, talk to Drew. Love you, Kenzie."

"Love you too." She blew me a kiss and dashed out the door. I hoped she could work it out with Drew. Especially since, starting next week, he was going to teach me how to bake bread.

I grabbed the croissants and propped my feet on the coffee table. I had about six hours before I had to start getting ready for dinner tonight, which was a lot of time to kill.

FINALLY, IT WAS time. This moment felt huge. Important. This would be the first time I spent time with Cole and the kids as an official couple.

When I pulled into his driveway to meet them for dinner, the garage door immediately slid open, and two excited teens ran out to meet me. I stepped out and waved at them with both hands over my head.

Cole followed behind them, stepping into the garage from the interior door. He looked so sexy in a dark blue suit and matching tie. A slow smile spread across his face when he noticed my wave.

"I love you," he mouthed, and I smiled.

I sent him heart hands since I was otherwise occupied with a chatty Nat and Ev, who wasn't chatty but seemed determined to listen to everything we had to say.

"Now, we don't have to worry about Dad being alone when it's Mom's turn with us because he has you to be with," she told me. "And you're perfect for him. I knew it the second I met you."

"I'm honored you feel that way." Tears filled my eyes, and I held my arms out, hoping they'd let me hug them, and burst into loud tears when they did. "We're going to be happy. All of us. I'll make sure of it."

"We know you will," Natalie whispered. "You've already helped me so much. For real, Madi." Tears shimmered in her eyes. "I love you."

I pulled away to brush them from her cheeks. "I love you too, sweetheart. And you too, Evan."

Cole looked like he was about to burst. His chest puffed up, and his grin was ear to ear. God, how I loved this man.

"Listen to me," I said, taking a deep breath to gather my composure before I went on. "I want you guys to know something right now. I know I'm not your mom. You have a mom, and I would never, ever try to replace her. But that doesn't mean you won't be my kids. I love your dad, which means I get to love you too. This means the world to me. It's a privilege to be in your lives, and I take it seriously."

"Okay. Yeah. I—" Evan scrubbed a hand beneath his eyes. "I never thought I'd have a stepmom before. This is pretty cool. I know you make my dad happy. He's been smiling again since you've been around."

Cole put a hand to the back of his neck and pulled Evan in for a hug. His eyes glowed with love as they met mine over Evan's head.

"I love you too," I murmured to him.

"Come here." He kissed me, soft like a whisper. "I'm going to make you happy here. I promise you, Madi."

"I know you will, Cole, because you already do."

**Can't get enough of Madi and Cole?
Turn the page for an exclusive
bonus scene!**

FALL – ONE YEAR LATER

The familiar sight of the TEN MILES TO COZY CREEK sign was my cue. Natalie and Evan snickered in the back seat as we approached because they were on board with my plan.

Okay, Natalie made the plan.

One year ago, Madi, in her ridiculous pink VW Bug, was stranded right here in this very spot, and today, I was going to add to that memory with a proposal.

Natalie had gone ring shopping with me a few weeks back, and in her purse was a one-carat, round diamond set on a platinum band. A halo of tiny diamonds surrounded it.

We were coming home from Colorado Springs, where we'd spent the weekend visiting Madi's mother and sisters. The kids loved being spoiled by them, and I just loved being with Madi, doing whatever made her happy.

I slowed the truck to a crawl when we approached the sign. The tires crunched through the brush as I came to a stop.

"Shit," I muttered.

"Are we out of gas or something?" Madi asked while the kids in the back seat attempted to keep everything under wraps. But their excitement was about to give us away. "Is something wrong?"

After putting the truck into park, I turned to her. "No. Everything is right."

The kids excitedly whispered to each other, then went silent.

"What's happening?" Her eyes lit up with excitement when she realized something was going on, and we were all in on it.

I took her hands in mine and a rush of pink stained her cheeks. A familiar bolt of awareness jolted between us, and my heart thundered.

"I saw you, Madi. Right here. One year ago today—you were waving your hands over your head, and all at once, right there on the spot, I knew you would change my life."

"Oh, my god. Cole—"

"You've been making it better in every way that counts since the day I met you. I want to spend forever making you as happy as you've made me. Will you marry me?"

Natalie passed me the velvet ring box from the back seat.

Madi gasped, nodding as her tear-filled eyes shone in the gorgeous Colorado sunlight.

I slid the ring on her finger. It fit perfectly.

"Yes, I will marry you!" she cried as she held her hand out. As the diamond sparkled in the sun, my heart filled with more joy than it could contain, and a deep feeling of peace settled into my soul.

"Dad," Evan whispered. "You were supposed to get her outside first. You didn't get down on one knee."

"Evan! Shh." I didn't see it, but Nat's eye roll came through loud and clear in her voice. "It's okay this way too," she insisted.

"I got excited and screwed this up," I confessed against Madi's lips, and she pulled back, smiling.

"We had big plans," Evan ratted me out.

"I guess I'm lucky Gigi's hot granddaughter said yes to me anyway."

Madi burst out laughing. "You could have proposed to me in a text message or a Post-It note on the fridge, and I would have said yes to you, Cole Sutter. I'm yours. But let's see those plans." She clapped her hands together and beamed at me.

"You got it, baby."

"Go, Nat," Evan said with a laugh. "You're first."

"Oh no! Dad. What are we going to do now?" Natalie's voice was deadpan.

"I think we're having car trouble!" Evan shouted. "Oh. I have a great idea. Have you ever looked at the view from the bluff, Madi? Let's check it out while Dad finds out what's wrong with the truck."

"No," her shoulders shook with laughter. "I haven't actually stopped to look." She turned to the kids. "Should we go out? What do you guys think?"

"I think you're already wearing the ring, but we can still get a great picture," Natalie answered, holding her phone up with the camera open, ready to go.

"Sounds perfect to me." Madi's eyes glowed with happiness as she took my hand. "I love this. Everything about it. I love all of you so much."

"We love you too," Evan said. "That's why this has to be right."

"You're a good kid, Ev," I told him as we exited the truck and took the short path that led to the bluff.

"Both of you are the best, and I'm a lucky lady."

Nat propped her camera up on the hood of my truck and set the timer.

I pulled them into my arms, Madi on one side and the kids on the other, and we smiled as our future unfolded before us.

ABOUT THE AUTHOR

NORA EVERLY is a lifelong bookworm. She started reading the good stuff once she grew tall enough to sneak the romance novels off the top of her mother's bookshelf and it has been nonstop ever since.

Once upon a time she was a substitute teacher and an educational assistant. Now she's a writer and stay-at-home mom to two small humans and one fat cat.

Nora lives in the Pacific Northwest with her family and her overactive imagination.

Find her at noraeverly.com